Fairy Tales

FOR

Fearless Girls

Retold by
Anita Ganeri

Illustrated by
Khoa Le

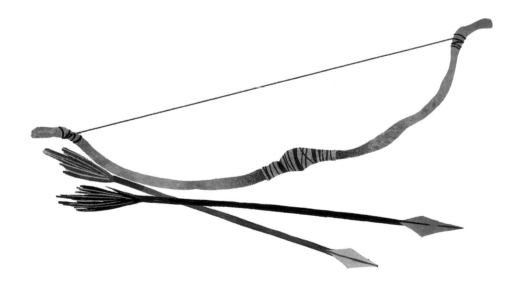

ARCTURUS

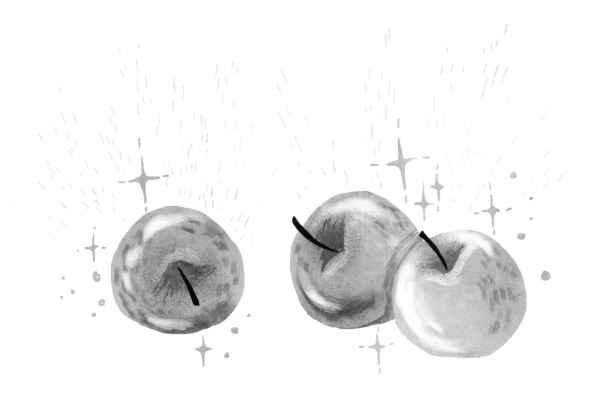

ARCTURUS

This edition published in 2020 by Arcturus Publishing Limited
26/27 Bickels Yard, 151–153 Bermondsey Street,
London SE1 3HA

Author: Anita Ganeri
Illustrator: Khoa Le
Editor: Donna Gregory
Designer: Ms Mousepenny

ISBN: 9781-78950-253-4
CH006953NT
Supplier 29, Date 1219, Print run 9971

Printed in China

CONTENTS

INTRODUCTION

Let's forget lovestruck Rapunzel, who waits patiently to be helped down from a tower by a handsome prince. Let's leave behind Snow White, who lies still in a glass box until a man comes by to rescue her. And let's ditch Sleeping Beauty, who's literally asleep for most of her own story. It's time to move on from stories about women who stand by, mark time, and twiddle their thumbs until other people take action.

This book isn't about the sort of girls that you usually find in fairy tales. These women are doers, not waiters. They have their own minds and take action. However, that's not to say that they're all virtuous figures. Amongst our protagonists, you'll find tricksters and thieves as well as noble heroes, and girls driven by revenge as well as heroism. These charismatic characters are just as varied as their male counterparts, with whom you may be more familiar—because in myths and folk stories about men, there's a Loki or Anansi for every Thor or Theseus. And it should be that way for women, too.

The fearless girls of our stories are free spirits who possess the same awe-inspiring qualities of self-confidence, strength, wit, and independence usually attributed to

heroes, not heroines. In our heroines' lives, love at first sight is a thing of myth. Love must be earned through acts of commitment and affection, and, vitally, by mutual respect. Our heroines are happy to be loved, but not at the cost of being claimed as someone else's property.

Of course, being free-spirited and independent-minded isn't always easy or popular. It never was. Strong women in fairy tales and folk stories are often painted in a negative light, as sinister stepmothers, evil stepsisters, wicked witches, or hideous trolls. Luckily, the girls in our stories couldn't care less what other people think. They've got their lives ahead of them, and they're going to lead them in the way they want to, whatever anyone says. After all, why shouldn't girls be as fearless, fabulous, and free as men? Why shouldn't girls be heroes too?

So, with all that in mind, get ready to meet some inspiring women who couldn't give two hoots about doing what was expected of them. And just as well. Thanks to their trailblazing and derring-do, they rescued their friends, family, and society in general from many a life-threatening scrape. There's amazing Atalanta, an expert shot with a bow and arrow, and so fast on her feet that no one could beat her fairly in a race. There's Tokoyo, the Samurai's daughter, who risked being drowned or devoured by a terrible sea monster to rescue her father from exile. There's Tatterhood, who dressed in rags and rode on a goat until people accepted her for who she was. And there's Unanana, whose children were kidnapped and eaten by a one-tusked elephant who hadn't reckoned with their fearless mother.

All of that's just for starters. The book is filled with tales of fearless women from all around the world. We hope that you'll enjoy dipping into their action-packed adventures, and also that you'll feel inspired by their examples to have some awesome adventures of your own.

The Tale of
Brave Bradamante
and Her Amazing Flying Horse

Long ago, there lived a mighty knight, the bravest woman in all of France. Her name was Bradamante, and her fame quickly spread far and wide. A fine and fearless warrior, she rode on a fabulous flying horse. It was a magical creature with an eagle's head, talons, and wings. What was more, she fought her enemies with an enchanted lance that unhorsed any villains who dared to fight unfairly. She wielded a sword so fiercely that it was a brave person who dared to take Bradamante on.

One day on the battlefield, Bradamante found herself fighting alongside two young men. They were named Melisso and Ruggiero. Melisso was strong and brave, but Ruggiero's fighting skills were so good, they almost matched Bradamante's. After fighting together for several days, Ruggiero and Bradamante fell in love and planned to marry.

However, Bradamante's parents had their sights set on their daughter marrying a wealthy nobleman, not a soldier. Despite her pleas, they refused to give their blessing to a marriage to Ruggiero. Finally, a determined Bradamante laid down a challenge—she would only marry a suitor who could match her in combat move for move and blow for

blow. If her parents could find her a nobleman who could do that, she would marry him. Her parents agreed, but Bradamante was sure that no nobleman in the kingdom could match her. To her parents' great alarm, her cunning plan worked perfectly. Suitor after suitor tried to win her hand, including Rinaldo, the son of the powerful sorcerer Atlantes. Each one was defeated. Bradamante could make her opponent fall with as little as one swing of her sword.

The only one to rise to the challenge was Ruggiero, as Bradamante always knew he would. Her parents had to admit defeat and give their blessing to the wedding.

After a fun-filled wedding day, surprisingly, both families became firm friends, and Bradamante and Ruggiero were looking forward to their happily ever after. Sadly, it was

not to be. Atlantes the sorcerer was furious that Bradamante had refused his son's offer of marriage, and vowed that he would have revenge.

As Bradamante and Ruggiero left their wedding party, Atlantes summoned a magical wind to kidnap Ruggiero and whisk him away to his enchanted castle. It stood on a high mountain, far away, and was made of glittering glass. Atlantes had filled it with tricks and illusions to confuse anyone who tried to enter it.

"They'll never be together now," Atlantes cackled.

However, he hadn't reckoned on fearless Bradamante. Riding her faithful flying horse, she followed Ruggiero to the castle, smashed through the glass walls with her enchanted lance, and rescued him.

Atlantes spotted them climbing onto Bradamante's horse together and was outraged. He summoned his strongest magic and put a spell on the horse. The loyal creature bucked Bradamante off, then picked up Ruggiero in its talons. To Bradamante's horror, it soared away through the sky.

Ruggiero kicked and struggled, but the horse did not let him go until it landed on a mysterious island in the middle of the sea, which belonged to the wicked witch Alcina. Alcina was beautiful, but she had a horrible habit of turning her unsuspecting visitors into rocks, trees, streams, and wild animals.

As Ruggiero glanced around, in quiet despair, he was surprised to hear a nearby myrtle bush speaking.

"Beware, beware," the bush warned. "Run for your life, young man, before it's too late. Wicked Alcina will fall in love with you and bewitch you with her beauty and charm, but she will soon grow tired of you. Then she will transform you into something to decorate her island. It has happened before and will happen again, mark my words. I was once Astolfo, a great knight, and now look at me. Your only hope is to find the enchanted urn that contains her magic and destroy it."

Ruggiero was only half listening. Despite Astolfo's warning, he strode straight off to find Alcina and once he found her, the unfortunate knight immediately fell under her spell. He forgot all about Bradamante.

Meanwhile, Bradamante was making plans to save her beloved Ruggerio. She had gone to visit Melisso, to ask him to help her. When Bradamante told Melisso the direction the horse had flown in, he guessed it had gone to Alcina's island, which he had heard of from some other knight friends. He brought his magic ring, which allowed the wearer to see through illusions and spells. Bradamante dressed herself as a young man in full battle clothes and called herself Ricciardo, as a disguise. They borrowed a boat and rowed across to the island.

When they got there, Astolfo the bush gave them the same warning that he had given Ruggiero. Bradamante and Melisso listened to him and they hatched a plan. They went to Alcina's palace together, to find Alcina and Ruggiero sitting next to each other on thrones. Behind the thrones bubbled an urn, the source of Alcina's magic. Melisso and "Ricciardo" introduced themselves as two young men who wished to compete for Alcina's hand in marriage.

Bradamante hoped that Ruggiero might recognize her voice, but she was dismayed to see that he was already so besotted with Alcina that he had forgotten all about her, their wedding day, and his previous life.

Alcina smirked at them both. "I already have the best man in the world," she said. "I don't need any more suitors. Although, I could do with some new rocks for my island."

She raised her hands to turn them into rocks, so Bradamante and Melisso ducked out of the door.

"We need to destroy her magic," Bradamante said. For the rest of the day, they watched, but everywhere Alcina went, she carried the urn with her. They knew they needed to distract her … but how?

Finally, while Bradamante watched Alcina, Melisso managed to get Ruggiero alone. Melisso valiantly tried to remind Ruggiero of his past life. He told Ruggiero about Alcina's wicked magic, and what had happened to all the others who had dared to cross her path.

At first, Ruggiero refused to believe him.

"If you're trying to trick me into leaving," he cried, "it isn't going to work. I love

Alcina with all my heart, and she loves me with all of hers. I'm going to stay here forever. And you can't stop me!"

To bring Ruggiero to his senses, Melisso took off his magic ring and placed it on his friend's finger so that Ruggiero at last saw things as they truly were. Instead of an enchanted island filled with babbling brooks and rolling hills, Ruggiero saw a harsh, stony desert haunted by howling monsters. And, as the spell was broken, he remembered Bradamante and his love for her.

"You must distract Alcina," Melisso told Ruggiero. "So that brave Bradamante can defeat her."

Together, they went back to the throne room. Alcina was lounging on her throne, not realizing that Bradamante was hidden behind a statue.

Ruggiero strode bravely into the middle of the room. "I don't love you and I wish to leave," he announced.

Alcina's anger was terrible. Summoning her most harmful spells, she called up every evil genie and spirit she could to stop him from leaving her. Bradamante leapt out from behind the statue, shook off her battle helmet, and defended Ruggiero from all the evil spirits. She dodged magical curses and, with a hundred swift swings of her sword, defeated all of the grasping monsters that Alcina could conjure.

Then, with a roar, Bradamante dived through the air, over Alcina's throne, and, with a sudden strike, smashed the urn into a million pieces. At once, Alcina's palace crumbled away into dust. Alcina herself sank into the ground, with a deathly wailing sound. The island was free of evil, at last. Ruggiero and Bradamante ran into each other's arms.

There was one last good deed to be done before they could leave the island—to transform the rocks, trees, streams, and wild animals of the island back into the people who they had once been. Among them was Astolfo, the knight who had been turned into the myrtle bush, and his son, Oberto, who had been turned into a ferocious cave lion. Melisso arranged to take all the newly transformed people home in the boat. Saying farewell to their friends, Bradamante and Ruggiero jumped on the back of Bradamante's flying horse and set off through the skies for home. They were looking forward to a life of happiness—and adventure.

Λτalaντa
the Fleet-Footed Huntress

Once upon a time, in the sunny land of Arcadia, in Greece, there lived a king and queen who had no children. They longed for a son to rule after them, and offered many prayers to the great gods to grant their wish. After a while, it seemed that their dreams had come true, when the queen gave birth to a beautiful, bouncing baby. The only problem was that the baby was a girl.

The king flew into a terrible rage: "I wished for a boy, and I got a girl," he fumed. "What good is a girl to me? She can't ride or hunt or learn to fight. And she can't be king of Arcadia after me. It's a complete disaster. There's only one thing to do."

With a click of his fingers, the heartless king summoned one of his men and ordered him to take the baby into the forest, far away on the border of his land.

"Leave her to be eaten by wild bears," he said. "It's the best way for us to get rid of the child."

So the man took the baby into the forest and left her under a tree. For a day and a night, the baby wailed for her mother, growing weaker and hungrier. Only the birds in

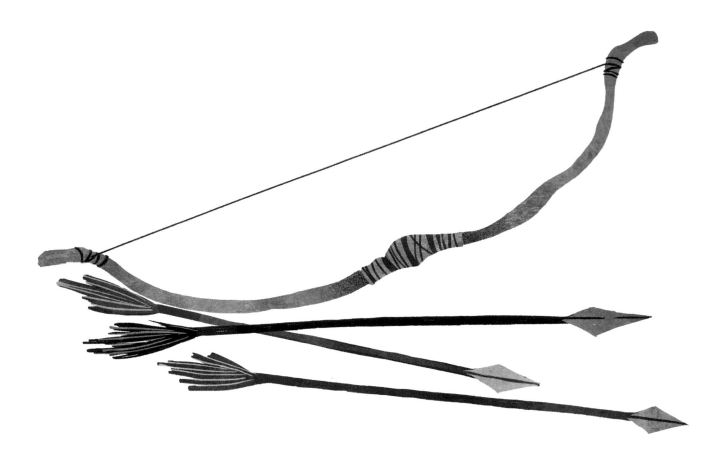

the trees could hear her cries. Then, the following evening, a mother bear came shuffling by. She heard the baby crying and wondered if it was a lost bear cub. Reaching down with her big, furry head, she gently nuzzled the baby's face. Cooing with delight, the baby reached up and touched the bear's shiny nose with her hand. Then the bear lay down beside the baby, and they both fell sound asleep.

The next day, the bear took the baby to her den in the woods, where they lived happily for several years. The little girl grew up fast and strong, trotting through the woods after her bear mother. Then, one day, a hunter came to the forest and stumbled across the bear's cave. The little girl was frightened, but the mother bear spoke soothing words: "You are growing up quickly," she rumbled sadly. "And it is time for you to move on from this place. From now on, your home will be with this hunter and his wife. They will look after you, dearest child, and teach you the skills you'll need in your life."

The little girl did not want to go, and cried for the bear who had been her mother for so long. The hunter and his wife were kind and welcoming, so it wasn't too long before she felt at home.

"We shall call her Atalanta," the hunter said. "And thank Artemis, goddess of hunting, who kept her safe in the forest until we found her."

As Atalanta grew older, the hunter and his wife gave her a fine hunting bow and a quiver full of arrows. They taught her how to shoot and hurl a hunting spear. Whenever they went out hunting, she came along, and proved herself to be an expert shot. She was nimble and strong and could outrun anyone. Soon, everyone in Arcadia had heard of Atalanta, the fleet-footed huntress.

The forest in which Atalanta lived lay on the borders of Arcadia and the next-door kingdom of Calydon. The king of Calydon, Oeneus, was wise and brave. He loved hunting and tending his vineyard. One summer, the harvest was particularly fine, and Oeneus decided to thank the gods for the bounty his kingdom had received by making offerings to them. In his excitement, Oeneus forgot to thank Artemis, goddess of hunting, and she did not take the slight well.

"I'll show them," she said angrily. "They won't forget me again."

The very next day, the largest boar anyone could remember came roaring out of the forest. It had two tusks, as sharp as knives, and gleaming, angry eyes. It tore through

the countryside, trampling crops, breaking down grapevines, and uprooting trees in the orchards. Then it killed all the sheep in the fields. The devastation went on for weeks as the boar never seemed to tire. Soon, the storehouses of Calydon stood empty, and people began to starve.

In despair, King Oeneus sent for his son, Meleager, who was the greatest warrior in the land. Together, they sent messengers to all the greatest hunters of Greece, asking for their help. The hunters came willingly, including Atalanta, who was armed with her mighty hunting bow, arrows, and spear.

"Your Majesty," she told the king, "the boar is destroying the forest where I live. I will go with the warriors on the hunt and kill it."

Some of the hunters who hadn't heard of her burst out laughing.

"What does she know about hunting?" one said.

"If she goes, I'm staying at home," said another. "Everyone will laugh at us!"

Prince Meleager had heard of Atalanta and he stepped forward.

"You're welcome to join us," he told her. "We're in dire need of your skills. As for the rest of you, shame on you. Are you afraid that Atalanta will prove a better hunter than you?"

The next day, the hunt began, and it was Atalanta who led the way. At last, they tracked the boar to a thicket—and it was a terrible sight to see. Its eyes shone red like fire, its mouth drooled and foamed, and it slashed its sharp tusks from side to side. Even before the warriors could load their bows, the boar charged, scattering men and dogs, leaving several of the heroes dead. Only brave Atalanta stood her ground. Carefully, she raised her bow, took aim, and let an arrow fly. It struck the boar straight between the eyes, and the great beast fell to its knees. Then Meleager finished the beast with his spear. It rolled over, dead.

When Atalanta went back to her old life, her fame spread far and wide. Her speed of foot, her courage, and her beauty became the talk of Greece. Many young warriors fell in love with her, but Atalanta preferred the freedom of the woods to being married. The trouble was that her suitors wouldn't take "No" for an answer, and more and

more arrived to woo her. Soon, Atalanta could stand it no longer, and called them all together.

"I will marry the man who can beat me in a running race," she declared. "But if I beat you," she continued, "you lay down your swords, bows, and arrows to me. No longer will you call yourself a warrior." One by one, the challengers came forward, and, one by one, Atalanta beat them all. None of them came close to winning, and so, she soon amassed a great mound of weapons.

Then, one day, a prince called Melanion arrived. He knew that he couldn't hope to outrun Atalanta, but neither did he want to lay down his sword. So he went to pray to Aphrodite, goddess of love, and she took pity on him. She gave him three golden apples and told him what to do.

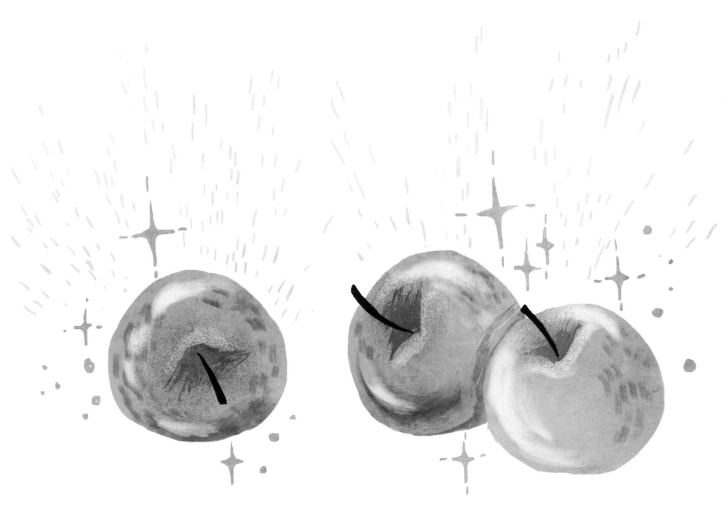

Atalanta gave Melanion a head start when the race began, but, swift as an arrow from a bow, she soon caught up and began to overtake him. Calmly, Melanion took out one of the apples, and threw it right in front of her. As the apple fell to the ground, it sparkled in the sun. Atalanta had never seen anything so beautiful and knew that she had to have it. As she stopped to pick it up, Melanion ran straight past.

Atalanta stood up and began to run again, and soon caught up with him. So Melanion took out a second apple, and tossed it into her path. It sparkled even more brightly than the first, and Atalanta stopped to pick it up. Again, Melanion ran straight past her, and again, Atalanta ran like the wind to catch him up. Atalanta started to figure out what Melanion was doing. *He is a clever prince*, she thought, *but he isn't going to get the better of me*.

However, just before the finish line, Melanion took out the third apple and threw it over his shoulder so that it rolled off the path. Not even thinking about what she was doing, Atalanta chased after it ... leaving Melanion to cross the line first.

Atalanta was annoyed. "You cheated! Those apples were enchanted!"

Melanion held her hand and kneeled on one knee. "I wanted to marry you so much that I took advice from Aphrodite herself. I cannot run as fast as you, but I can love you as strongly as any man ever could. I won't hold you to your promise of marriage, because we hardly know each other. I only ask that you allow me to spend a few days in your company. If you prefer, I will put down my sword and leave now, although it will pain me to do it."

Atalanta knew that Melanion must have lived quite a life to receive the blessing of Aphrodite, so she decided they would spend a few days together in order for her to hear all of the stories she felt sure he could tell. A few days stretched into weeks, and then months. Soon, she realized that she had fallen in love with him, and after a couple of years, Atalanta and Melanion married. They lived happily together for very long time, but they never raced each other again.

Nana Miriam
and the Horrible
Hippopotamus

In a village by the great River Niger, in West Africa, there once lived a man called Fara Maka, and his daughter, Nana Miriam. They belonged to the Soroko people, who were famed and feared as great warriors, and Fara Maka was one of the bravest and best.

Now, Fara Maka was built like a giant, and was so strong that he could uproot a baobab tree with just one hand. He was also said to be ugly. His daughter, Nana Miriam, was incredibly strong like her father, but she was also beautiful and clever. Fara Maka was proud as could be of his daughter, and taught her everything he knew. Together, father and daughter roamed the land and paddled along the river, with Fara Maka pointing out all the different fish, plants, and animals, teaching Nana Miriam their natures and names. There was one other thing that he taught her—magic. Before long, Nana Miriam knew more magic than her father, though she didn't tell anyone, not even him.

At that time, a huge, monstrous hippopotamus—who also knew magic—lived in

the River Niger. It was always ravenously hungry, even after a meal. Every year, just as the Soroko people were about to harvest their precious rice crop, the hippo splashed out of the river, waddled onto the land, and gobbled down every single rice plant. It munched its way through harvest after harvest until there was nothing left for people to eat and famine gripped the land.

Hunters from the village tried time and again to kill the beast, but the hippo kept outwitting them, transforming itself into a crocodile, a water snake, or a giant fish, and quickly swimming away. One day, Fara Maka himself went out to hunt the monster, carrying seven of his sharpest spears.

"These spears have never failed me before," he said. "When I return, the beast will be dead!"

When at last he tracked down the hippo, he pulled his arm back, took aim, and threw. Seven times, he hurled a spear, and seven times, he failed to hit his target. For, suddenly, the hippo made seven pots appear from thin air, filled with fire. One by one, Fara Maka's spears landed in the pots, burst into flames, and melted in the fire. After Fara Maka ran out of spears, the seven pots filled with fire disappeared, and the hippo cackled, "You will never kill me! I have magic too and I am unbeatable!" The monstrous and terrible hippo transformed again and swam away. Proud Fara Maka was forced to admit defeat and return to the village empty-handed.

To save face, Fara Maka knew that he had to do something. He marched to the next village to ask for help from Kara-Digi-Mao-Fosi-Fasi, a hunter whose reputation almost matched his own.

"Will you help me to hunt this beast?" asked Fara Maka.

"I will," replied Kara-Digi-Mao-Fosi-Fasi. "And I'll bring along one hundred and twenty of my finest hunting dogs."

Each hunting dog was the size of a horse, with fearsome fangs, and eyes that glowed in the dark. They made Fara Maka nervous, but he didn't like to admit it. Before long, they'd tracked down the hippo—it would have been difficult to miss—and Kara-Digi-Mao-Fosi-Fasi turned his trusty dogs loose. Fangs gnashing and chains rattling, they

made a terrifying sight, or at least so Fara Maka thought. The hippo thought otherwise. It laughed when it saw the baying pack.

"I'm not scared of a few scrappy dogs," it boomed. "You'll have to do better than that."

The monstrous creature grabbed each of the one hundred and twenty horse-sized hunting dogs by the tail and gobbled them down, one by one. Then it turned its back on the horrified hunters and lumbered off to raid another rice field.

Fara Maka and Kara-Digi-Mao-Fosi-Fasi ran as fast as they could, all the way back to Fara Maka's house. There they were met by Nana Miriam, and they told her what had happened, leaving out the bit about running away.

"What a brute!" Fara Maka said, trying to stop his voice from trembling. "We tried everything, and nothing worked."

"That's right," continued Kara-Digi-Mao-Fosi-Fasi. "And if we couldn't stop it, then nobody is likely to. After all, we are the best hunters in the land."

Nana Miriam listened to their story and decided it was time for her to take things into her own hands, and get rid of the hippo once and for all.

"Well," she said, smiling. "There's nothing else left to do. I'll have to go and see this beastly creature for myself!"

Fara Maka was beside himself.

"No, no, no," he cried, taking her hand. "My beloved daughter, you are wise and strong. There can be no doubt about that. But our greatest warriors have tried to kill this beast, and nobody can touch it. You are my only child—I beg you not to go."

Kara-Digi-Mao-Fosi-Fasi just snorted at her. "What nonsense. You wouldn't stand a chance against such a monster. Listen to your father, that's my advice, and stay at home, where you belong."

His words simply made Nana Miriam more determined. She'd show him. Calmly grabbing a spear, and her leather juju bag, in which she kept her magic powders and charms, she turned her back on the two men and strode off in search of the hippo.

Before long, Nana Miriam found the hippo. It had left a trail of destruction along the riverbank, and was busy devouring yet another rice field. It looked up as it saw Nana Miriam approaching, and grinned through its terrible teeth.

"Ha, they've sent a child to kill me," the hippo sniggered. "That's the funniest thing I've ever seen."

"We'll see about that," replied Nana Miriam, holding herself straight and tall.

"What makes you think you can do it?" asked the hippo. "When the strongest and cleverest hunters in your village and beyond have failed. Even one hundred and twenty hunting dogs couldn't stop me. What have you got to say about that?"

Nana Miriam gave the hippo a long, hard stare.

"If you're ready to do battle," she challenged him, "I'll show you what I can do."

"Ready when you are," chuckled the hippo.

"I'm ready," replied Nana Miriam.

So the battle began between the hippo and Nana Miriam. Hoping to catch her off guard, the hippo made the first move. With a deafening roar, it set the rice field alight, and then created a giant wall of fire between them. Nana Miriam acted quickly. She reached into her juju bag. She pulled out a pouch of magic powder, which she flung onto the flames. At once, the fire turned into water, which soaked harmlessly into the ground.

"You'll have to do better than that," she taunted the hippo.

"Oh, don't worry," it replied. "I haven't finished with you yet."

The hippo gave another deafening roar, and this time an enormous, gleaming iron wall grew up between them. The hippo looked pleased, but it didn't last long. Once again, Nana Miriam reached into her juju bag and pulled out a magic hammer. With all

her strength, she pounded the hammer against the iron wall, and had soon smashed it into pieces.

"Anything else?" called Nana Miriam. "Or have I won?"

For the first time, the monstrous hippo looked worried. It wasn't used to coming second, and decided to run away before it was beaten. It transformed itself into a raging river that hurtled into the Niger at full speed. Nana Miriam was ready. She reached into her juju bag, pulled out a bottle of magic potion, which she then sprinkled over the hippo-river. In an instant, the river dried up, and turned back into a hippo again.

Just at that moment, Fara Maka appeared, with Kara-Digi-Mao-Fosi-Fasi at his side. Fara Maka wanted to check up on Nana Miriam and he was curious to see if his daughter really could kill the hippo. Distracted by their sudden arrival, the hippo forgot all about her, and charged straight at the two men.

Nana Miriam was ready. As the hippo roared past her, she leapt out and grabbed its back leg. Then, summoning all her strength, she swung it three times around her head, before hurling it across the River Niger. It smashed into some rocks on the other side of the bank, and crashed to the ground, stone dead.

All three hunters returned to the village, to dance, feast, and sing the story of Nana Miriam's great deeds. And from that day on, the Soroko enjoyed many rich rice harvests and were no longer starving—all thanks to Nana Miriam.

The Amazing Adventures of Tokoyo

Many centuries ago, in Japan, a powerful emperor, called Hojo Takatoki, ruled over the country. One day, a great Samurai lord, Oribe Shima, offended the emperor and found himself banished to the Oki Islands, a wild, rocky, and hard-to-reach group of islands stretched out along the coast.

Oribe was forced to leave behind his beloved daughter, Tokoyo, in the care of his family. Heartbroken, Tokoyo mourned the loss of her father. She longed for him to be pardoned, but that day never came. Finally, when she was almost grown up, she made a vow to herself:

"I will go and find my father," she said bravely. "Or I shall die trying."

Then she sold all her belongings and set off on a long journey to the coast. From here, on a clear day she could see the island where her father had been exiled. When she tried to persuade the local fishermen to take her across the sea to the island, they just laughed at her. It was against the law to visit those who had been banished, they said, and breaking the law meant certain death.

Tokoyo had not come all this way to give up now. With her last few coins, she bought food, and under cover of night, went down to the shore, where she found a small boat. She pushed the boat into the water, and started rowing as hard as she could. It was a risky crossing, across storm-tossed water, but Tokoyo had been brought up by the sea, and it held no fear for her. Besides, luck was on her side. A stiff breeze and a strong current carried her across the ocean, and the following evening she washed up on a rocky shore. Shivering with cold and exhaustion, she found a sheltered spot on the beach, lay down, and went to sleep.

The next morning, Tokoyo began her search for her father as soon as she woke up. The first person she came across was a fisherman.

"I am the daughter of Oribe Shima, the great Samurai lord," she said. "I've come a very long way in search of my father. Can you tell me where he is?"

"I can't help you," replied the fisherman. "I don't know your father, and you'd do well to stop asking so many questions about him. It will only get you into trouble."

So Tokoyo was forced to wander from place to place, across the island, and back again. By now, all her money was gone, and she was forced to beg for food. One evening, she came upon a little shrine, perched on a rock a little way offshore. After swimming out to the shrine, and bowing before the image of the Buddha, she prayed to him and asked him for help in her search. Then, exhausted, she lay down and fell sound asleep, right in that holy place.

Sometime during the night, Tokoyo was woken up by the curious sound of clapping, and someone crying. By the moonlight, she saw an old monk clapping his hands while chanting a prayer, and a young girl sobbing. Both were dressed in flowing white robes. When the prayer was over, the monk stopped clapping and led the girl to the edge of the rocks. He was about to push her off the rock and into the sea when Tokoyo jumped up, rushed over, and grabbed the girl's arm—just in time to save her life. The old monk looked at her in surprise.

"It seems that you are a newcomer to this island." He sighed, sadly. "Otherwise, you would understand why I have to do this terrible deed. Our island is cursed by an evil spirit, a serpent called Yofune-Nushi. He lives down there, at the very bottom of the sea. Every year on this day, he demands that we throw a young girl into the water as a sacrifice to him. If we neglect to do this, he sends great storms, and our crops fail, and our fishermen drown, and our people starve for the rest of the year. So, you see, giving this one life saves many others."

Tokoyo had been listening carefully and thinking hard.

"Holy monk," she said, "I understand now, and I am sorry for you all. Let this girl go, and let me take her place. I am the daughter of the great Samurai lord Oribe Shima, who has been exiled to this island. I came here to search for him, but I cannot find him

anywhere and my heart is broken. I have nothing left to stay here for. All I ask in return is that you take this letter to my father."

With this, brave Tokoyo kneeled in front of the shrine and prayed to Buddha for courage and strength. For, she did not simply intend to become a sacrifice, but to kill the evil serpent and rid the island of his menace once and for all. Then she pulled a small pearl-handled dagger from her waistband. It had belonged to her father, and his father before him, and was the last thing of value that she owned. Holding it in her teeth, like a pearl diver, she jumped into the sea and vanished from view.

Down and down Tokoyo swam through the clear water, cutting through like a fish until she reached the bottom. There, she found herself in front of a cave glittering with pearls and seashells. As she peered into the darkness, she could just see a man standing inside. Fearing nothing, she swam farther in, holding her dagger ready to strike. Still, the figure did not move, and Tokoyo realized that it wasn't a man after all, but a wooden statue of the emperor who had banished her father.

At first, Tokoyo was angry. She raised her dagger, intending to take her revenge out on the statue, but what good would that do?

No, she thought, *rather than destroying the statue, I shall repay evil with good and rescue it instead.*

So she untied the sash of her robe and wound it around the waterlogged statue. Then she tied it to her back, and began to swim strongly out of the cave. Just as she reached the entrance, a terrible sight met her eyes—a hideous, yellow-eyed monster, with the body of a snake, sharp claws, and glowing scales along its back. It could only be the evil Yofune-Nushi, ready to devour the girl who was his due.

Slowly, the monster slithered toward her, and Tokoyo braced herself for the attack. As it lunged at her, with its enormous jaws agape, she swiped with her dagger and put out the creature's right eye. Writhing in agony, the monster tried to reach the safety of his cave, but blinded by the loss of his eye, he could not find his way back. Tokoyo took full advantage, swiftly stabbing him in the heart, and with a last tormented gasp, Yofune-Nushi died.

Tokoyo was delighted that the monster was dead and the island was safe again. With the very last of her breath, she tied the other end of her sash around the monster's neck, and towed him up to the surface. Standing on the cliff edge, the monk and girl were astonished to see a figure struggling to rise from the rushing waves.

"Why, it's Tokoyo," the girl cried. "The girl who took my place. I recognize her robe. But she seems to have a man and a giant snake with her."

By this time, the monk had rushed down to the shore and was pulling an exhausted Tokoyo out of the water.

Soon, the whole island heard the news—Yofune-Nushi was dead! Now the celebrations could begin. The emperor's statue and the monster's hideous head were brought into town, and Tokoyo was given a hero's welcome. A report was dispatched to Emperor Hojo Takatoki himself, telling him of Tokoyo's death-defying feat. On hearing this, the emperor, who had been suffering from a strange illness, suddenly found that he was cured.

"A curse was put on your statue before it was thrown into the sea," one of his wisest advisers told him. "Now that the statue is found, the curse is lifted, and we have Tokoyo to thank for that, too."

"And who is this Tokoyo?" asked the emperor. "I owe her a great deal."

"The daughter of Oribe Shima," came the reply.

"Oribe Shima?" the emperor smiled. "Then he must be released at once."

And so, thanks to Tokoyo's daring and courage, she and her father were reunited. Both were overjoyed to see each other again. They returned to their home with the emperor's blessing, and with very generous rewards of treasure and land. And they were never apart again.

How Little Molly Whuppie Outwitted the Giant

Along time ago, in England, there lived a man called Mr. Whuppie and his wife, Mrs. Whuppie, who had too many children to feed. So they took their three youngest girls, Katy, Jane, and Molly, and left them all alone in a deep, dark wood.

Holding hands, the three little girls wandered here and there, hoping to find their way home, but soon were hopelessly lost. They were frightened and hungry, and it was getting dark. Just then they spotted a light shining through the tangle of trees.

"Look over there," said Molly Whuppie, who was the youngest, but was as brave as a lion. "It must be a house. Perhaps they'll give us a bed for the night, and some food." So they knocked on the door and were amazed when it was opened by a woman who was enormously tall and enormously wide.

"What do you want?" she asked, peering down at them.

"We're lost and hungry," Molly replied. "Can we come in and have a bite to eat?"

"I wouldn't dare," said the woman. "My husband's a giant, and he'll kill you and eat you all up if he finds you here."

"Please," begged Molly. "We're so hungry. Let us stay for a while. We'll go before your husband comes home."

The giant's wife took the girls in, and they'd just sat down by the fire with some bread and milk, when the giant crashed through the door. He was so tall that his head scraped the ceiling, and his hands and feet were as big as shovels.

"Fee, fie, fo, fum," boomed the giant, "I smell the blood of some earthly ones! So, wife, who have we got here?"

"Oh, just some wee lassies," his wife replied. "They'll be gone once they've finished their snack."

The giant gave a great big gap-toothed grin. Then he slumped down in his chair and ate a huge supper—enough for twenty usual-sized men. Afterwards, he belched loudly and stared at the three terrified girls.

"You poor things," he growled. "You look frightened and exhausted. Stay a few days, I insist. I'm a great baker, and I'll bake you something nice tomorrow."

The giant's wife led them up some wooden stairs to a dusty attic, where there was a great wooden bed.

"Sleep tight," she cackled as they climbed in.

Then she stomped back downstairs.

Although they were very scared, they were really very tired, and soon, all the girls were sound asleep, except for Molly Whuppie. She guessed that the giant was up to mischief, and, quiet as a mouse, she slipped out of bed. She overheard him in the kitchen downstairs, chuckling as he sharpened his carving knife.

"He means to eat us after all!" Molly whispered to herself. She knew that there was no time to lose, and woke her sisters up. They had to escape before the giant came back upstairs. Molly thought quickly. If she could just distract him and lead him away from the stairs and the front door, they might have a chance.

Clever Molly took one of her shoes and hurled it out of the attic window so it landed with a thump outside. She heard the giant muttering that there might be a tasty deer out there. He stomped round to the back of the house to look.

Hand in hand, Molly and her sisters crept downstairs and out the front door, then ran and ran through the woods. They found a curious bridge made of a single hair, but decided to cross farther downstream. By morning, they'd reached a fine-looking house, which turned out to belong to the king.

"We can't go in there," Katy said. "We haven't even brushed our hair and you only have one shoe."

However, Molly had other ideas. Without even stopping to knock on the door, she walked straight in and told the king their sad tale.

"Well, well, well, little Molly Whuppie," the king said at last. "You're a very brave girl, no doubt. But this particular giant has been hurting my people for years, and I think you could do even better. Go back and steal the great sword that hangs above the giant's bed. If you do this, he'll be less of a danger to the people, and I'll give your eldest sister, Katy, anything that is within my power to grant."

"I'll certainly try," replied Molly Whuppie, bravely.

The next day, wearing new boots given to her by the queen, Molly traced her footsteps back to the giant's house, and, while the giant was out hunting and his wife wasn't looking, she hid under their enormous bed. She waited and waited without making a sound, until the giant and his wife had eaten their supper, and were asleep, snoring loudly. Then she crept out, stood silently on the bed, and reached over the giant. Just as she grabbed the sword, it clattered against the headboard, and woke the giant up. Molly ran as fast as she could, until she reached the bridge made of just

one hair. She was so light that she could run straight across, but the giant was too heavy to follow. Left behind, he shrieked with rage, and shook his plate-sized fists.

Molly gave the giant's sword to the king. Katy declared her wish for the hand in marriage of the king's eldest son, whom she had been getting to know while Molly was stealing the sword. Katy and the king's eldest son were soon happily married, but the king hadn't finished with Molly yet.

"Well, well, well, little Molly Whuppie," he said with a big smile. "You've done very well, but you can do even better. Go back and steal the magic coin purse that the giant keeps under his pillow. If you do this, your middle sister, Jane, can marry my middle son if she wants to."

"I'll certainly try," replied Molly Whuppie, and off she went.

Once again, she crept back into the giant's house and hid until the giant and his wife went to bed. Then she slipped her hand under the giant's pillow. Just as she snatched the purse, the coins inside clinked and woke the giant up. Once again, Molly ran as fast as she could, until she reached the bridge of hair. And, once again, she skipped across, while the giant stood shaking his fists.

Molly gave the purse to the king. Shortly afterward, Jane and the king's middle son were married. The king had one final task for Molly.

"Well, well, well, little Molly Whuppie," he said, "you have done very well, but you can do even better. Go back and steal the gold ring that the giant wears on his finger. If you do this, you can marry my youngest son."

"I'll certainly try," replied Molly Whuppie, ready for her toughest test yet.

Back Molly went to the giant's house, and hid under the bed, until the giant and his wife were snoring. Then she picked up the giant's hand, and, as gently as she could, pulled and pulled until she got the ring off. Just as she slipped it onto her wrist, the giant woke up and grabbed her hand.

"Got you at last, Molly Whuppie," he raged, "and this time, you won't get away. I baked you some delicious cakes, but you rudely ran away without even trying them, and then you stole my sword and purse. Now, what will your punishment be?"

"If it were up to me," Molly said quickly, "I'd put you in a sack with a cat and a dog. I'd add a needle, thread, and scissors, and hang the sack on the wall. Then I'd go into the woods and find a big stick and beat the sack to teach you a lesson!"

"An excellent plan, young Molly." The giant smirked. "Then, that's exactly what I'll do to you!"

So the giant fetched a sack and put Molly inside with a cat, a dog, a needle, thread, and scissors. Then he hung the sack on the wall. Leaving his wife to guard it with her life, he set off into the woods.

"Oh, what an amazing sight," cried Molly, from inside the sack.

"Why, what is it?" asked the giant's wife.

"The most beautiful thing I have ever seen," said Molly.

"I want to see it too," begged the giant's wife.

"But you'd have to be in the sack with me," replied Molly.

"I daren't take the sack down," groaned the giant's wife.

"Then I'll help you up into it," sang Molly.

Molly took out the scissors and cut a hole in the sack, only just big enough for her to squeeze through. Then she jumped out, holding the needle and thread. Molly helped the giant's wife up into the sack, then sewed the hole behind her until it was closed.

From inside the sack, Molly could hear the wife complaining that she couldn't see anything. Molly took no notice, and hid behind the door. Before long, the giant came home, a great tree trunk in his hand. He took the sack down from the wall and began to beat it.

"Stop! Stop! You fool!" his wife, cried. "It's me, your wife! It's me inside!"

46

However, over the loud sounds of the cat's meows and the dog's howls, the giant couldn't hear what she said. It was only when he spied Molly running out the door that he stopped beating the sack. He chased after Molly, once again, until she reached the bridge of hair. And again, she leapt across, light as a feather, stranding the giant on the other side.

"You stole my sword, purse, and ring," he raged. "And now you tricked me into beating my wife. Woe betide you, Molly Whuppie, if you ever come anywhere near here again."

"Don't worry," laughed Molly. "I'm never coming back."

Then she took the ring to the king.

"I'm sure your son is very nice, but I don't think I want to be anyone's wife," she told him. "However, I would like a job."

The king made her his new Explorer in Chief. Molly Whuppie roamed the vast kingdom for the rest of her days, defeating monsters and discovering all sorts of new things and interesting treasure to bring back to the king. She never saw the giant again, but stories of her cleverness and courage were still being told for many years to come.

How **Mizilca** **Tricked** a **Sultan**
and Saved Her Father from Disgrace

In Romania, long ago, there lived an old knight who was also a master of magic and sorcery. One day, a messenger arrived at his castle, sent by the sultan. The sultan was gathering an army for his latest war, and demanded every knight in his kingdom to serve him for a year and a day. Failing that, each knight must send a son in his stead—otherwise they would be disgraced and put to death.

The old and noble knight was too frail to go himself, but he had no sons to send. His three beautiful daughters were his pride and joy, but girls weren't allowed to fight. In despair, the knight stopped eating or smiling, even when his daughters were around. He took to his bed, sighing deeply and shaking his head.

His eldest daughter, Stanuta, came to him.

"Dear Father, whatever is the matter?" she asked gently. "Are you ill? Or have we done something wrong?"

"No, no, my child," the knight replied sadly. "It's not your fault, and I'm not ill."

He told her about the sultan's request, asking her to keep it a secret from her sisters.

"Don't worry, Father," Stanuta smiled. "I am tall and strong. If I dress like a man and cut my hair short, I can be your son! I'll ride by the sultan's side, and no one will know the difference."

The old knight was horrified at the thought of his daughter setting off for the sultan's court. Headstrong Stanuta would not change her mind, so he decided to use his magic to dissuade her. Stanuta had her long hair cut off, and her father gave her the finest horse from his stables, his sturdiest shield, and his trustiest sword, and watched her ride away. Then, ignoring his many aches and pains, he jumped on to his own horse and galloped across the fields until he came to a bridge at the boundary of his lands. There, he used his magic to turn himself into a blue boar, and hid in the woods beside the river.

Soon, Stanuta came riding up and had almost reached the bridge when the boar charged straight at her, snorting smoke through his nostrils. Stanuta screamed in terror and pulled on the reins to turn her horse around. She galloped back to the castle.

Next, the knight's second daughter, Roxanda, came to see her father.

"Dear Father, we're so worried about you," she said softly. "You still seem so very sad. Whatever is the matter?" Her father told her about his dilemma, and, like her sister, she begged to go to the sultan's palace, disguised as a boy.

"Please, Father," she pleaded. "I'll ride straight to the palace, and I won't let any boars get in my way." Roxanda immediately cut off her long hair, and her father gave her his second-best horse, his second-best sword, and a dented old shield. Then she set off down the road. And, as she did so, her father jumped up from his sickbed, mounted his horse, and galloped off, across the fields, until he came to the bridge. There, he used his magic to turn himself into a red lion, and hid among the trees.

When Roxanda reached the bridge, the lion leapt out at her with a bloodcurdling roar. Terrified, Roxanda gave a loud scream and pulled on the reins to turn her horse around. Then she galloped home as fast as she could.

The old knight's youngest daughter, Mizilca, was the bravest of the three sisters. She went to her father and asked for his permission to ride off to serve the sultan.

"Dearest Mizilca," her father replied fondly. "I cannot allow you to go. Your sisters are older and stronger than you, and they have failed. How do you hope to succeed? Stay at home and keep me company in my old age." Mizilca was not ready to give up. She knew that her father doted on her, and that, eventually, she would get her own way.

"Father, please let me go," she begged. "Boars and lions don't frighten me."

"I absolutely forbid it," grumbled her father.

Mizilca kept begging and pleading, until he couldn't stand it any longer. He agreed to let her go, but he only gave her his rustiest sword, his oldest lance, a battered shield, and an ancient horse that hadn't been ridden in years. Mizilca was too excited to care. She cut her long hair, put on her boyish disguise, and prepared to set out. As she left the castle, her father was already on his way. He raced across the fields and reached the bridge, where he used his magic to turn into a green dragon. Then he hid in the woods and lay in wait for her.

Before long, Mizilca came riding by the bridge, and at once, the dragon rushed at her, breathing out great clouds of fire. Mizilca was not like her sisters. She didn't panic or turn her horse around. She galloped straight at the dragon, holding her sword, ready to fight. Before she could strike a blow, the dragon turned on its heels, and fled. The old knight was very relieved to get back to the castle in one piece that day.

Instead of going after the dragon, Mizilca crossed the bridge and rode, not stopping until she reached the sultan's palace.

There, she approached the sultan and bowed low.

"Your Majesty," she said, "I am the old knight's son, and have come to pay my father's debt to you."

The sultan looked her up and down. He thought she looked like a girl dressed as a boy, but he couldn't be sure about it. So he welcomed her warmly into his band of knights.

As the weeks passed, Mizilca proved that she could ride and shoot a bow just as well as any of the sultan's knights. Yet still, the sultan had his doubts. So, he went to see an old wise woman and asked her advice on finding out if Mizilca were a girl or a boy.

"That's easy," cackled the wise woman. "While this knight is out hunting, have merchants come to the palace. Tell them to set up their stalls in the great hall. On one side, they should lay out their finest clothes and embroideries. On the other side, they should lay out their finest daggers and swords. If the knight is a girl, she'll choose the pretty clothes. If he's a boy, he'll go for the weapons."

The sultan wasn't so sure. But he did as the wise woman said, and summoned merchants to set out their wares. Mizilca had never really been particularly interested in fashion, though, so she walked past the fine clothes and went straight to the weapons.

Still, the sultan was not convinced, and went to see the wise woman again.

"Have your cook make some buckwheat porridge," she told him. "Then mix in some pearls. If the knight is a girl, she'll pick out the pearls and save them. If he's a boy, he'll throw them away."

However, the wise woman was wrong. Mizilca, like lots of other girls, had never

developed a taste for precious stones and jewels. She took her bowl of porridge, picked out the pearls, then tossed them under the table as if they were worthless stones.

The sultan paid one final visit to the wise woman, for he still was not certain.

"Scatter flowers all over the floor of the great hall, and call your knights in," she said. "If the knight is a girl, she'll step lightly over the flowers, or pick them up and make a bouquet. If he's a boy, he'll stamp on them and squash them."

Again, the sultan did as the wise woman advised. However, Mizilca was reading a particularly good book on the way to dinner and she didn't even notice the beautiful flowers as she crushed them underfoot.

At last, a year and a day had passed, and it was time for Mizilca to head home. She took her leave of her fellow knights, and mounted her old horse. The sultan himself came out to say farewell.

"You have served me well," he said to her. "Your father should be proud of you, and his debt is paid. But before you go, I have one last question—are you a boy or a girl?"

"Mighty sultan," she replied respectfully, "does it really matter? I served you as well as any of the boys, did I not?"

"But," pleaded the sultan, "if you are a woman, then how did you pass all my tests?"

Mizilca hadn't even realized the sultan had been testing her! She asked him what the tests were. When the sultan told her, she burst out laughing. She laughed and laughed until tears of joy streamed down her face. She laughed so hard that her hat fell off, and her long hair, by now grown back, tumbled over her shoulders.

"You old-fashioned fool. Haven't you realized?" said Mizilca. "Women are no more alike than men—and a great many of your male knights love fine clothes and pearls too!"

Then, spurring on her horse, Mizilca galloped off toward her father's castle, where a sumptuous feast had been prepared. And, from that day on, every knight in the land showed Mizilca, and all women, the greatest respect.

Tatterhood
and Dacia

Along, long time ago, in Norway, there lived a king and a queen who had no children, and this made them both very sad. The queen often complained to her husband how lonely and dull life was in the palace without any children running around. In despair, the king suggested that they invite their two little nieces to stay. And soon the palace rang with laughter, and the queen smiled, at last.

One day, the queen was watching her nieces in the palace courtyard, playing and picking flowers together. Just then, a beggar woman came by, with a little girl dressed in rags. The little girl began playing with the queen's nieces.

"You shouldn't be playing with my nieces," the furious queen cried. "Now shoo, whoever you are."

"You wouldn't say that if you knew about my mother's magic powers," the beggar girl said.

"And what powers might those be?" asked the queen, scornfully.

"She can help people to have children," said the beggar girl.

"Tell your mother that I want to speak to her," the queen said. "Now!"

So the girl fetched her mother, who was selling eggs at the palace door.

"Your daughter tells me that you have special powers," the queen said. "And that you could tell me how to have children of my own."

"Well," said the woman. "I could do that. But it'll cost you, and I'll want payment in gold."

The queen counted out five gold coins.

"That'll do nicely," said the woman, rubbing her hands. "Now, I do know a spell that might help you. But you must follow the instructions carefully."

"Yes, yes," said the queen, nodding eagerly.

"Before you go to bed," continued the woman, "have your servants bring two pails of water. Wash yourself in each, then pour the water away under your bed. When you look under the bed in the morning, you'll see two flowers—one red and lovely; the other brown and like a weed. Eat the red flower and leave the brown one be."

The queen did exactly as she was told, and by the next morning, two flowers had bloomed. The queen ate the red flower. It tasted so sweet that she couldn't stop herself and she ate the brown one as well.

Not long afterward, the queen found that she was pregnant with twins, and soon enough, it was time for her babies to be born. The first baby was a strange-looking little girl holding a wooden spoon, and riding a goat. As soon as she was born, the child started bawling, "Mama! Mama!"

"If I'm your mama," said the queen, "I pray to God to help me mend my ways."

"Oh, don't worry," the little girl piped up. "There's another one coming after me— you'll like her much better!"

Sure enough, the second baby was also a girl, but this time, she was pretty and sweet, like a proper princess.

The sisters were as different as night and day. The younger twin was polite and gentle, while her older sister was loud and clumsy. Her mother named her firstborn

Tatterhood, after the ragged clothes she wore, and she called her secondborn Dacia. The sisters loved each other dearly, and were never apart.

One Christmas Eve, when the twins were about nineteen, a terrible crashing and banging broke out in the corridor outside the queen's sitting room.

"What's all that noise?" asked Tatterhood.

"Oh, it's nothing," replied the queen. "Don't worry about it."

However, Tatterhood kept asking, until the queen gave in.

"It's a pack of trolls," she said, angrily. "Every few years, they turn up and cause mischief. It's always at Christmas, but there's nothing we can do about it. "

"Nonsense!" replied Tatterhood. "I'll get rid of them."

"You'll leave them well alone," cried the queen. "They're dangerous little beasts."

"I'm not afraid of a few pesky trolls," replied Tatterhood, hopping on to her goat and brandishing her wooden spoon.

She told the queen to keep all the doors tightly shut, then set off to face the trolls. She whacked them so hard with her wooden spoon that they turned around and ran away.

Just then Dacia opened a door the tiniest bit, and peeked out to see how things were going. And, POP!, up jumped an old troll, and cut off the princess's head. In its place, the troll stuck a cat's head on her shoulders, and she ran back into the queen's sitting room on all fours, meowing pitifully.

"I've got no choice," Tatterhood fumed when she came back. "I'll have to go and get her head back."

Tatterhood stormed off to her father's office and asked for a good boat, and supplies for a long voyage. Then, she headed off for the land of the trolls, taking her unfortunate sister with her.

Under Tatterhood's expert command, and with a fair wind, they quickly reached the land of the trolls. Then, leaving Dacia on board, Tatterhood rode her goat to the trolls' house. One of the windows was open, and through it, Tatterhood spied Dacia's head, hanging on the wall. Still on her goat, she leapt through the window, grabbed the head, and galloped back to the boat. A shrieking pack of trolls came after her, swarming around her like angry bees. But the goat butted them with its sharp, pointed horns, and Tatterhood bashed them with her wooden spoon, until the trolls were forced to give up. Once she was safely in the boat, Tatterhood put Dacia's head back in place, so that she went back to being a girl.

Rather than sailing straight home, the sisters decided to explore the world together. One day, they reached a beautiful kingdom. When the king and his two sons saw the strange boat, they wondered who it belonged to. The king's eldest son hurried down to greet the strangers. As soon as he saw Dacia, he fell in love with her.

"Will you marry me?" he asked the princess.

"Only if my sister is getting married too. I won't leave her by herself," Dacia replied.

The prince looked at Tatterhood. He thought she looked wild and dirty. Who would want to marry her? He thought quickly and invited the sisters to the castle for a feast. Then he spent the rest of the day begging his younger brother to look after Tatterhood. The younger prince also thought Tatterhood looked grimy and the last thing he wanted to do was marry her, but he agreed to give her a chance, for his brother's sake.

Back on board the ship, Dacia put on a new dress and brushed her hair until it shone.

"Why don't you borrow one my dresses?" she asked her sister, but Tatterhood refused to change out of her rags.

"No, thanks," she replied. "I'll go as I am."

The king sent his sons to accompany the princesses, as well as a pair of fine white horses for the sisters to ride. While Dacia rode beside the elder prince, looking splendid, Tatterhood followed, next to the younger prince, on her faithful old goat.

"You don't say much," said Tatterhood.

"What is there to talk about?" replied the prince, glumly. "Unless," he added, quickly, "it's to ask you why you ride that ugly goat."

"Is it an ugly goat," answered Tatterhood, "or the finest horse you ever saw?"

At once, the goat turned into a magnificent horse.

"I see," said the prince, astonished. "Well, why do you carry that wooden spoon? What on earth is it good for?"

"Is it really a wooden spoon," replied Tatterhood, "or a magic wand?" At once, the wooden spoon turned into a ruby-tipped magic wand. The prince was even more surprised.

"One final question," he said. "Why do you wear that ragged hood instead of fine clothes like your sister?"

"Is it really a ragged hood," came the response, "or a golden crown?"

At once, the ragged hood turned into a glittering crown of gold and pearls.

For a while, they rode on in silence, until, at last, Tatterhood spoke.

"Aren't you going to ask me why my clothes are covered in mud and soot?" she said.

"No," replied the prince, smiling. "You have chosen to wear them, and that's good enough for me. If you wish to change them, you can, but I don't want you to be anyone except yourself."

At once, Tatterhood's muddy clothes turned into a grand silver gown, with no sign of mud or soot anywhere.

Dacia turned around and gasped. "Tatterhood, why have you changed?"

Tatterhood smiled at her. "I've always been this way, but you're the only one who's always loved me just as I am."

The younger prince was so entranced that he proposed marriage right away, but Tatterhood gently turned him down. "The man who truly loves me would love me when I am riding a goat with tattered clothes, for looks are the least important part of me."

With that, she bade her beloved sister and the princes farewell and rode away to have another adventure.

Princess **Imani** and the **Magic Fan**

Long ago, there lived a king in India called King Girish. He had two daughters, called Kupti and Imani. "Daughter," he asked Kupti one day. "Do you trust me with your life and fortune?"

"Of course I do, Father," replied the princess. The king then asked his younger daughter, Imani, the same question, but he got a different reply.

"No, Father," she cried. "I'd like to make my own way in the world."

"Hmm," said King Girish with a frown. "We'll have to see about that." Determined to teach her a lesson, the king sent for a poor, old holy man who lived in a tumbledown shack.

"My younger daughter wants to make her own way in life," King Girish told him. "You are old and frail and can hardly walk. I'm sure you'd be glad of some help. So I'm sending my daughter to look after you."

Before too long, the princess and the holy man reached the shack where he lived. It was hardly a suitable home for a princess, but Imani had a plan.

"Do you have any money at all?" she asked the holy man.

"A penny," he replied.

"Give it to me," said the princess. "Then go and see if you can borrow a loom and spinning wheel."

The holy man hobbled off into the village, while Imani headed to market to buy oil and rough flax yarn. Back home, she rubbed the oil onto the old man's troublesome leg. Then she sat at the spinning wheel and spun the finest thread ever seen. Next, she sat at the loom and wove the thread into the finest cloth.

"Take this cloth to market," she told the holy man. "And sell it for two gold coins, nothing less."

At the market, Princess Kupti came by, and spotted the beautiful cloth. She happily paid two gold coins for it, and the holy man headed home again.

Every day after that, Imani bought oil to treat the holy man's leg, and wove cloth for market. Slowly, the old man's leg got better, and her cloth became famous. They repaid the kindly woman who had lent them the loom and the spinning wheel, and they bought a sturdy new set for themselves. Imani discovered she was very talented at designing pretty new patterns in cloth that proved even more popular at the market, and soon the hole in the floor where they kept their money was overflowing with gold coins.

"We have enough to build a new house," said the princess, and she sent for the builders, who built one of the finest houses in the kingdom. And when King Girish asked who owned such a house, he was told that it was his daughter's.

"Well, well," exclaimed the king. "She's done it—she's made her own fortune."

A few months later, King Girish had to make a journey to the faraway kingdom of Dur. Before he left, he asked Princess Kupti what she'd like him to bring as a gift.

"A ruby necklace!" she answered.

King Girish sent a messenger to ask Imani, who was busy untangling a knot on her loom. When the man asked her what gift she wanted, she replied, "Patience!" Now, she meant that he should wait until she had finished, but the messenger took this as her answer and hurried back to the king.

"Patience?" said King Girish, puzzled. "I don't know where I'm going to buy that."

The next day, the king left on his travels. His business done, he bought a ruby necklace for Kupti, then sent his servant to market to find some patience for sale. The stallholders laughed at the servant, and told him to stop being such a fool.

Soon, word of the servant's curious request reached the ears of the young king of Dur. He sent for the servant, and listened to his story.

"If it's patience the princess wants," the king said with a smile, "I know where there is some, but it's not for sale."

Now, the king of Dur's name was Subbar Khan, and Subbar means "patience," but the servant did not get the joke. Desperately, he began telling the king how clever, talented, and hardworking Princess Imani was, in the hope that he would change his mind and give him some patience to take to King Girish.

"Enough, enough!" laughed King Subbar Khan. "I'll see what I can do."

With that, he fetched a golden casket that contained a fine feather fan.

"This casket has no lock or key," the king said. "It can only be opened by the person who truly needs what's inside. That person will receive the gift of patience, though it may not be the sort of patience they were expecting."

Delighted, the servant took the casket, and tried to pay for it, but King Subbar Khan would take no money.

When Kupti and Imani's father returned home, he sent his messenger to take the casket to Imani.

"What's this?" said Imani, in surprise. "I didn't ask for anything."

However, she took the casket and showed it to the old holy man who tried his best to open it. Then he handed it back to the princess, and at her touch, the lid sprang open immediately. Inside lay the fan. Imani took it out and began to fan herself with it.

After three strokes, a figure appeared out of nowhere—King Subbar Khan of Dur!

"And who may you be, sir?" asked the old man.

"King Subbar Khan of Dur," the king replied. "The princess has summoned me."

"I haven't summoned you," cried Imani. "I've never seen you before in my life."

The king explained how the messenger had come to buy patience, and how the king had given him the casket and fan.

"The fan has magical powers," he explained. "With three strokes, you can summon me. Then, with three taps on the table, you can send me home again."

Princess Imani wanted to send the king home there and then, but the holy man was delighted to have such a guest, especially one who was good at chess. The king and Imani had lots of long talks, and they both learned a great deal from each other. Imani found herself summoning the king more and more often, until eventually she gave him his own room in their house.

When Princess Kupti heard about the handsome and clever young king that had been visiting her sister, she was jealous. She went to see Imani, pretending that she wanted to look around her new house. Later, she slipped secretly into Subbar Khan's room, and scattered poisoned splinters of glass under his bedsheets. Then she went home as if nothing had happened.

That evening, Subbar Khan was summoned as usual, and they played chess and talked late into the night, when he headed to bed. As soon as he lay down, the thousands of tiny splinters of glass pricked him all over, and he began burning from head to foot. In the morning, he still felt terribly sick. However, he said nothing, and waited until Imani tapped the fan to transport him home. All the best doctors in the kingdom were sent for, but none could work out what was wrong. For weeks, he grew worse and worse, until, eventually, he lay close to death.

Meanwhile, Imani and the holy man were worried. However often they waved the magic fan, Subbar Khan never appeared. The princess could stand it no longer and decided to go to Dur herself disguised as a young holy man. One evening, she came to a dense forest and lay down under a large tree to sleep. She found sleep was hard to come by, and she lay awake, listening to two monkeys chattering in the tree.

"Good evening, friend," said one of the monkeys. "Where are you from, and what news do you bring?"

"I come from Dur," replied the other. "And the news is bad—our king is dying. Word is that he was poisoned by splintered glass."

"It's a shame his doctors don't know about a bath potion made from the berries of this very tree," said the first monkey. "Mixed with hot water, it would cure him in three days, at most."

Imani waited until it was morning, then gathered up the berries from the tree and walked as fast as she could to the market in the city of Dur.

"Medicine for sale!" she cried. "Cures anything, or your money back."

"I wonder if it could help the king?" one man said.

"It's worth a try," replied his friend.

They took her to the palace and announced that a new doctor had come to try to cure the king.

When Imani saw the king she was shocked at how thin and pale he had grown. She quickly prepared the potion and gave it to the king's attendants, instructing them to bathe the king with it. To everyone's astonishment, it worked so well that the king had his first good night's sleep in weeks. The next day, the king asked for something to eat. By the third day, he was well but weak; and by the fourth, he was up and sitting on his throne.

"Bring the doctor to me," he told his servant. "I want to thank him for saving my life."

When Imani appeared, the king didn't recognize her and was astonished that such a young man could be so talented. He tried to reward the doctor with money and precious jewels, but all the doctor would take was the king's signet ring and a pretty silk scarf.

Back home, Imani told the holy man what had happened, then waved her fan and summoned Subbar Khan. He explained about his illness and why he had stayed away so long, full of praise for the brilliant young doctor who had finally cured him.

At that, the princess opened a cupboard and took out the ring and scarf.

"Are these the rewards you gave to the doctor?" she said, with a smile.

"They are indeed," the king replied, in surprise.

Then, understanding all that had happened, the king asked Imani and the holy man to move to Dur. Imani could train to at the Royal University to be his royal doctor, and he and the holy man could play chess every night. They agreed and lived happily ever after.

Maada and the Mountain Dweller

On an island off the coast of Canada, there lived a princess of the Haida people, the daughter of the village chief. Her name was Maada, and she was proud and spirited. Too spirited, some thought. Her parents wanted Maada to get married and settle down, but Maada had other ideas. She loved being free to run barefoot along the beach, and roam the mountain trails. Suitors came regularly to the village to ask for her hand, but Maada turned them all down.

Now, Maada's grandmother was the keeper of a special box filled with dried herring roe on kelp, which the Haida call k'aaw and consider a great delicacy. She was supposed to keep the k'aaw for visitors, but she had a soft spot for her granddaughters, and she was always slipping slivers to Maada and her little sister Kilsa, then pretending that one of the dogs had eaten them. One day, she'd just fed the girls the last delicious morsels of that year's roe, when news came that another suitor and his family had arrived on the shore, by way of a beautifully painted canoe.

Maada's father sent his men to take the visitors to his handsome cedar wood house. Then, dressed in his finest robes, he ordered the traditional Dance of Peace and Welcome

to be performed. His wife went to fetch some k'aaw for his guests to chew on, until the proper feast was ready. When she asked for the k'aaw, the grandmother told her that the last of it had gone.

"The dog ate it," the grandmother said, as usual.

"Really?" said the chief's wife, suspiciously, eyeing her two daughters, who were sitting nearby. "Have you two seen anything?"

Maada and her sister couldn't answer—their mouths were too full.

"Open your mouth!" their mother shouted at Maada, and saw the k'aaw inside.

"Such a greedy girl!" she raged. "You may as well marry the horrible old Mountain Dweller—his house is always crammed with food."

Maada was angry and hurt by her mother's harsh words. That night, when she went to bed, she whispered to her sister.

"I'm going to marry Mountain Dweller," she said. "At least he lives far away from our mean mother and all these annoying suitors."

"If you're going, I'm coming with you," said Kilsa.

So the sisters laid long wooden dishes in their beds, covered in fur robes to look as though they were tucked up in bed. Then they crept out of the cedar house and into the dark woods. When the girls did not appear the next morning, their mother went to wake them.

"Get up," she said as she shook one of the piles of furs. "Our guests are starting to wonder where you two are."

She pulled one fur cover back, then the other … only to find that the beds were empty. The princesses had run away. At once, a group of hunters was sent in search of them, but the sisters managed to hide up a tree, and stay out of their way. Then, when the hunters had moved on, Maada set off up the mountain at breakneck speed.

"I'm famished," her little sister said.

"There'll be plenty to eat when we get there," replied Maada.

Tired and hungry, the girls carried on up the steep slope. Before long, they came across a little mouse trying to get onto a big tree stump.

"Poor little mouse," said Kilsa, wearily.

"There you go," said Maada, gently lifting it up onto the stump.

Just then they heard a small, squeaky voice.

"Come in, come in," the voice said. "Welcome to my humble home."

The girls noticed a tiny house, lavishly decorated with intricate carvings.

"Mouse Woman!" the little princess squealed in delight, for Mouse Woman was famous. She was known for her great wisdom and for being a guide to wayfarers.

"You helped me," said Mouse Woman. "Now it's my turn to help you."

She gave them cranberries and roasted salmon to eat.

"Now, my dears," she asked. "What brings you to the mountain?"

"My mother said I should marry Mountain Dweller," Maada replied, blinking back tears. "Because she thinks I'm greedy, but I'm not. I'm going to get away from her."

"I'll take you to Mountain Dweller," squeaked Mouse Woman, nose twitching. "But be warned. His house is guarded by terrible beings."

"Terrible beings?" wailed the little princess. "I want to go home."

Maada had no intention of turning back now.

"Mouse Woman, please tell me of the dangers," she said, much more bravely than she felt inside.

"I will tell you about three of the dangers," Mouse Woman replied. "And give you the magic to overcome them. But I'm afraid I can't tell you about the fourth—you'll have to deal with that by yourself."

Mouse Woman told Maada about the hunting dogs, floating waterweed, and crushing rocks that guarded Mountain Dweller's house. Then she gave Maada three gifts—a magic knife, a knife-sharpening stone, and a magic fish—which Maada put safely in the pouch at her waist.

Just after sunrise the next morning, Maada boldly headed out along the trail, with Kilsa following behind. Before long, two snarling hunting dogs rushed at them, ready to pounce. Maada threw the magic fish at them, and they quickly gobbled it down. Immediately, they turned into playful puppies, chasing each other's tails, and the girls were able to slip straight past them.

Soon, they reached a mountain lake that was completely smothered with long, green strands of tangled waterweed. A canoe was waiting for them, next to a tree covered in thick moss. Using her magic knife, Maada cut off a large clump of moss and tucked it in her boot. As they paddled across the lake, the strands of waterweed began to close in from both sides, threatening to capsize the canoe. Maada tossed the moss into the water, and, at once, the strands moved aside to let the canoe pass.

They weren't out of danger just yet. On the other side of the lake rose the crushing rocks, ready to crash shut if they tried to pass through. As the rocks began to move, Maada hurled the magic knife-sharpening stone into the gap. At once, the rocks shrank back on either side, and the girls raced safely through.

They found themselves in a flower-filled valley, where Mountain Dweller's splendid wooden house stood. Just then a young man appeared from the trees. He was dressed in fine skins and furs, and carrying a hunting bow.

"Welcome, princesses," he said. "What brings you so far from home?"

"I've come to marry Mountain Dweller," replied Maada.

"I am Mountain Dweller," the young man said.

Maada was surprised; he wasn't old at all, and he seemed quite nice. She smiled at her sister as he led them to his house.

Inside, Mountain Dweller's house was even more magnificent than it looked from the outside. It was decorated with stories in fabulous carvings and paintings, and strewn

with huge chests of precious furs, not to mention piles of food boxes and bowls. Soon, they were tucking into the most delicious meal they'd ever eaten.

"I'm off hunting," Mountain Dweller said later, picking up his bow. "Please make yourselves at home. But don't look behind that screen, whatever you do."

He pointed to a large screen that stretched across one corner of the room. The girls looked at each other. They were both thinking the same thing—the fourth danger! As soon as Mountain Dweller had gone, the princesses heard noises from behind the screen and smelled meat roasting. But there was something else in the air, which made them shiver and pull their furs more closely around them.

"Perhaps it's an evil old woman, cooking?" whispered Maada.

"But we're not going to look," whimpered Kilsa. "Are we?"

Mountain Dweller did not return until late in the evening, and then early next morning, he headed back out. Again, the sisters heard noises and smelled cooking from behind the screen. It was the same for the next four days.

"We can't carry on like this," Maada sighed. "We'll have to face the fourth danger, whatever it is."

Then, taking a deep breath, and gripping a stout stick of firewood, she pushed the screen aside. Behind it stood a hideous old woman, with long, white hair and evil, red eyes. As the woman reached a clawlike hand out to grab the princess and throw her on the fire, Maada bashed the crone with her stick, knocking her into the cooking fire. The woman went up in a big cloud of choking black smoke, which turned into a thick cloud of gnats.

When Mountain Dweller returned that night, he was overjoyed.

"You've rid us of the evil that's plagued these hills for so long," he cried. "I can't thank you enough."

Then, all four dangers over, he guided them back to their family's village, bearing lots of gifts of food and fine furs. When they were nearly home, they heard the distinctive sounds of mourning. What had happened? Then they saw their brother, who shrieked as if he'd seen a ghost.

"My sisters!" he cried, racing back to the family longhouse. "I've just seen them!"

"You can't have," replied his mother, her face streaked with tears. "They've been away for so long now, they must be dead."

At that very moment, the princesses reached their family house, accompanied by Mountain Dweller. Clinging to their mother, they promised never to run away again.

"But I thought we were getting married?" Mountain Dweller asked Maada.

"We were." Maada smiled. "But it wouldn't be fair on either of us to marry just to teach my mother a lesson. I hope we can still be friends?"

Mountain Dweller agreed, and so, with no hard feelings, he went back to his valley, promising to visit from time to time. And Maada went back to doing what she did best— running barefoot on the beach, roaming the mountain trails, and eating k'aaw with her grandmother.

Sumac and the Search for the Magic Lake

Long ago, there was a powerful Inca emperor who only had one son. The prince had been sickly ever since he was born. Despite the royal doctors' best efforts, the prince's health got worse and worse as he grew up. In despair, the emperor went to the temple to pray.

"Great gods," he prayed. " I beg you to cure my son. I am an old man, and am not long for this world. If my son dies too, who will look after our people?"

Then he waited quietly for an answer. To his great surprise, he heard a voice coming from the sacred fire that burned in front of the altar.

"Listen well," said the voice, faint but clear. "Send for a cup of water from the magic lake that touches the sky at the end of the world. If the prince drinks this water, he will be cured."

As the voice faded, the fire sputtered and went out, and among the ashes, a golden drinking flask appeared. The emperor and his wife were filled with hope for the first time in their son's short life. But how would they get the water?

The emperor was too old and frail to go on such a long journey himself. So, he sent out a proclamation. Whoever could fill the flask with water from the magic lake would be handsomely rewarded. Many brave men answered his call. They searched far and wide, but none could locate the lake. And so weeks and months passed by, and the golden flask stood empty.

In a village far away from the palace, there lived two poor brothers, Anku and Roca, with their little sister, and their parents. They scraped a living by farming corn and potatoes. Hearing the royal trumpet, they went to see their parents.

"Dear Mother and Father," said Anku. "Please let us go and search for the magic lake, so we can heal the prince and claim the reward. We'll be back before the harvest."

Reluctantly, their parents agreed.

For months, the brothers searched every corner of the country, carrying their buckets, and found many lakes, large and small. However, none were magic, and none touched the sky. Soon, it was harvest time, and the brothers had to go home.

"We can't go back empty-handed," said Roca.

"Don't worry," replied Anku. "We'll get some water from the next lake we pass. It's not like anyone, not even the emperor, would know the difference. Hopefully the prince will get better anyway, and we'll get our reward."

Back at the palace, Anku and Roca presented the lake water to the grateful emperor. He filled the golden flask, but the water vanished as soon as it was poured in.

"Your Majesty," the High Priest told the emperor. "The flask will only hold magic lake water. It's telling us that you've been tricked."

In a terrible rage, the emperor threw the brothers into the palace dungeon and forced them to drink the lake water they'd brought back, to remind them of their lies.

Once again the emperor sent messengers to every part of his empire, but this time, he doubled the reward. The brothers' little sister, Sumac, was looking after her llamas. She hurried home and begged her parents to let her go and find the magic lake.

"No, no," cried her mother. "You're far too young. Look what happened to your brothers. I don't want to lose another child."

"But if no one finds it, the prince will die," replied Sumac. "And perhaps the emperor will pardon my brothers as my reward."

Eventually, her parents agreed, and Sumac set off at once, with her youngest llama for company. Her father packed her a bag of toasted corn kernels to eat on the journey.

On the first night, Sumac snuggled up to her llama and went to sleep. In the night, she heard the cries of a hungry puma, and was worried that the llama would be eaten. When morning came, she sadly sent the llama home and carried on her way. That night, she climbed a tree, out of reach of the puma. She shared her corn with some hungry sparrows, then went to sleep.

The next morning, she was woken up by the sound of the sparrows' voices.

"Poor little thing," one bird twittered. "She'll never find the lake like this."

"We must help her," chirped another.

"Yes," a third chirruped. "After all, she shared her corn with us."

"Oh, please help me," interrupted Sumac. "I don't know where to start looking."

Each of the sparrows gave her one of their wing feathers, and the first sparrow told her to hold them all together like a fan.

"The feathers have magic powers," the sparrow said. "They'll take you wherever you want to go and protect you from harm."

"The magic lake is guarded by three monsters," the second sparrow added. "But don't be afraid. Hold the fan in front of your face and they won't be able to hurt you."

Thanking her new friends, Sumac tied the feathers together with a ribbon from her hair. Then she held the fan to her lips and whispered, "Magic fan, please take me to the lake at the end of the world."

Sumac found herself carried off by a gentle breeze. Up and up it swept her, until she was soaring over snowcapped mountain peaks. Then, at last, it set her down on the shore of a beautiful lake at the end of the world, where the water touched the sky.

Fan in hand, Sumac ran to the lake's edge. As she reached the water, she realized that she had left all her belongings behind in the forest, including a flask for carrying the water in.

"I wish I'd brought a flask," she groaned.

Then, hearing a soft thud, she looked down. On the sand lay a golden flask—the very same one that the emperor had found in the ashes.

As she kneeled down to fill the flask with water, she heard a hissing noise behind her. Turning around, she saw a huge crab snapping its enormous claws.

"This is my lake," the crab growled. "Now buzz off or I'll pinch you."

Quick as a flash, Sumac spread the fan in front of her face. At once, the crab closed its eyes and fell fast asleep.

Again, Sumac kneeled to fill the flask, and this time, she heard a slapping sound coming from the lake. There was a gigantic green alligator beating its tail on the water.

"This is my lake," the alligator snarled. "Now buzz off or I'll bite you."

Sumac again held the fan in front of her face. The alligator yawned loudly, then sank into a deep sleep.

A third time, Sumac kneeled by the water, and this time, she heard a loud shrieking sound coming from the sky. It was a terrifyingly huge, flame-breathing, flying serpent, with bright red scales.

"This is my lake," hissed the serpent. "Now, buzz off, or I'll set you on fire."

At this terrifying sight, Sumac spread out her fan, and once again, it saved her from harm. The flying serpent dropped to the ground, folded its wings, and dozed off on the sand.

With the three terrible beasts snoring loudly, Sumac quickly filled the golden flask with water. Then, holding the fan to her lips, she whispered:

"Magic fan, please take me to the emperor's palace."

No sooner had she spoken than she found herself in a room in the palace. The prince lay on a huge bed, ghostly pale and still. His parents stood by his side, weeping, because he was close to death.

Sumac went straight to the prince and gave him a few sips of water. At once, the magic began to work. The sickly prince opened his eyes and smiled weakly. Within just a few minutes, he was sitting up in bed.

"I'm feeling better already," he beamed. "And I'm starving! What's for dinner?"

"I can't thank you enough for saving our son's life," the emperor said to Sumac. "We can never truly repay you. Please ask for whatever you want."

"You are very generous, Your Majesty," Sumac answered. "I have three wishes that I beg you to grant. Firstly, I wish for my brothers, Anku and Roca, to be forgiven and set free."

"Your wish is granted," said the emperor, and freed the brothers immediately. "What is your second wish?"

"I wish for the magic fan to be returned to the sparrows so they can have their feathers back," she replied.

However, even before the emperor could grant her wish, the magic fan spread itself open, and fluttered out the window toward the forest.

"And your last wish, brave Sumac?" asked the smiling emperor.

"I wish for my parents to be given a bigger farm and a better house to live in," she said. "And enough money to live the rest of their lives comfortably."

"Your wish is granted," the emperor nodded. "But you haven't asked for anything for yourself. What would you like, Sumac?"

Sumac declared that the only thing she wished for herself for now was to go back to her family, though she asked that she might be given an interesting job at the palace when she was old enough. The emperor agreed, and sent his own guards to accompany her and her brothers safely home.

Meanwhile, back at the palace, the golden flask never grew empty again, however much water was drunk from it. Thanks to Sumac's courage, the prince and his descendants all enjoyed the best of health.

Feng Mian,
the Head of the Family

Many years ago, in the Chinese countryside, there lived an old farmer and his three sons. Two of his sons were married, and the family all lived together in the one tiny, ramshackle house. The farmer's daughters-in-law, Ying Yue and Ru Shi, came from a lively and beautiful village quite a long way away. They had been best friends since they were babies, and while they both loved their new family, and were happy to have each other, they often felt lonely and homesick for their own parents and siblings.

According to the custom, they had to ask their father-in-law's permission every time they wanted to visit their old homes. Unfortunately, they asked so often that the farmer began to get very annoyed. Eventually, he decided to find a way to put an end to their pleading, once and for all.

"You're always asking me to let you go off to visit your parents," he told them. "And you think I'm being hard-hearted when I say no. So, I'll let you go on one condition—that you each bring me back something precious."

"Of course, Father," they both answered, quickly.

"Very well," he said. "I want one of you to bring me some fire, but it must be wrapped in paper. The other must bring me some wind, also in paper. If you can't get these for me, you can go to your villages, but you must never come back here."

Without really thinking, the women nodded their heads in agreement. They excitedly packed their things, and almost immediately set off for their village, before their father-in-law could change his mind.

It was a long walk, but the women chatted happily about all the things they would do when they reached home. They had walked a long way, when disaster struck, and the strap on Ying Yue's sandals broke. As they sat by the roadside, trying to mend it, they suddenly realized what they had agreed to do. There was no way they could bring back fire and wind, wrapped in paper. But then, they would never see their beloved husbands again. In despair, the women began to cry.

Sometime later, a young girl came by, riding a water buffalo. Seeing their sad faces, she stopped and asked if she could help.

"No one can help us," they wailed. "Our father-in law has set us an impossible task."

The girl insisted on hearing their story, and when they'd finished, she smiled.

"I can definitely help you," she told them. "If you come home with me, I'll show you how to find what he wants."

So off the daughters-in-law went to the girl's home, where she showed them a paper lantern with a candle inside, and a paper fan.

"When you light the candle, you'll have fire, wrapped in paper," the girl said. "And when you wave the fan, you'll have wind in paper."

"Oh, thank you, thank you," the daughters-in-law cried. "How can we ever thank you enough? We are so happy we met you!"

Then they went cheerfully on their way to their village. After a happy stay, they bought a paper lantern and a fan and headed back home to their husbands.

The old farmer was surprised to see them coming down the road.

"I told you not to come back," he scolded. "Unless you brought the things I asked for."

"But, Father," they told him. "We've got them, both of them!"

They handed him the lantern and fan.

"How did you solve the riddle?" he cried in astonishment. "Tell me!"

They told him about meeting the girl on the water buffalo, and how she had helped them.

"She sounds like a very clever young woman," the farmer said to himself. "She might just make an excellent match for my youngest son."

So he sent a message to the girl's family to see if they would agree. And when everything had been arranged, the wedding celebrations took place.

However, this was to be no ordinary marriage.

"Because my youngest son's wife is so clever and wise," the farmer announced to his older two sons and their wives. "She will now be head of the family. You must ask her advice in everything, and do as she says."

For the time, this was highly unusual—the head of the family was usually a man. But the new head of the family, whose name was Feng Mian, quickly took matters into her own hands. She told the farmer and his sons that they must never go to or from work empty-handed. Each morning, they were to take fertilizer to the fields, and, in the evening, bring back any sticks they could find. By doing this, the family soon had fields full of crops, and were never short of firewood to burn. And when there were only a few sticks of wood left to collect, Feng Mian told them to bring back stones for building, which they piled up outside the house.

One day, a gem dealer rode by and spotted the pile of stones. When he stopped to take a closer look at them, he noticed that one of the stones contained a large lump of precious jade. At once, he went to the house and asked for the head of the family. Imagine his surprise when Feng Mian replied! He was even more surprised at her sharp bargaining skills, and left, agreeing to pay a high price for the stones. Of course, he said nothing about the jade, but promised to come back in a few days to pay.

Feng Mian guessed at once that the gem dealer was trying to cheat them. She told her father-in-law to invite him for dinner and draw him into a conversation about precious stones and how to identify them. Feng Mian listened from behind a curtain. Then she went outside, found the jade, and hid it in the house.

The next day, the gem dealer returned with the money, and saw to his horror, that he'd been found out. Feng Mian agreed to sell the jade to him, if he also bought the pile of stones—but only for a much higher price than he had offered before. The money she earned made the family rich, and they built a grand new house, with a sign on the gate that read "No Sorrow."

A few days later, a government minister came by. He stopped when he saw the sign on the gate.

"That's a very boastful sign," he said, angrily. "Every family has its fair share of sorrow. I shall fine you for your arrogance."

"We have a happy home and family," replied Feng Mian, politely. "The sign is simply to ask visitors to leave their sorrows behind at the gate."

"Even so," raged the minister. "As punishment, you can weave me a piece of cloth as long as this road."

"Of course, Your Excellency," said Feng Mian, with a deep, respectful bow. "Just as soon as you have found both ends of the road and told me the exact length."

The minister realized that he'd been outwitted, and it made him even angrier.

"And you can also bring me as much oil as there is water in the sea," he fumed.

"With pleasure, Your Excellency," said Feng Mian, with an even deeper bow. "Just as soon as you have measured the ocean and told me the exact number of gallons you need."

"If you're so clever," the minister replied, "perhaps you can read my mind. If you can, I'll drop the fines. See this songbird perched on my finger? Now, tell me this. Am I planning to squeeze it to death or let it fly away safely?"

"Your Excellency," answered Feng Mian. "You are an important minister, and I'm just a humble girl. If you don't know more than me, you shouldn't fine me at all. Now, I have a question for you. I'm standing with one foot on one side of the door, and the other on the other side. Tell me, am I planning to come in or go out? If you can't read my mind, you shouldn't ask me to read yours."

Of course, she knew that the minister wouldn't able to guess, and he was forced to admit that she was right. Tutting loudly, he took his leave, and the family, with its wise and clever head, lived without sorrow for many years to come.

Unanana and the Elephant

There was once a woman called Unanana who lived in a village in South Africa. In the Zulu language, there's a saying "Unanana-bosele," which means "as stubborn as a frog." Unanana was well named—she never gave up, no matter what life threw at her.

Sadly, Unanana's husband died, leaving her a widow on her own. But, true to her name, Unanana was determined to make the best of things. She lived with her two children, in a tumbledown hut near the forest, where many wild animals lived. Every day, people from the village passed their hut, on their way to collect firewood from the forest. And every day, they would stop by the hut. "What beautiful children you have, Unanana," they would say. "You must be very proud of them."

One morning, Unanana set off into the forest to collect firewood. She left her children playing a game of pebbles with their older cousin. She could hear their happy shouts as she disappeared among the trees. And when they got tired of playing pebbles, they made little huts from sticks and leaves.

Suddenly, they heard a loud rustling, and a baboon ambled into the yard.

"Whose children are these?" the baboon asked the cousin, in its incredibly deep, booming voice.

"They are Unanana's," replied the cousin, with a smile.

"Well, well, well," the baboon said. "I've never seen such beautiful children before." Then it scampered back into the forest, and the children went on with their game.

A little while later, they heard the snap of a twig and saw a gazelle staring at them with its big, brown eyes.

"Whose children are these?" the gazelle asked the cousin, in its soft, gentle voice.

"They are Unanana's," she replied, as before.

"Well, well, well," the gazelle said. "I've never seen such beautiful children before." Then it bounded back into the forest. This time, the children didn't go back to their game. They were hot and thirsty. Their cousin gave them each a small gourd to use as a cup, which they filled from the water pot by the door.

Just then, they heard a rumbling roar and saw the spotty body of a leopard. The cousin was so frightened that she dropped her water gourd.

"Whose children are these?" asked the leopard, in its low, growling voice.

"They're Unanana's," the cousin replied, trembling.

"Well, well, well," said the leopard. "I've never seen such beautiful children before."

Then it turned around and slunk back into the forest.

After this, the children didn't feel like playing anymore, and they didn't want any more visitors. All they wanted was for Unanana to come home, and soon. But, instead of their mother, an enormous elephant, with only one tusk, came lumbering out of the trees. It stood staring at the terrified children, who tried to hide behind a large rock.

"Whose children are these?" the elephant bellowed, in the loudest voice they'd ever heard.

"Th-th-th-they're Unanana's," stuttered the cousin, too frightened to move.

"Well, well, well," said the elephant. "I've never seen such beautiful children before. I think I'll take them back with me!"

With that, the elephant opened its mouth wide and swallowed the two children down with a gigantic, very noisy gulp. Then it stomped back into the forest.

Their cousin screamed, ran back into the hut, and slammed the door. How was she going to explain to Unanana that she had lost her children?

It was not until much later in the day that Unanana returned, carrying a large bundle of firewood. The cousin came running out of the hut, in a terrible panic. It took a while for Unanana to understand what she was trying to say.

"I'm sorry!" sobbed the cousin. "Couldn't stop it. Elephant. Took the children. Oh no! Oh no! Whatever shall we do?"

"I'll just have to go and find them," Unanana replied. "But I'll need a few things first."

She went into the hut and put a potful of beans over the fire to cook. When the beans were soft and ready, she let the pot cool, then balanced it on her head. Next, she found a long, sharp knife and tucked it in her belt. Then, leaving the cousin to look after the hut, she set off into the forest to look for her children.

The first animal she met was a baboon.

"Baboon! O baboon!" she called. "Have you seen an elephant with one tusk? It has eaten my children, and I need to find them."

"I know you," replied the baboon, in its deep, booming voice. "You're Unanana. I will help you. Follow this track until you reach some tall trees and white stones. There you will find the elephant."

Unanana thanked the baboon and set off down the track, but there was no sign of any tall trees anywhere, nor white stones, nor elephant. In fact, the only animal she saw was a gazelle.

"Gazelle! O gazelle!" she called. "Have you seen an elephant with just one tusk? It has eaten my children, and I need to find them."

"I know you," replied the gazelle, in its soft, gentle voice. "You're Unanana. I will help you. Follow the track until you reach some tall trees and white stones. There you will find the elephant."

Unanana thanked the gazelle and carried on down the track. She walked and walked until she was tired and hungry. But she didn't eat the beans in her pot—they were for her children. On and on she went, and on and on, until, around a bend in the track she came across a leopard.

"Leopard! O leopard!" she said, in a weary voice. "Have you seen an elephant with one tusk? It has eaten my children, and I need to find them."

"I know you," the leopard replied, in its low, growling voice. "You're Unanana. I will help you. Follow the track until you reach some tall trees and white stones. There you will find the elephant."

Unanana thanked the leopard and staggered off down the track, hardly able to put one foot in front of the other. Suddenly, in front of her, and on her last legs, she spied some tall trees and white stones. And, lying contentedly in the shade, was an enormous elephant with only one tusk.

Unanana looked the elephant square in the eye.

"Are you the elephant that ate my children?" she asked.

"Don't be silly," boomed the elephant. "Why would I do that? It must have been another elephant. Now, if you just follow the track … "

"Tell me the truth!" yelled Unanana. "Did you eat my children?"

"No, I did not," lied the elephant. "As I said, if you just follow … "

At that moment, Unanana rushed at him, waving her knife, and screaming, "Where are my children? Tell me NOW!"

Then the elephant opened its huge mouth wide, as if to reply, and … swallowed Unanana, her cooking pot, and knife down in one gulp. Little did the great beast know that this was exactly what Unanana wanted. She slipped down the elephant's throat,

down and down, into the darkness, and landed in its stomach, where an astonishing sight met her eyes. The walls of its stomach were like rolling hills, and dotted around she saw all sorts of people and animals, and her own two beautiful children.

"Mother! O Mother!" they cried as she hugged them. "We're really scared. And really hungry."

Unanana took the cooking pot off her head and gave the beans to the children to eat. Soon, crowds of people had gathered around.

"We're hungry, too," groaned the people. "Please can we have some of those beans?"

"How can you be hungry?" Unanana replied. "You can get milk from your cows and goats, and eggs from your chickens. Cook the eggs over a fire, but make sure the fire's good and hot."

So the people made a blazing fire and began to cook their eggs. As they did so, the elephant started to roar in pain. He made so much noise that the other forest animals rushed over to see what was the matter.

"My stomach's killing me," the elephant groaned. "It feels as if it's on fire—it must be something I ate."

The burning pain grew worse and worse, until, before long, the elephant rolled over, dead. Quickly, Unanana pulled out her knife and hacked out a doorway between the elephant's ribs. Out stepped Unanana and her children. Out stepped the cows, goats, dogs, and chickens. Out stepped the people, who couldn't thank Unanana enough for saving them. They gave her all sorts of gifts so that Unanana and her children were no longer poor.

When they got home, the cousin was overjoyed to see them, safe and sound. They celebrated with a party for the whole village, and lived happily ever after.

The **Warrior Queen** and the **Wizard**

Once upon a time, a kingdom in Russia was ruled by a woman called Queen Maria Morevna. She inherited her kingdom from her father, who not only taught her to rule wisely and well, but trained her in warfare. She was married to a young prince called Ivan. He was good and brave, and came to live in Maria's palace with her.

Then, one day, a messenger galloped through the palace gates. He brought news that Prince Ivan's kingdom was under attack and that the prince should come home at once.

"I'll come with you," said Maria, smiling. "You'll need someone to look after the kingdom properly while you're away."

So the two set off for Ivan's palace, where he assembled his army for war. Then he said goodbye to Maria, with these words of warning.

"You have all the keys to the palace," he said. "But the door to the room in the tower must be kept locked at all times. Don't go up there, I beg of you."

Maria was instantly curious, though she was very busy for a few weeks ruling the kingdom. One holiday weekend, she found herself with some time to explore, and, despite Ivan's warning, she climbed the stairs to the tower.

"I'll just take a quick look," she said to herself. "Surely that won't do any harm."

She unlocked the door and stepped into the room. There was an old man with a long white beard and long white hair, chained to the wall.

"Dear lady," the old man begged. "I'm so thirsty. Please bring me some water. In return, I will spare your life one day."

Taking pity on the old man, Maria fetched three large buckets of water, which he gulped down, one by one. As he did so, he grew stronger, until he was strong enough to snap his chains apart.

"Thank you, Maria Morevna," he laughed. "You have made an old man very happy."

"But who are you?" cried Maria.

"Koschei the wizard," the old man replied. "Years ago, Prince Ivan's father captured me and locked me up in here. To get rid of evil, he claimed. Now you have set me free, and you will never see the prince again."

Then, with a hideous cackle, he flew out the window and far away, until he found Prince Ivan and his army. He swooped down, snatched the prince from his horse, and flew away with him, to his fortress by the sea.

When evil Koschei had gone, Maria knew that there was no time to lose. She was the great Maria Morevna, after all. At once, she leapt on her warhorse, and rode off to rescue her husband.

Many days later, Maria reached Koschei's fortress. She hid in the forest until she saw the wizard riding off on a magnificent black horse. Sword in hand, she crept into the fortress, where she found Ivan deep in a dark dungeon. Overjoyed to see each other, the two began to plot their escape. But it wasn't going to be easy—Koschei's horse could run like the wind. They couldn't hope to overtake it, and if Koschei caught them, he would kill them both.

"But we can't stay here," said Maria. "It's a chance we'll have to take."

So they headed back to the forest and raced off on Maria's horse as fast as it could carry them.

Meanwhile, Koschei's great horse suddenly stopped in its tracks.

"What's the matter, you lazy, good-for-nothing?" shouted Koschei.

"Maria Morevna has rescued Prince Ivan," it snorted.

"Well, what are you waiting for?" Koschei shrieked. "Get after them, or I'll have you turned into dinner for the dogs."

Flying across the ground, the horse quickly drew level with Maria and Ivan. The wizard seized them and carried them off to his fortress.

"How dare you try to cross me?" screamed Koschei. "Now, prepare to die."

As he raised his sword to strike, Maria called out:

"You once promised to spare my life," she said. "Remember?"

"Very well," sneered the wizard. "I won't kill you this time."

Instead, he sealed Maria into a large barrel and threw it into the sea. Then he took Ivan back to his palace.

Luckily, a few days later, a hawk, an eagle, and a raven flew by and spied the barrel bobbing in the waves. With their sharp beaks and claws, they pulled it ashore and tore it open. To their great surprise, Maria crawled out.

"Thank you," said Maria Morevna. "But I've no chance of rescuing Ivan now, inside the barrel or out!"

"If Ivan can find out where the wizard got his horse," the birds squawked, "you can try to get another one its equal."

Maria set off for Koschei's fortress. Once more, she waited for the wizard to leave, and crept in to find Prince Ivan. She told him what the birds had said, then left, promising to come back the next day.

That evening, when the wizard returned, Ivan asked him about his horse.

"I've never seen such a superb creature," he began. "Where did you get him from?"

"From an old Baba Yaga," Koschei replied, flattered. "She has a herd of magical horses, which I once tended for her. The horse was my reward."

"But how did you find Baba Yaga?" exclaimed Ivan. "That can't have been easy."

"Only someone as clever as me could manage it," boasted the wizard, pulling a red silk cloth from his cloak pocket. "She lives by the far seashore. First, I had to cross a river of fire. So I waved my magic handkerchief, and a bridge appeared. Simple, really."

He beamed at Ivan and puffed out his chest, very pleased with himself.

Later that night, as the wizard slept, Ivan slipped out of the dungeon and stole the handkerchief.

The next day, Ivan gave the handkerchief to Maria, and told her what Koschei had said. Maria set off on the long journey to Baba Yaga's house, using the handkerchief to conjure up a bridge over the river of fire.

On she walked, hungry and thirsty, when she saw a mother bird with her chicks. One of those would make a good meal, she thought. But the mother flew around, squawking loudly, begging her not to eat her little ones.

"Leave my chicks be," the mother bird said. "And I will help you, one day."

Maria had a kind heart, and walked away.

Later, she found a wild beehive. The thought of honey made her mouth water. But the bees pleaded to be left in peace.

"Leave our honey," they buzzed. "And we will help you, one day."

So Maria went on her way again. She walked until she reached the seashore, where she caught a crayfish on the rocks. Dinner, at last! But the crayfish cried:

"Spare my life, please, and I will help you, one day."

So, of course, Maria did.

At last, Maria spied a strange-looking hut, built on four tall stilts—Baba Yaga's house. She climbed a ladder and knocked on the door. It was opened by a bent-over old woman with a wizened face and sharp, brown eyes.

"Come in, Maria Morevna," she croaked. "Tell me, what is it you want?"

"I've come to tend your horses," Maria said, cautiously. "So that I may earn one of them, as a reward."

"Well, why not?" said Baba Yaga. "If you care for the horses well, I'll give you the fastest and finest. But, if even one of them goes missing, I'll kill you, mark my words."

Baba Yaga gave Maria a place to sleep, and something to eat and drink. The next morning, Maria opened the stable door, and let the horses out to graze. At once, they galloped off in every direction. In seconds, they were all out of sight. All day, Maria looked for them, but they were long gone. As she was about to give up, a flock of birds appeared in the sky, led by the mother bird whose chick Maria had spared. The birds found the horses and pecked them so hard that they ran back home again.

Baba Yaga was secretly furious. She had ordered the horses to run away, so that she could kill Maria, and now her plan had been foiled. The next day, she sent them deeper into the forest. Maria followed, wearily, but they were nowhere to be seen. Then, suddenly, a swarm of bees filled the air. They found the horses and stung them until the beasts fled back to their stable.

Baba Yaga hadn't finished yet. The next day, she sent the horses down to the sea and told them to swim until they were out of sight. A dejected Maria sat down on a rock—her quest to find Ivan seemed hopeless. Then something nipped her finger—it was the crayfish.

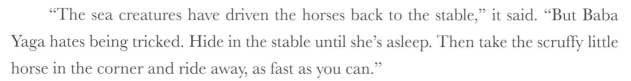

"The sea creatures have driven the horses back to the stable," it said. "But Baba Yaga hates being tricked. Hide in the stable until she's asleep. Then take the scruffy little horse in the corner and ride away, as fast as you can."

Maria did as the crayfish said. Late at night, when Baba Yaga slept, she came out of her hiding place, saddled the scruffy horse, and galloped off. After crossing the bridge over the river of fire, she let the horse graze in a meadow filled with lush, green grass. After a few days, the horse grew large and powerful—a match for the wizard's horse. In no time at all, they reached Koschei's fortress, where Ivan was waiting. He climbed up behind Maria and they fled.

When Koschei learned of their escape, he exploded with rage and leapt straight on his own great horse.

"After them, you useless, lazy beast!" he cried, giving the horse a sharp lash with his whip. "Faster, faster! Go faster. We'll never catch them like this."

The horse ran like the wind, until it drew level with Maria and Ivan. But as Koschei lifted his sword, the horse bucked, throwing his cruel master to the ground. With a few well-aimed kicks, the horse sent the wizard limping back to his fortress, never to be seen again. Then, having seen that Maria was kind to all creatures, the horse turned to Maria and let her get on his back.

So Maria Morevna and Prince Ivan finally returned to their kingdom. They were overjoyed to be reunited, but it wasn't long before Maria was riding off, again, at the head of her army. After all, once a warrior princess, always a warrior princess.

Fallon,
the Girl from the Northland

Long, long ago, the freezing Northland of Finland was ruled by old Louhi and her daughter, Fallon. One bleak morning, Louhi heard a very strange sound coming from the bank of the nearby icy river. She hurried to untie her little boat, and rowed downstream, where she found an old, silver-haired man standing on the bank, howling like an injured wild animal.

"Who are you, stranger?" called Louhi. "And where do you come from?"

"I come from the Land of Heroes," the old man replied. "But I'm completely lost."

"Come to my house," said Louhi. "At least you can get warm and dry."

He thanked her for her kind offer, and helped her to row back upstream. As they sat beside the fire, he told Louhi of his troubles.

"My name is Vainamoinen, but my friends all just call me Vaina," he began. "I am known as a singer of songs."

Now, Louhi had heard of Vainamoinen, and she knew he was no simple singer, but a famous and powerful magician.

"Silly old fool that I am," he continued. "I came here to find a wife. But it has been one long disaster, and all I want is to go home."

"And what will you give me if I help you?" asked Louhi.

"Gold and silver?" suggested Vaina. "Jewels? Furs?"

"The only thing I want," said Louhi, "is a Sampo—a special magic mill that can grind flour, salt, and coins, all from thin air. Get me this, and I'll give you a horse and sled to take you home. Oh yes, and whoever makes me a Sampo can marry my daughter, too."

"Alas, I don't have the skills to make you a Sampo," Vaina sighed, sadly. "But I know someone who does. He is Seppo Imarinen, the master smith of the Land of Heroes. I will send him to you."

As Vaina set off home on his new sled, Louhi had a warning.

"Keep your head down until you reach home," she said. "Don't look up, or bad luck will surely follow."

Vaina hadn't gone far, when he heard a sharp, clacking sound. Forgetting Louhi's warning, he looked up and, to his surprise, saw a rainbow. And sitting on the rainbow was a young woman weaving on a loom. She was old Louhi's daughter—Fallon, the Girl from the Northland.

"Your mother says we shall marry when I next return. Will you have me, Girl from the Northland?" he asked.

"I'll think about it," Fallon said, laughing. "If you can tie an egg in knots without breaking the shell, and split a horsehair with a knife."

114

"That's nothing," boasted Vaina, climbing out of the sled. And he did exactly as she asked.

"Now peel a stone, and chop a block of ice into pieces with your bare hands," Fallon said.

Again, Vaina did exactly that.

"Clever," said Fallon, admiringly. "But can you make a boat from the pieces of my loom and launch it without touching it?"

"Easy," replied Vaina, and set to work. For hours, he chopped and shaped planks of wood, until, suddenly, his saw slipped and sliced deep into his leg. Could this be the bad luck Louhi had warned him about? When he looked up, both the Maid and the rainbow had gone.

Summoning up his most powerful healing spell, Vaina stopped the bleeding, and bound his leg with a bandage of moss. Then he hobbled back to his sled and drove south as fast as he could.

When Fallon reached home, Louhi scolded her for playing tricks on Vaina.

"Well, you shouldn't have offered me as a reward," Fallon replied scornfully. "I don't want to get married at all, especially not to an old man like that!"

"You could do a lot worse," said her mother. "He's promised to send a smith to make a Sampo for us."

Back in the Land of Heroes, Vaina wasn't so sure he could keep his promise. What if Seppo didn't want to go? Then he had a brilliant idea. Using all his magic, he began to sing. As he sang, a tall pine tree with golden needles sprang up, reaching high into the sky. Its branches were scattered

with twinkling stars, with a full moon perched on top. Then he went to find Seppo, and explained his dilemma.

"But I don't want to go the Land of the North," the smith said, wielding his huge hammer. "It's full of monsters, and freezing cold."

"It's not that bad," said Vaina. "Come and see what I brought back."

He took Seppo to see the golden pine tree, and encouraged him to climb to the top. As Seppo did, Vaina began to sing up a howling gale that carried Seppo off through the air and dropped him right on old Louhi's doorstep.

Seppo was furious at being tricked, but Louhi and Fallon made him welcome, especially when they found out his name.

"Well, well, well, Vaina kept his promise," Louhi said. "A master smith like you should have no difficulty making a Sampo. And, in return, perhaps my delightful daughter might agree to marry you."

"In your dreams," muttered Fallon, behind her back.

Several weeks later, Seppo finally finished making a magnificent magic Sampo. When Louhi pressed a lever, it ground out flour from one side, salt from another, and coins from a third. His task complete, Seppo turned to Fallon.

"I've made you a Sampo," he said. "Now will you marry me?"

"No, thank you," she replied, firmly. "I don't want to get married."

A dejected Seppo returned home, but he couldn't get Fallon out of his mind. He had fallen head over heels in love with her. He had thought she had started to change her mind about marrying him after all, and was disappointed that she had said no again.

When he told Vaina what had happened, the magician was secretly pleased.

"She must want to marry me after all," he said to himself. "And is sorry for playing her tricks on me. I'll finish making the boat she wanted, and it will be the finest, strongest boat ever seen."

When the boat was finished, Vaina painted it red and gold. Then, very early one morning, he hoisted a great red sail. He hoped to slip away without being seen, but Seppo's sister, Annikki, spotted him, as she was washing clothes by the seashore.

"Where are you going, Vaina?" she called.

"Fishing for salmon," he replied.

"But you haven't got any nets or lines," she said.

"Hunting wild geese, then," he tried again.

"But you haven't brought your bow and arrows," she said.

"Okay, okay," admitted Vaina. "If you must know, I'm going to the Land of the North to ask the Maid to marry me."

Immediately, Annikki dropped her washing, and raced off to find her brother, to tell him about Vaina's cunning plan. For she knew that Seppo still pined after Fallon. Without delay, Seppo put on his finest clothes, harnessed his best horse to the sled, and set off at top speed.

In their farmhouse in the Land of the North, Louhi and Fallon watched as Vaina's boat pulled up on the shore, and Seppo's sled slid over the snow. Fallon was secretly delighted that Vaina had come back, as she had missed his company, and come to realize that they made a good team.

"I know I said I wouldn't," Fallon told her mother, "But I think I would like to marry Seppo after all."

"Are you absolutely sure you wouldn't rather marry the rich, powerful wizard? No? Well, Seppo's got to do more to prove he is worthy of my only child," said Louhi. So, she called for Seppo, and set him an impossible task.

"To prove you're worthy of marrying my daughter," she said. "You must clear the Field of Snakes."

Seppo turned deathly pale. He was terrified of snakes, but he desperately wanted to impress Louhi and Fallon.

"Don't worry," Fallon whispered. "Forge a coat made of chain mail, iron boots, and iron gloves for me, and I'll do it for you. The snakes can't bite through metal, and I'm not scared of them, anyway."

Seppo made Fallon the most beautiful chain mail coat with sturdy boots and gloves, and she tilled the field in neat, straight strips without being bitten once. But when Seppo returned to the farmhouse, his hopes of marrying Fallon were about to be dashed again.

"That doesn't count, since you didn't do it yourself," said Louhi. "So, now you'll have to do another task. Catch the Great Pike that swims in the river, but don't use a net or line."

Seppo trembled at the thought of the Pike's terrible teeth, but once again, Fallon came to his rescue.

"Forge a giant bird from fire, with claws of iron," she said. "It will catch the Pike, and you won't be harmed."

So this is exactly what Seppo did.

"Now, please may I marry your daughter?" Seppo asked Louhi, handing her the Pike's head for the pot.

"Yes, you may," interrupted Fallon, before her mother could find anything else for him to do.

The PRINCESS, the Merchants, and the Very Unusual Cupboard

In Sudan, there was once a powerful Sultan who lived in great luxury, with a fabulous palace, with exquisite gardens, hundreds of servants, and a treasury full of gold. The Sultan was not good at managing his money—he left all that to his wife. He had a daughter, Amira, who was as clever and shrewd as her mother, which was just as well.

One sad day, when Amira was about twenty years old, the Sultan's wife fell ill and died. The Sultan was heartbroken. In deep despair, he mourned his wife, refused to take any part in affairs of state, and shut himself away in his rooms. The palace fell into dreadful disrepair, and the gardens became choked with weeds, but the Sultan was too sad to instruct the workmen or gardeners. Worse still, he started to spend money as if there were no tomorrow. Eventually, he squandered all his money, until his once overflowing coffers lay completely empty.

Now, the Sultan also had a very large strongbox, full of gold ingots, which his wife

had put aside for a rainy day. When all his other funds were gone, he remembered the strongbox, and began to work his way through the ingots, too. Luckily, Amira kept a close eye on her father. Every time he opened the strongbox, she secretly removed an ingot, and buried it in a deep hole in the ground. As time passed, the strongbox also lay empty, but, by now, Amira had a large store of gold hidden away. And, with the palace running short of food, and the servants needing their wages, she dug up one of her ingots, and took it to market to sell.

Amira went straight to the most important merchant in town and asked him to buy her ingot for what it was worth. The merchant was so dazzled by the princess's charm that he instantly fell in love with her.

"Beautiful princess," he said. "If you agree to be my wife one day, I will pay you twice what your ingot is worth."

Amira didn't want a husband, and she certainly didn't want to be bought as a wife. She refused his offer, to his great shame and dismay. And when she asked for her ingot back, he replied that he didn't know what she was talking about.

Angrily, Amira went to see the next merchant. She told him what had happened, and asked for his help in getting her ingot back. To her annoyance, this merchant, too, decided that he was madly in love with her.

"Beautiful princess," he said. "If you agree to be my wife one day, I will pay you four times what your ingot is worth."

The same thing happened with a third merchant. And with a fourth. Eventually, Amira could stand it no longer, and went to sit in the shade of a nearby tree. As she sat there, sighing, an old wise woman passed by.

"Why do you look so sad, Princess?" she asked. "It's too lovely a day to be in a bad mood."

Amira told her the story of the ingot, and the way the merchants had spoken to her, as if she was an object they could buy.

"They need to be taught a lesson," cackled the old woman. "And I know just the thing. I will gladly help you, if you give me just half of the ingot, in return."

"I will give you what you ask for," agreed Amira. "If you help me get it back."

"Then listen carefully," began the old woman, and she told Amira what to do, then bade her farewell.

Back at the palace, Amira summoned the court carpenter. As the wise old woman had instructed, she asked him to make a big cupboard, with four doors. Each door had to open into a compartment large enough for a person to fit inside. The carpenter had never been asked to make anything like this before, and worked on it, day and night for a week. When it was finished, he installed it, proudly, in Amira's sitting room.

With the cupboard in place, Amira went back to the market, and headed straight for the first merchant's shop.

"Good Sir, I beg you to give back my ingot," she said. "I have great need of it—it is the only thing of value that my father and I have left."

"In that case, dear Princess," the merchant replied. "Accept my offer. I will pay you twice what your ingot is worth, if you agree to be my wife."

"I agree," smiled Amira, to the merchant's astonishment. "But there's no time to lose. Come to the palace tomorrow, at midday exactly, and wait for me in my sitting room."

"I'll be there," promised the lovestruck merchant, handing back both the ingot and twice its value in coins.

Delighted, Amira went to see the second merchant.

"Dear Sir," she added. "Could you do something for me? Get my ingot back from your friend, and bring it to me. I have great need of it—it is the only thing of value that my father and I have left."

"I will gladly give your ingot back," the merchant simpered. "And give you two ingots of my own, if you agree to be my wife."

"I agree," smiled Amira. "But there's no time to lose. Come to the palace tomorrow, just after midday, and wait for me in my sitting room."

Dancing with joy, the merchant gave her two ingots, and promised to be there on time. Then, Amira went to see the third merchant, and the same thing happened. In return for two of his gold ingots, she promised to marry him. She told him to come to the palace the next day, a few minutes after the second merchant. Lastly, she visited the fourth merchant, and arranged for him to arrive at the palace a few minutes after the third man.

With nine gold ingots in her hands, Amira left the market, and skipped back to the palace. She gave the gold to her father, on the condition that he mend his ways. The Sultan smiled at his clever daughter, sadly.

"Your mother would have been proud of you," he said. Then he summoned his ministers for a meeting, and began issuing instructions for getting the palace roof fixed, and the gardens watered.

Before the Sultan left, Amira asked for his help. He was to hide in the next room,

and, each time he saw someone enter her room, he was to knock on the door. He must do this every time someone arrived, until all four merchants were there.

Next day, exactly at midday, the first merchant arrived at the palace. Amira welcomed him warmly, and showed him into her sitting room. The merchant couldn't believe his luck. He was just admiring the princess's new cupboard, when, to his alarm, there was a loud knock on the door.

"Quick, you must hide. My father will not approve of our marriage," said Amira. She went to the cupboard, and opened the first door. She told the merchant to get in. Then, she locked the door behind him, and put the key in her pocket.

A few minutes after midday, the second merchant arrived. He was about to sit down and make himself comfortable, when there was a loud knock on the door.

"We must avoid my father until we are married, for he will not approve," said Amira. "Please hide in here." She opened the second door of the cupboard, hid him inside, and locked the door. Then she put the key in her pocket.

The same thing happened with the third merchant, and the fourth. And, when all four merchants were locked inside, Amira called some porters to take the cupboard off to the auction house. There, it caught the eye of her childhood friend, who was now a Sultan from a nearby kingdom, and he offered a high price for it. Amira was happy to sell it, on one condition.

"Great Sultan," she told him. "If you promise not to regret what you find in the cupboard, I shall not regret selling it to you."

"Agreed!" the Sultan replied, and Amira handed him the keys.

The Sultan was planning to take the cupboard straight home, but curiosity got the better of him. As a crowd gathered to watch, he opened the first door, and found the first merchant, cramped and red-faced inside. Then, he opened the second door, then the third, and the fourth, until all four merchants had scrambled out. The crowd clapped, and roared with laughter, at the merchants' embarrassment.

"Tell me, Princess," asked the Sultan, admiringly. "How did you manage to lock four merchants in a cupboard? It's the cleverest thing I've ever seen!"

So, Amira told him all about the gold ingots, and how the merchants had tried to trick her into marrying them. She turned to the merchants. "You all tried to buy me, so instead I sold you. It serves you right!"

She gave each of the merchants the same number of gold ingots as they had tried to buy her with. They all scurried home and nobody in the kingdom ever tried to cross clever Princess Amira again.

The
Englishwoman's House

The Duchess of Devonshire's bedroom at Chatsworth House.

The
Englishwoman's
House

Edited by Alvilde Lees-Milne
Photographed by Derry Moore

Collins
Grafton Street, London, W1
1984

William Collins Sons and Co Ltd
London · Glasgow · Sydney · Auckland
Toronto · Johannesburg

Designed and produced by Breslich & Foss
Middlesex House
34–42 Cleveland Street
London WIP 5FB
Designer: Tony Garrett

British Cataloguing in Publication Data
The Englishwoman's house
    1. Interior decoration—England
    I. Lees-Milne, Alvilde
    643'.7'0942   NK2043
    ISBN 0-00-217344-1

First published 1984
Reprinted 1985
Text and Design © Breslich & Foss
Photographs © Derry Moore

Set by Fakenham Photosetting Ltd, Fakenham, Norfolk
Originated by Dot Gradations Ltd, Essex
and printed by Grijelmo, Spain

Endpapers: *Fabric 'Khayyham' reproduced by courtesy of
Arthur Sanderson and Sons Ltd, Berners Street, London.*

Contents

Foreword by HRH
Princess Michael of Kent

As a very un-Englishwoman I feel privileged to have been asked to write a foreword to this book.

I am, however, lucky enough to live in two quintessential English houses, Nether Lypiatt Manor in Gloucestershire and a part of Kensington Palace on four floors. Both are full of English furniture, legacies of my husband's grandmother, Queen Mary, an adoptive Englishwoman with legendary taste and knowledge of the decorative arts; and my late father-in-law, Prince George, Duke of Kent, who shared his mother's passion for collecting.

I have always disliked the term 'decoration' and have carefully contrived to have any house I have lived in not looking 'decorated'. The English houses, many of them included in this book, that I most admire have successfully avoided the stamp of a particular designer and instead reflect their owners' taste, fantasy, whims and way of life.

Nearly twenty years ago I came to England to study, in particular, the eighteenth century English house, and so I hope I have restored both our houses in a style to which they were once accustomed. If only this book had been written sooner many of the mysteries of the English house would have been unfolded to me much earlier.

Marie Christine

A mirror in Barbara Cartland's house reflecting and surrounded by many of the original paintings for covers of her novels.

Introduction

Today one has to be cautious in discriminating between the sexes. Men and women are supposed to share the same sensitivities and sensibilities. Nevertheless, when it comes to a house, women do as a rule show a livelier interest than men in making it attractive. They also have a more positive approach in its arrangement.

So-called women of taste in the 1920s and 1930s were rather frightened of colour. They were inclined to favour pastel shades, beige and *eau de Nil*, which they considered safe and respectable backgrounds. Today all this has changed. As in cooking, stronger flavours prevail.

The purpose of this book is to demonstrate how twenty-eight women have coped with the different problems of creating homes for themselves and their families, while revealing their candid likes and dislikes in decoration.

The decision whom to invite to contribute to the book has not been an easy one. I have tried to collect different types of houses, large and small, in town and country. Each owner has written about her favourite rooms and objects with genuine affection. Indeed, enthusiasm seems to be the keynote of every chapter.

The contributors take us on a personally conducted tour, sometimes only to one room, sometimes to several. They regale us with personal anecdotes and explain the multifarious problems which beset them. Some of these are amusing. All of them are instructive and provide us with ingenious hints and practical advice how to set about creating our own homes when that critical moment of life comes, which it inevitably must, to all of us.

This is a book of constructive thought and original ideas. Some contributors have had to modernise large, stately homes untouched for years; others have reconstituted old rectories and cottages of various dates and styles. Others have tackled London flats, and one has even adapted an old dairy. They all have something different to tell us. Whether you admire their taste, or not, you cannot fail to be intrigued by the diversity of their ideas. The reader can really feel that he or she gets inside the houses, and furthermore to know the writers individually. Their personalities come through so forcibly.

I wish to thank Her Royal Highness Princess Michael of Kent, whose interest in interior decoration is well known, for writing the Foreword. I am also of course deeply grateful to all those whose splendid cooperation and patience have made this book what it is.

Thilde Lees-Milne

Soft aquamarine and apricot are used in the little Regency sitting-room, decorated as a print-room.

Laura Ashley

RHYDOLDOG HOUSE
Rhayador, Powys

Rhydoldog means water running over stones. This could either be a reference to the two beautiful waterfalls which tumble for two hundred feet down the hill behind the house, or perhaps to some stepping stones across the streams which flow through the pastures below. One of the streams was diverted over two hundred years ago and the bed made into an impressive driveway lined with cedars in place of the old farm cart track which approached from behind the hill.

In fact the house, like most old buildings, has seen lots of changes, even in this case to the extent

of moving the front entrance to face three different directions in three different centuries.

Rhydoldog was built in the seventeenth century as a group of stone farm buildings with a farmhouse comprising living-room, dairy and bedrooms above. The front door faced into the hill for shelter and also for the convenience of running across the yard to the extensive farm buildings. Early in the eighteenth century the story goes that a group of smugglers from Kent, fleeing the Customs men, came with their families to hide in the Welsh hills. One of them bought Rhydoldog farm

The drawing-room is mainly crimson; the original grey marble fire-place and mirrored overmantel have been put back.

and turned the little house back to front to give a
Georgian façade with the additions of dining-
room, sitting-room, an elegant staircase, some
more bedrooms and a good wine cellar. Most
importantly, the front door now faced the view
down the Wye valley, and with the new carriage-
way made from diverting the river bed one could
sweep in style right up to the new front terrace.

Then at the end of the nineteenth century
another great change took place when the house
was turned around once again to face north east by
putting a new Gothic porch at the side, a new
entrance hall with stained glass doors, encaustic
patterned tiles, a gun-room, flower-room, library
and brand-new large drawing-room. Upstairs,
there were now dressing-rooms and eleven bedrooms plus a large schoolroom.

When our family took over the house in 1971
it was in a very good state of repair and we were
fortunate in that the same local building firm had
looked after it as long as anyone could remember,
so that they knew exactly where all the various
pipes and electrical fittings, boilers, etc., were.
We just had to get down to the redecoration of all
the rooms.

My own attitude towards decorating an old
house is to find out all one can about the history of
the house and even, if possible, the original
colours used. I have no prejudices about colour
but prefer to stand in a room and feel what it is
asking for, especially insofar as its original building date is concerned. This house, however, was a
complete mix of old Welsh farmhouse, Georgian,
and finally and probably dominantly, Victorian
Gothic. The only answer was to decorate each
room exactly to its own period, and this we did.

The first hallway is Victorian and is wallpapered with an Owen Jones print coloured in
browns and greys to match the old tiles and blending with the lines of old books on the shelves and
on into the library, which is in plums and burgundy on cream with curtains in a paisley stripe
and a faded rose carpet. The heart of the house,
with its elegant early eighteenth century staircase
and polished oak floor, is wallpapered in a
Regency stripe in soft aquamarine and apricot;
these colours follow through into the little
Regency sitting-room, which is decorated as a very
fashionable looking print-room. The wallpaper
here is a moiré print which gives the effect of fabric
on the wall and the striped curtains have a zigzag

A pretty bedroom looks over the Wye Valley.

pelmet taken from one of the rooms at the Brighton Pavilion. Through the green baize door into
the back hallway, which has not very much light,
there is white linoleum and a pale grey and white
wallpaper to give maximum light effect. The large
old kitchen itself has terracotta/cream 'Shepherd's
Purse' wallpaper and curtains which look very nice
with the scrubbed tables and tiled floor and cooking range. The dairy and laundry follow through
mainly in creams with touches of terracotta.

The dining-room started its life as a Georgian
room with a fire-place of the period flanked with
arched open shelves for china displays. Then at
the turn of the century an Edwardian bay was
added with large glass doors to the terrace. We
decided to decorate it in Edwardian style with a
wonderful old wallpaper print of the period in
deep browns with matching curtains. Very dark
you might say, yet in candlelight with a brightly
burning fire it is stunning and in summer it looks
cool and makes a frame for the wonderful view.

However, it was the drawing-room which
gave the greatest challenge. It was not as if the
house as it stood was an architectural masterpiece
(people have actually burst out laughing at the
sight of it), and so it was very straightforward to
obtain planning permission for what I had in
mind—to take out the ugly drawing-room windows and build a conservatory right along the
terrace. It seemed strange in fact that the house
hadn't got a conservatory already and now that it

Stepping down from the drawing-room into the conservatory.

has everyone imagines it has always been there, it looks so right. So I used our local builders, gave them my plans, which were a composite of all the Gothic style conservatories I had ever seen, and we tiled the floor, made doors for each end with low handles which were a copy of our front door handle and shaped the roof and windows to suit. We discovered a company who were reproducing iron seats to an old pattern and after that it was no problem to add a riot of ferns, lilies, palms and aspidistras as well as a statue and other pieces of sculpture. The upholstery, cushions, tiles, etc., are in an Owen Jones print in a fresh green and white. This conservatory was one of the most satisfying things I have ever done and was especially poignant for me because I knew I was going to have to leave the house very soon afterwards.

But we mustn't forget the drawing-room,

Another part of the drawing-room with Gothic bookcase.

The Gothic style conservatory looks as if it had always been part of the house.

which now looked totally a part of the conservatory since one stepped straight down from it. Naturally it had to be decorated in Gothic style and seemed to want to be crimson (although I still long to do a room in Gothic blue and gold). A friend of mine possessed a very ancient rug which both of us loved but was really in tatters. So we persuaded a carpet company to reproduce the same design and its border in a smart Brussels weave, keeping the original colouring of shades of crimson on a sand background. This looked magnificent when laid in our drawing-room. We had at the same time put back the original heavy grey marble fire-place and mirrored overmantel and removed from the room every stick of furniture, which consisted of the usual eclectic mix of comfortable sofas and family paraphernalia (because you have to be singleminded when decorating and I do know about sulking husbands and children, etc.). A huge Gothic side table was the first find and it cost so little money that the family groans became even louder. Then a splendid bookcase was installed plus extraordinary chairs that most people wouldn't want, some antlers for the wall, various feathers and shells under glass domes, more sculptured heads of poets and politicians, and the room looked magnificent. I forgot to mention that the wallpaper is printed in the same colourings as the carpet and was from an old design found at Harewood House in Yorkshire; the motif for the curtains came from the footboard of an old bed and the design for the pelmets was copied from an old upholsterer's book. I am particularly fond of these old tradesmen's books and the very elaborate, quite theatrical interior designs they portray—and why not live with swags and tassels? Anyway, the drawing-room now looks distinctly like the interior of a hunting lodge in a Walter Scott novel.

For seven years I lived between this Welsh house and a family house in London and I left Rhydoldog for ever on an early April day when the wild daffodils were smothering the banks of the old water garden and thousands more nodded to me all the way down the lovely driveway to say farewell.

I now live in Brussels and in France in quite a different way, but that is another story altogether.

Laura Ashley

Gothic side table in the drawing-room. ☞

Ana Ines Astor

A COTTAGE
Wiltshire

A few years ago, I needed to find a house in the country large enough to have children and grandchildren to stay, easy to look after, in nice country and in pleasant surroundings.

Having looked at endless unsuitable places and been 'gazumped' whenever there was anything vaguely adaptable, I was about to give up when I happened to look at some old copies of *Country Life*. There, staring out at me, was the cottage I needed. It looked charming, unspoilt, with all the necessary requirements, and the price was extremely attractive. But the fact that it had

remained unsold for many weeks made me uneasy. There must be some terrible drawback. I found out that the problem was a right of way, which led from one end of the village to the other, allowing people and riders to go by at all times. But this 'drawback' has been a pleasure for me—I enjoy people walking by and riders returning from the local hunt, but *they* must be plagued by my unending swearing, in every language I know, as I struggle in my garden. At one time the right of way became one of the most popular dog lavatories within two miles. It has now been gravelled, and

The Garden Room.

this seems to be the answer.

The cottage is thatched, with very thick walls and low ceilings, and is about three hundred years old. There were some additional buildings at the back which I have since joined to the centre building. It had originally been a pub, overlooking the village green. One of the downstairs bedrooms had a bread oven, a large beam going across the ceiling with three very strong hooks, and, when the workmen started putting the heating in, they found a well at the far corner of the room, by the window. It had to be filled in, but I did regret it the summer of that terrible drought.

The house had a happy feeling about it and you could sense that the previous owners had loved it and been content there; and there were no inglenook fire-places.

A tiresome friend, now a firm acquaintance, remarked that it was rather 'twee'. 'What a joy', said I, 'then I can fill the garden with gnomes and put "private eye" faces on them.' Undeterred by gloomy friends, I settled down to organise it. Taste is not only personal but relative. As a rule, houses have characters of their own which dictate how they would like you to live in them—that is unless they are irretrievably uncooperative.

It took a long time, sitting in every room at different angles and in different lights, plans in hand, studying all features and adapting them to taste and needs. Still sensitive to the 'twee' remark, contemplating what small proportions I had to work with, I decided then and there to turn it into a sort of nursery cottage. Not being British by origin, I could not aspire to the perfection of a Mrs. Tiggywinkle ambience so decided to try for the third bear style. A rather feminine third bear.

There were lots of alterations to be done, outside and inside. One of them was integrating an upstairs bathroom which I took off the end of a very long bedroom. As the ceiling below seemed tired and sagging, I was advised by the local builder to put in a plastic bath-tub to alleviate the burden. With a plastic bath-tub you tend to lose the heat of the water; and if you have a large guest you inevitably hear, as the walls are thin upstairs, a funny noise of body rubbing against wet plastic, sounding a bit like a seal.

I have never used an interior decorator. I came to this country during the war when there were none to be had, so followed my own taste, making endless mistakes as I went. In my time, I have tortured many builders. I always believe in using local professionals and started with the most expensive, as there was a lot of rewiring to be done and heating to be installed. A few years later, when I joined the outbuildings to the main house, I thought I would be clever and do it on the cheap. Felled by the charm of a man whose magic words were of how everything was possible and could be done immediately, I gave in, only to find a few years later that I had to go back to the expensive one as the roof leaked and the windows and doors rotted.

The entrance hall had to be altered so that a large larder could be integrated into it, so I had to get the right proportions in order to house gum-boots, baskets and the general paraphernalia of winter outdoor wear. Being in a hurry to move in, I chose to whitewash all walls. I found, in a town nearby, very nice carpeting in an off-white,

A pen-and-ink drawing of the back of the cottage by Mrs. Astor.

smooth tweed easy to shampoo, and I used it for all the downstairs rooms.

The sitting-room faces south. Two large thick beams run all the length of the room, under the ceiling, from fire-place to the opposite wall; these beams were supported by an upright wooden post. As the ceiling sags, I was advised by the builders to add another supporting post in the middle of the room, about two feet from the other one. It was then difficult to know what to do with the awkward space between them, so I placed a small round table there and covered it with a patchwork cloth of different patterns of red, pink, greens, blues and pale blues on a white background. On this table I placed a lamp which lights up the centre of the room. In between the windows, facing south, I put a desk, and on the opposite side a large and long settee to seat large-sized bears. The big stone fire-place had a Breughel look about it but the cold wind invariably howled down and it always smoked. I installed an old-fashioned iron wood-burner, called the 'Resolute'. It is effective, clean and warms a great deal of the house.

The curtains are hung by rings from plain dark wooden poles. I have used a very old-fashioned chintz, unobtainable now, of moss rose buds with green leaves on a white background speckled with light brown spots, and these are edged on the side facing the light in bright pink. The same chintz covers the large settee. By the fire-place under the window, there is a smaller settee covered in 'Amanda' Jonelle cotton, the overall colours of pale green and pink blending in with the rest of the room. I like mixing different prints in the same room, providing they have something in common, and have gone as far as covering an armchair with three different samples

The small window on the stairs is fitted with late Victorian stained glass.

The chairs and sofas in the sitting-room are covered in a mixture of gaily-coloured prints.

Mrs. Astor's bedroom.

The beamed sitting-room with south-facing windows.

I had bought to try out. It makes everything more varied and fun. All sofas and armchairs have needlework cushions with flower, butterfly or animal motifs, all colours and shapes blending into the room. By the fire-place there is a flowered bell-pull in needlework, and all side tables are white and low. Over the very large sofa there is a Venetian mirror, falling to pieces but still holding a lively reflection of the French door going into the garden. All paintings are done either by myself or members of my family. I do not have anything of value.

Sometimes in a room there is what I call the

Bermuda triangle, a fatal bit which will not come off, no matter how much you move the furniture around. There is one at the side of this room where I have two bookcases; in between the books I have photographs, bits of china and paintboxes. I am a clutterer by nature—much as I try to keep a room clear, within twenty-four hours it is full to the brim again.

A Venetian mirror hangs over the large sofa in the sitting-room.

By the fire-place on the left, there is a door which leads to a winding staircase. Halfway up there is a small window. My daughter gave me some stained glass from a church, late Victorian in alternating squares, some with primroses, others with cyclamen, with a deep red and green surround; it just fitted and looks very attractive.

The stairs are a bit narrow. They were painted black, and at night the light isn't too good. After a few falls it was obvious I had to sacrifice local norms for practicability, so I vandalised the stairs. I asked our local decorator to paint them

and the passage upstairs flamingo pink. It has created a great deal of comment, it gives the place some life, and I never fall now.

The bedrooms upstairs have very large beams going across and at an angle; they too were painted black. When I had the cracks in the walls done I painted all the beams white and it instantly made the rooms larger. I wallpapered walls and ceiling in a tiny, pale green flowered print on a white ground; you barely notice the print and it gives an overall colour without driving you mad. The paper came from Tesco's, and I have it in other bedrooms in different colours contrasting with the colours of the curtains. One particular bedroom has the curtains, dressing table, bed and buttoned Victorian armchair all covered in a Jonelle cotton named 'Loreta'; it is printed all over in different shades of reds and pinks relieved by a little pale green. The flowers have a distinct Eastern feeling. There is a square needlework rug with a deep pink background and a crown of white flowers in the middle with white initials inside it. All carpets upstairs are off-white. To give the bed some protection from the door I have hung from the ceiling, on a thick, round, brass rod, a curtain which runs round the foot of the bed. The chest-of-drawers is painted white and stencilled in a design of leaves in bright pink. I have used this design in different ways, alternating up and down, and it now looks very dressy, ready to go to a party. In this bedroom and in the passageway I have hung paintings by my grandchildren and children when they were young. I find them colourful, funny and artistic.

I don't think one's taste really changes; it expands as one acquires better ideas, through living. The cottage was decorated in two stages —when I first moved in and about six years later, when it needed repairs. By then my life was more relaxed and I had learnt many lessons.

We live in peace with each other—I love it. My cottage is my castle.

Chiquita Astor

Isabel Colegate

MIDFORD CASTLE
Bath, Avon

Our house is built in the shape of a clover-leaf, or trefoil. A magazine article in 1899 suggested that it was the ace of clubs, and that the original owner, Mr. Henry Disney Roebuck, had won a fortune on the turn of a card and commemorated it by having a house built for him in the shape of the winning card. It seems more likely that a fortunate inheritance from a rich uncle provided the wherewithal and that the design was taken from the *Builders Magazine* of 1774. In this John Carter, a Gothic enthusiast who had made various drawings of Horace Walpole's 'small cap-

ricious house' at Strawberry Hill, published a plan for 'A Gothic Mansion to be Erected on an Eminence that Commands an Extensive Prospect'. The ground plan of Midford follows John Carter's, though the builder who carried out the design added a storey and enlarged the basement.

There are three rooms round a central diamond-shaped hall. The pattern is repeated on the two upper floors, with landings in place of the hall. The stairs go up one of the straight sides between the turrets in a kind of square spiral. It is a surprisingly practical and convenient design.

The castle from the north-east side.

The library showing the tall pointed windows.

Part of the hall.

Over the library fire-place the imaginary eighteenth-century landscape by Richard Bampfylde.

dusty yellow colour, but when we considered the ceiling and the cornice we felt we should never be able to decide how to do it and what to pick out in what colour, so we asked the decorator Peter Hood to help us. He dug back through the layers of paint and found the original colour. It was dusty yellow, a colour much used in eighteenth century Bath, he told us, because it was supposed to go well with Bath stone. He painted the ceiling in paler tones, picked out the cornice in terracotta and painted the woodwork flat white and grey. To make it perfect we still have to aspire to the red curtains he recommended for us.

I spend a good deal of my time in the library, where my desk is. The other room on the ground floor used to be the drawing-room. The kitchen is to the side of the house, a fairly discreet stone box which was built on in 1938, when the basement kitchen must have been finally pronounced too

A view of the nineteenth-century Chapel Tower through a quatrefoil of the castle.

Less practical and convenient is the basement on which the whole thing is raised, and which extends in front of the house, underneath the strip of lawn and the balustrade, to emerge at ground level further down the hill. So determined was Mr. Disney Roebuck to build his house on just that slope of the steep hill that it had to be raised up on this strange platform, underneath which the servants, kitchens, horses and carriages were originally housed in what must have been, for the humans at least, some discomfort. Mr. Disney Roebuck secured his extensive prospect; the view over the Midford valley is essential to any idea of the house.

To one side of the house, and slightly lower, is a picturesque building put up about thirty years after the main house in order to accommodate the horses and carriages, and by that time the priest, in more comfort than the basement could afford. The Conolly family who bought the house in about 1810 were Roman Catholics, and at right angles to the stables they built a chapel whose tower remains although its walls have crumbled; the ruins have become incorporated in the garden. This building, like the view, is part of the effect of Midford. Like the house itself it is a curious mixture of fantasy and common sense.

None of the rooms in the house is large, although they are high. They all have pretty plasterwork on the ceilings and cornices. When we came to decorate the dining-room we thought of a

inconvenient. The drawing-room is known to us as the orange room because when we first came we painted it that colour (there used to be a book of historic colours which you could get from Parsons Paints, and this as far as I remember was Majolica Yellow). In those days it was a children's room. The children are nearly all grown-up now but the room doesn't seem to have become any tidier; it is certainly nothing so decorous as a drawing-room.

From the tidiness point of view, the disadvantage of my having my desk in the library is outweighed by the fact that underneath the

The diamond-shaped hall looking through to the dining-room.

curved walls. There is a table under one of the bookcases in the library which he made, and another long thin table, lacquered red, which goes behind the sofa and is usually covered with books. The walls here, above the panelled dado, are blue, and have a silk screen pattern in purple, making a sort of Gothic frieze above the level of the new bookshelves. This was designed by Ed Gilbert and Lucy Barlett who were then in partnership, and there again perhaps we were too cautious when it came to choosing the colours, because the purple only just shows up on the blue and in some lights you can hardly see it at all. On the other hand, I quite like that. The trouble with a house which has pretty architectural features is that you sometimes wonder if it wouldn't look best of all if you whitewashed the walls and left it empty.

All the rooms on the ground and first floors have three tall pointed windows, and we decided we didn't want to lose this shape by covering it with big curtains at night. Nor did it seem right to overpower a fairly small room with elaborate drapes over the tops of the windows. In the end we had the curtains cut to fit the arch, sewed them onto tape and tacked the tape onto the inside of the arch. The curtains are drawn by two strings running through rings at the top. We have used this design in all the rooms except those where we only have shutters.

Over the fire-place in the library we have an imaginary landscape by an eighteenth century painter called Richard Bampfylde. It belonged to my parents but turned out to be wholly appropriate for this part of the world, for Bampfylde was a West Country squire who was a friend of Henry Hoare of Stourhead, where there are a number of his pictures. Beneath it there is a little dark moonlight picture by John Crome the Younger which I bought in a sale in Bath some years ago. It needs cleaning. So does everything really. This was the first room we decorated when we came here twenty-two years ago, and it needs doing again. Whatever happened I should want it much the same; but that's because I dislike change rather than because I think it's perfect.

original glass-fronted bookcases on each side of the room are capacious recesses which look like drawers but are much deeper because of the thickness of the stone walls. Great heaps of papers of various kinds can be swept into these at a moment's notice; eventually, if left there long enough, they may be eaten by the mice. The bookcases presented us with what we thought was a problem. We wanted more book space but were nervous of diminishing or somehow throwing off balance the existing bookcases. Eventually we decided to put up the plainest possible shelves painted the same colour as the walls, and we had the ones between the windows made first. Even so, it was some time before we asked Alex Roberts to make the other two; as soon as they were up we wondered what we had been worrying about.

Alex Roberts is a furniture designer who lives and works in part of the stables here, and he has made several pieces of furniture for us to fit the

Isabel Colegate

Marian Brudenell

DEENE PARK
Northamptonshire

When I first visited Deene in January 1955 it was pathetically dilapidated and horribly uncomfortable.

There was a house party of twenty-four for a local dance and the warmth of the welcome from Mr. and Mrs. George Brudenell, my future father- and mother-in-law, obliterated the penetrating cold in the house. We were divided up into dormitories full of small iron beds with rocklike damp mattresses brought in from the stables. The sheets were grubby and I later discovered they were unwashed between visits but the top part ironed; the blankets had probably been at Balaclava and were crawling with maggots—it was like a ward at Scutari.

We were woken at dawn by the apparition of an ancient bandy-legged tramp who shambled into the room with logs to get the fire going. This proved not to be a ghost but Jo, who had started work here in 1903 and remained except for naval service in the First World War until his death in 1971.

Just as during the Civil War the house was plundered and extensively damaged by Cromwell's troops and needed restoration and refurnishing afterwards, so it was in 1945. Throughout the war the house was occupied by soldiers, British as well as Czechs, Poles and Indians, and by 1945 it had reached the nadir of decay. As Mr. and Mrs. Brudenell were quite unaware of decoration or of modern comforts it fell to my husband Edmund, while still in his teens, to persuade them to install electricity and some bathrooms. His father had held a three-day sale of the contents when he inherited in 1917 and more furniture was sold in 1948 to pay for installing electricity.

Deene is a large Elizabethan/Georgian house which has been home to thirteen generations of Brudenells and has reflected the changes in fortune of the family who over the centuries have enlarged, altered and patched it up so often. We wondered if we could ever manage to make it more habitable and continue to live in it and decided we couldn't bear to abandon it.

Deene Park.

We knew it would mean not only redecoration but extensive plumbing and electrical work, installing central heating and curing dry rot, not to mention buying furniture, carpets and curtains. The cost was inestimable and we would have to do it very slowly, just one room at a time and there were nearly a hundred!

My father- and mother-in-law (with whom we were to share the house for nearly seven years) gave us the Bow Room as our drawing-room and let us do it up how we liked. As it was the first of the eighty-six rooms we have done we particularly love it. It faces south with big French windows looking out to the garden and park and has bookcases on three walls, one of which is rounded with a fire-place in the centre. It had last been decorated in 1922, when the bookcases were painted iron grey and the walls a sickly yellowy beige. I was twenty-one, expecting twins and feeling rotten, and had no idea how to begin, so we con-

The oval drawing-room.

Lady Cardigan's brass four-poster is now back in her bedroom, together with prints and photographs of her and the hero of the Charge of the Light Brigade.

Part of the large drawing-room.

sulted Tony Howes who suggested that we should avoid the sombre colours traditionally used in libraries and take the softer colours from the Van Dyck school portrait of the first Lady Cardigan hanging over the chimney-piece. Coles made a damask-patterned wallpaper in quite a strong, rather dirty pink which admirably counteracts the heaviness of the old leather bindings. The bookcases were painted white and we kept the old dull brown plush curtains although we altered the deep box-pleated pelmets. We bought comfortable sofas and chairs to replace the old backbreakers with horsehair seats and arranged them so that people could talk to each other instead of shouting across an open space.

We bought lamps with silk shades which give a warmer light than the old barley-sugar standards with dark parchment shades. Now, twenty-seven years later, the room has changed a little. The Van Dyck has been replaced by a Reynolds of a later Lady Cardigan and we have improved the quality of the furniture.

By 1948 the Victorian pale blue silk on the drawing-room walls was rotten and hung down in faded yellow festoons, but unfortunately it was then replaced by a most dreary wallpaper. We enlisted the help of Oliver Ford, who found a lovely silvery blue American wallpaper reminiscent of the old silk and combined it with palest blues, greens and yellows on chairs and carpet. It is now a peaceful room dominated by the seventeenth century portraits. The furniture here is mostly mediocre French—unfortunately good French furniture was quite beyond us in price. We were however very lucky to have started in the fifties before prices went mad and when you could still find bargains in back streets. We bought masses of furniture, lots of china, usually chipped, and rescued quite a few pictures of ancestors which turned up in the salerooms.

It was great fun hunting things down and rearranging the rooms for them. Finding the right place is important but not always easy or obvious. If everything in a room is all of the same date and too carefully matched it has that clinical effect frequently seen in museums and houses open to the public. As Deene dates from Tudor to Regency times with rooms of all sizes we have had ample scope to avoid boredom, but we have always considered what the original use and appearance might have been and tried to use materials that are

Small ante-room full of pretty things.

either old or don't look glaringly new. Nothing has been regilded and whenever possible things have been repaired. Thank goodness we had a skilled and cooperative house carpenter who became adept at picture-hanging and altering panelling and doors, and a team of willing hands who heaved the furniture up and down and round about trying to find where things looked best; we put picture rails in every room so that pictures could hang from chains and be moved without leaving the walls scarred. Edmund used to get very irritated by this 'earthquaking' and always wanted everything put back by dinner.

The most important room in the house is the Elizabethan Great Hall with its hammerbeam roof. It is very much the heart of the house and the

Left: *Seventeenth-century portraits hang on the silvery-blue walls of the peaceful drawing-room.*

Below: *Painting of the dining-room by John Sergeant, 1982.*

The dining-room today.

Country Life *photograph of The Great Hall, 1909.*

first room visitors see. In old photographs of 1909 and 1915 during the lifetime of the notorious Lady Cardigan it was an astonishing clutter of Victorian carved oak and leather chairs, oil lamps, stags' heads, mementoes of Balaclava and a whole stuffed tiger standing snarling menacingly on a gilt Queen Anne table. Above him on the oak panelling hung a magnificent Louis XIV clock which, together with the fire-place and the panelling from the other three walls, was sold in the twenties. The room degenerated into a barn, with brown silage paper on the walls and frosted glass replacing the seventeenth century stained glass in the windows. These were restored in 1959, and in 1963 the massive coarse fire-place dated 1571 was moved in from the billiard-room, the walls were plastered and painted, and the huge sofas with carved figures on the arms were brought back. Lady Cardigan, dressed in white satin even in her eighties, used to play the piano here and sing torrid love songs after dinner to the assembled, usually male,

company. She had been the adoring wife of the hero of the Charge of the Light Brigade whose junior she was by twenty-seven years. She died in 1915 after forty-seven years of merry widowhood at Deene only interrupted by a short-lived marriage to a Portuguese count. Her reputation was such that few ladies ever came here. Lady Cardigan was an accomplished, high-spirited woman, an excellent linguist and with a sharp wit, but her lively eccentricity shocked society. She wore Lord Cardigan's uniform trousers for bicycling, proposed marriage to Disraeli, wore thick white make-up and a blonde wig, had steeplechases over the gravestones in the churchyard and kept her coffin in the house, sometimes lying in it and asking how she looked! Some years ago her bed was offered back to us—my father-in-law had sold it in 1918—and of course we accepted with alacrity. It is a pretty brass four-poster and is now back in her bedroom covered in fine turquoise cotton. The room is full of prints and photographs of her and Lord Cardigan as well as a signed picture of the Pope, who rather surprisingly gave them an audience on their honeymoon. We used a Swiss wallpaper with a little all-over pattern and bought an old Scotch carpet in the perfect colours for two pounds ten at a sale.

Of all the Lady Cardigans Adeline must have been by far the most beautiful and amusing but her extravagance, with houses at Cowes, Newmarket, Melton and London as well as Deene and a yacht called the *Sea Horse*, led to the arrival of the bailiffs and the sale of her clothes, carriages and horses.

The bailiffs returned in 1928 and removed more things from the house, but luckily none of the family portraits without which the house would look depressingly bare. Though there are no great masterpieces they do give a valuable sense of continuity and are certainly decorative. We have had years of happiness and fun bringing the house back to life and pray that no disaster will cause the bailiffs to return or the contents to be dispersed again.

I hope that our descendants will live here and look after the old place and save it from the dreaded dead hand of a Committee or Institution.

Marian Brudenell

Barbara Cartland

CAMFIELD PLACE
Hatfield, Hertfordshire

In 1275 a knight called Camfield bought a few acres of ground near Hatfield in Hertfordshire and apparently retired there.

Later, in the reign of Queen Elizabeth I, a very beautiful Tudor manor house was built on the ground, with dovecots and fishpools as was customary in those days.

But the land had earlier been known to the Romans, and there is a Roman road going through the estate as well as a gravel-pit from which, from Roman days on, gravel was extracted for building.

In the eighteenth century Capability Brown was asked to landscape the park. It sloped down to a winding stream which eventually, after passing a great deal of woodland, reached the river Lea. This has now been enlarged to form two lakes.

In 1867 Edmund Potter, a rich industrialist from the North, pulled down most of the Tudor house and rebuilt Camfield Place. His grand-daughter Beatrix Potter often stayed with him there, and in her biography there is a whole chapter written by her on 'The place I love best'. She undoubtedly wrote *The Tale of Peter Rabbit* about Camfield and illustrated some parts of her

'The most beautiful bed in the world'—a carved French four-poster dated 1650.

Above: *The library, containing over six thousand books, has deep blue panelling picked out in white.*
Below: *The kitchen forms an attractive setting for colourfully produced dishes.*

Favourite 'Egyptian' colours of Nile blue and bright coral pink are used in the bedroom.

grandfather's garden.

The door in the wall which the little rabbit couldn't squeeze underneath is still there, so is the goldfish pond where the white cat sat twitching his tail, and the potting-shed in which Peter Rabbit hid in a watering-can. In fact Mr. McGregor's garden is very much the same today as it is in her book.

In another part of the garden there is an oak tree planted by Queen Elizabeth I when she was a prisoner as a girl at Hatfield, to commemorate the spot where she shot her first stag. The acorns and leaves from this tree, which I have dipped in gold, are considered very lucky and people write from all over the world to tell me what benefits they have brought them.

The outside of the house is not very attractive, being late Victorian, but fortunately the inside was transformed by the previous owner, Lord Queenborough. He had two American millionairess wives, one of whom was the mother of Lady Baillie who owned the magnificent Leeds Castle. They put Georgian cornices in all the large, high rooms designed by Mr. Potter, added exquisite Adam mantelpieces, parquet flooring throughout the house and ten bathrooms. I have twelve, so there is no excuse for anybody to be dirty at Camfield Place.

What I have, which is unique and could not be found anywhere else, is a picture gallery which is actually a passage running right across the house; part of it belongs to the old Tudor manor, and it is entirely decorated with the original paintings done for the covers of my novels.

There must be over five hundred of these now. My first artist, Frances Marshall, whose designs have a special magic, is now unfortunately dead, but the work of two other artists decorates the walls and the only trouble is that I am beginning to run out of space!

During the war I altered the colouring of some of the most secret R.A.F. stations in England and it was proved that in doing so I improved morale. I am a tremendous believer in colour and my two favourites are Nile blue and bright coral pink, which I chose from the lovely Egyptian murals in the Valley of the Tombs of the Kings in Luxor. Wherever I have lived I have had these colours. While they are purely Egyptian in my bedroom, in the drawing-room the walls are a little more jade, as is the carpet, but the curtains are still a brilliant pink.

My library is to me one of the most important rooms in the house because it contains all the books that are absolutely essential to my work. For every novel I write I read twenty to thirty history books; it is very important that the background to every story should be correct as I am read in schools and universities all over the world. This room, which has a deep, almost peacock blue panelling picked out in white, contains over six thousand books. The carpet is a special shade of pink while the curtains and sofa are sunshine yellow.

Because I write between twenty and twenty-five books a year my secretaries' office is of paramount importance, and here again the walls are covered with some of the best and most beautiful of Frances Marshall's covers for my novels. The filing cabinets are all red, and so are the typewriters.

When my husband and I first came to Camfield Place in 1950 immediately after the war, there were heavy restrictions on how much decorating and improvements you could do. As Lord Queenborough died when he was eighty-eight, there was a great deal that wanted doing. I managed, however, to bring colour and beauty into every room and I collected the furniture I particularly love from antique shops for what seem now bargain prices.

One piece of furniture of which I am particularly proud and which is, in my opinion, the most beautiful bed in the world, I acquired in the most amusing manner.

I was motoring down from Scotland and stopped at Harrogate. I told somebody there that I wanted a four-poster bed and was informed there was one for sale in York. My son and I drove into York and I saw the shop I wanted to visit while we were stuck in a traffic jam. I left him, jumped out, went into the shop and saw an exquisite French four-poster dated 1650 which was beautifully carved. It had a sunburst of angels surrounding the Blessed Virgin over the bedhead. The original gilding was still on the canopy overhead, also the hook from which a lantern had been hung. I took one look, said I would have it, and ran back to my son.

The traffic jam was still outside so I took over the wheel of the car while he went into the shop, agreed it was exactly what we wanted, and was back in the car before the traffic had started to move.

I have had a great deal of the bed regilded and I myself, with plastic wood, mended the very few places on the canopy which needed it. There are two carvings of its original owner, one wearing his armour and the other his ordinary clothes. I feel because he was a Frenchman he would appreciate how much we all love and admire his bed.

It is always difficult to know what to do with caricatures. I shall never have as many as the Earl Mountbatten of Burma, who had half-a-dozen passages ornamented with his. But I have collected them all together and have them hung in the

The gentlemen's cloakroom houses an extensive collection of original Barbara Cartland caricatures.

gentlemen's cloakroom, where they amuse every guest who comes to the house. It seems a perfect place for them, and although it is not very easy I try whenever I am caricatured to buy the original from the artist.

As I am President of the National Association of Health, I believe good food is the foundation of good health. Therefore my kitchen is very important. It is, I think, beautiful; digestion starts with the eyes, and just as my dishes are lovely, many of them being a picture on the plate and as colourful and attractive as I can make them, so is where they are cooked. The wallpaper and the curtains are the design of the Bird of Paradise.

More than anything else what one needs in one's house is the right atmosphere, and when I came to Camfield Place I asked the local Rector who, fortunately, had lived in Jamaica so that he understood what was required, if he would bless my house. He blessed every room including the kitchen, which is most important, and I can confidently say that the house now has a lovely and peaceful atmosphere.

It was not until some years after we moved

here that Margaret Lane published the biography of Beatrix Potter and revealed that she had been frightened by ghosts in the hall and when she went up the stairs.

The only ghost we have now—and as I lived in a ghost house when I was a girl I dislike having them around me—is that of a black-and-white cocker spaniel which I had to have put to sleep because he had cancer.

I was the first person to see his ghost sitting under a table in the hall. My live dogs were frightened of him because at first he went for them ferociously when they tried to eat their dinner. Now he leaves them alone. Almost everybody in the house has seen him at some time or another.

He was a very sweet, quiet little dog and I think he stays with us because this was where he was happy and he does not wish to leave those he loved.

The garden is a bird sanctuary and the birds come every morning to eat the nuts which I put outside my bedroom window.

Apart from the pheasants we breed and my own free-range chickens, the estate is full of wild-life, even though we are only seventeen miles from London.

There are barking deer, foxes, squirrels, badgers and an inordinate amount of moles and, of course, we can never get rid of the 'Peter Rabbits'. Unfortunately they eat every flower I put in the garden with the exception of geraniums, and I therefore fill the flower-beds all around the house every year with bright coral pink geraniums, and hope the 'Peter Rabbits' will ignore them.

But they are, of course, part of Camfield Place and have 'owned' it for far longer than we have.

Diana Cooper

Little Venice, London

I think I will write about bedrooms, of which I have had quite a number in my long life. It is the room in most houses to which I'm the most attached—offering repose, sleep, privacy, or receiving of friends, clustered or singly, round a bed in which I weightless lie.

This is my life today and nearly every day and has been since I lost my independence—independence being my faithful little mini car, which I am too old to drive. Thus one comes back to one's beginning, but without independence or agility and with failing senses—consciously

worsening instead of the unconscious bettering from earliest childhood.

Like all my contemporaries, I spent two-thirds of my early life, together with a sister, in the night-nursery, the first unremembered in a small house in Bruton Street, still standing but now shop-fronted. (Once, many years ago, alone in my car, I followed a sirening fire engine quite a long way for fun, and found our flaming goal to be the house of my birth!)

In a little country house I suppose my family had taken for the five of us, there were curiously

Part of the drawing-room which has a very French atmosphere.

Lady Diana Cooper's present bedroom. The pale yellow french wall-paper is covered with small pictures.

A pretty arrangement of objects with a 'trompe l'oeil' in the background.

enough no country sports, so for my father, who enjoyed fishing, shooting, clubs, women and entertaining, there was nothing to do. At Hatley there were not even neighbours, no electric light or taps, or, of course, baths, only the silly tin slipper-shaped tubs in front of the fire-place.

We would often be taken to my grandfather's castle, called Belvoir, where life was much the same, no light or running water on the first floor, but watchmen indoors and out at night, who shouted most comfortably. Every hour one would hear a gravelled footstep and then, 'Past twelve o'clock—all's well'.

Suddenly everything changed—a child died! Then, with Nanny and a governess for the older children, it was settled to expand in London, where a very beautiful enormous house, decorated by William Kent, was bought. We were all sad— change often saddens—a new night-nursery,

habits unaltered—but, oh! the unexpected wonder of it! electric light and hot water you could
turn on and off, and real long baths.

I spent more time in bed because I developed
a muscular disease which lasted me three or four
years. Stairs were forbidden, so my next bedroom
was about as beautiful a reception-room as you
could hope to find: mirrored walls, massively but
delicately garlanded with chains of metal-gilded
flowers. Here I slept with a criminal called
'Fraulein', only getting up at lunchtime and being
carried to my mother's bed next door—another
reception-room not half as gorgeous as mine, but
both had two enormous windows looking onto
Green Park where a military band played Gilbert
and Sullivan once weekly. My mother's bedroom
had a concealed proper bathroom, so we were
complete.

Messenger boys, aged elevenish, took my
mother's notes to her friends for sixpence and I
went out all afternoon by hansom cab at half a
crown an hour. In the mornings I had daily treat-
ment, still in bed. The evening was pretty often
the theatre, generally Shakespeare, including
rehearsals at His Majesty's, the Beerbohm Tree
family being interwoven with ours. I was cured by
the age of eleven and lost my sensational reception
bedsitter in disfavour of the schoolroom, looking
onto a huge cobbled courtyard alive with cab and
private horses stumbling away noisily.

Belvoir had become my father's, and my
mother had decked it with light and water and I
had my first real bedroom of my own—black-
painted walls, a scooped alcove washing basin,
self-painted to look as if under water, with a stone
cockleshell (protruding) to hold the soap and
swags of 'everlastings' in little bunches, and the
narrowest, highest, reddest four-poster to the ceiling.

The whole arrangement was made more
incongruous when I tell you that bang in the
centre of the small, narrow room was a real
punchball which I would punch by the hour in
order to fight fat or to imagine I was chastising a
lady I was not in favour of.

I was an adult at 14, making a bit of money by
sewing a kind of chiffon 'top', to the knee, designed
by the great Poiret (and lent me by a fashionable
rich Parisian lady) and edged with silver braid, for
three pounds, it costing me no more than fifteen
shillings thank the Lord.

Another corner of Lady Diana Cooper's bedroom.

A brilliant few seasons in weekend 'stately
homes'—two nights weekly in variable
bedrooms—were followed by the utter change of
Guy's Hospital, for the Great War was enforcing
us all to work. I had a little room to myself, of
which I was not master, for the essential light
blazed you awake at 7 am and blacked you out at
10 pm, so I really have no memory of the room.

Peace, then marriage and looking for a house.
I found one in a quarter of Bloomsbury, a quarter
not yet the legend it became. It cost ninety pounds
a year with Adam mantelpieces and the right
window-panes—all-important to me, who could
or would not live behind plate glass—and a
charming garden with forest trees.

After a hundred identical bedrooms while
theatrically touring America, my husband's career
took us to Admiralty House. There was an outlook
almost as sensational as the Green Park one, with a
view of Whitehall and St. James's Park, and a bed
held and rocked by golden dolphins, designed by
Rex Whistler. Naturally I liked the bedroom best,
though the ground floor was also crowded with

The small hall has silk on the walls.

golden dolphins. Downstairs was duty; my bedroom was bliss.

The next bedroom I remember was in Singapore in a charming little house deliberately built, except for the bedrooms, without doors or panes in windows. Again, in spite of the 'tick-tock' bird that hindered sleep, my refuge was my bedroom. The Japanese ousted us and so back to our Bognor home, sleeping to the lullaby of sea waves.

Peace was looming distantly and Algiers was our next mission—a new agony for me to be torn from happiest farming duties. There we found ourselves in a huge Arab house shared by another couple—Arctic cold in winter, no staff at all, washing at Harold Macmillan's next door, sleeping *in* my valuable mink coat. Yet it was still a joy to go upstairs to an agreeably proud bedroom.

Looking out of my window one spring morning I was surprised to see a semi-nude Arab crucified, with string, not nails, but frying in the violent sunshine, having been caught stealing. 'No', I was told, 'he can't be freed till midday.' So at midday he was brought down from his cross and left to return to his stealing.

The bedroom, as usual, became the club, with Randolph Churchill and Evelyn Waugh breakfasting on my bed; but still a refuge room.

Peace! And from peace to Paris as Ambassa-dor's wife. Panic! Everything that I most disliked, the only delight the most wonderful bedroom, said to have been Pauline Borghèse's (Napoleon's sister), repudiated, God knows why, by usual ambassadresses—probably because there was no bathroom, but I got one in a flash, fashioned like a tent in a space outside the door. The bedroom itself was sensational—walls, curtains, screens, sofas and chairs all of the same crimson red silk and a vast bed of the same silk crowned at all but cciling height by an imperial eagle and supported by *retour d'Egypte* figures. A few of the chairs' seats were beginning to wear, and I suggested to what was then called the Office of Works that they order a hundred metres of the identical silk to be kept for future dilapidation at the Embassy. My surprise was total upon discovering that the identical material came not from Lyons but from Macclesfield, England.

After two or three years in the country's service, wearying, but restored by the bed, we moved out of Paris to a very pretty little house within the walls of the park of Chantilly, where from my bedroom I looked south onto well-tended grass sloping down to an important lake, fed by an even more important cascade. No traffic, no tourists—only woodland groves, peopled by beautiful silent statues.

I came home after about ten years, alas! alone, and found myself a house I would exchange with no other in the best of all quarters—Little Venice—whose bedroom, whence I scribble now, I still find the room of the rooms in the house I like best, with forest trees in thc garden, a big bed and tiny dog—still, and as always, a *refuge*.

Diana Cooper

The Duchess's four-poster bed has an arched cornice and painted fluted posts. The chintz bed hangings match the window curtains.

Deborah Devonshire

CHATSWORTH
Bakewell, Derbyshire

I f you are a woman who finds herself married to the hereditary owner of what used to be known as a stately home and is now called a historic house, you soon become aware of the unwritten rules of primogeniture.

You live in furnished rooms, surrounded by things which do not and never will belong to you. You are also aware that if you should become a widow you move, pronto, and the familiar things stay.

All interest is centred on the eldest son and his family. Younger sons are looked on as a sort of

long-stop insurance but the birth of a daughter is greeted with sighs from the family solicitor. This situation is taken for granted by Englishwomen. It is the way of primogeniture and it is the reason that, in spite of savage taxation, there are still wonderful interiors in English houses, hundreds of which can be seen by paying a pound or two in the season. I have seen it from both sides, having married a younger son who became his father's heir through the depredations of war. It is part of the Great Unfairness of Life, but it works.

At Chatsworth there is ample evidence of the

Looking to the fire-place of the small sitting-room. The walls are hung with dark green watered silk.

system. Furniture and pictures from abandoned Cavendish houses (Devonshire House and Chiswick House in London, Compton Place at Eastbourne and Hardwick Hall in Derbyshire) crowd the attics and give so much to choose from that, as well as rearranging most of the rooms here, I have furnished two country hotels.

In 1957 we began to think about moving back into Chatsworth. The family had left in 1939 and a girls' school moved in with the war—three hundred girls and their teachers lived there in discomfort till 1946, sleeping in passages and state rooms and doing their lessons in any suitable space. After that the house was empty. My mother-in-law made the huge effort to get it reopened for people to see round in 1949 and the staff of ten Hungarians she engaged did magnificent work cleaning and making ready the rooms on the public route round the house. They did not have time to do much to the rest and it was very depressing to come over from our own house in the village a mile away and look at the shuttered rooms, so shabby and having that special stale, closed-up smell.

When we decided to come and live here we considered which bit of the house we would use. There are a hundred and seventy-five rooms at the last count so the possibilities were endless but we soon settled for the traditional rooms used by the family. These are on the first floor facing south and west. We have never regretted it.

Work went on for nearly two years. We put in seventeen bathrooms and central heating. (Till 1939 there was one bath and lavatory for seven visitors' bedrooms on the east side of the house.) This meant water going long distances to rooms which it had not reached before. Slowly the smell of emptiness and decay gave way to the smell of paint and now it is only by an effort that I can remember how squalid and dingy the rooms were after being shut up for years.

Because of the shape (and size) of this house it is wonderfully convenient to live in when it is open in the summer. The people who come to see round go straight from the ground floor to the second floor where the state rooms are. You can sit in the drawing-room on the first floor and be unaware that a thousand other people are in the house at the same time. So well built is it that the faintest murmur, like a distant sea, is all you hear.

I was lucky when I started work on the house

A mixture of old and new pictures against the slub silk walls of the bedroom.

in 1958 because Andrew gave me a free hand so I only had to please myself. I think the role of a professional decorator must be very difficult. He has to please his client and can rarely do just what he wants, but when the job is finished his name is connected with it however much he may regret the decisions of the client. I can't imagine employing a decorator, partly because I am too mean but mostly because I love looking for the materials and other necessities myself. It is like hunting, and is nearly as exciting when, after drawing blank for days, you suddenly find the stuff you want.

Because of the vast size of the house (the roof is one and a third acres) I will try and describe the two rooms I spend most time in, or I shall overrun my allotted space by thousands of words.

In 1958 the Duchess's bedroom still had a peeling blue wallpaper left from the 1930s and the doors and paintwork were of the dreariest, dirtiest buff. The four-poster bed was so shrouded in dustsheets (and dust) that you could not guess what it was like. It had been a classroom during the war but the bed was left as there was nowhere else to put it.

When we unpacked the bed it revealed an arched cornice painted with flowers and painted fluted posts. We found the bed hangings, which match the window curtains. They are made of a chintz with bunches of flowers as 'filling' and wide borders of huge peonies and chrysanthemums, a pattern which is repeated in other bedrooms in the house. I have never seen it anywhere else. It is strikingly beautiful and is of Chatsworth scale and quality. The silk-covered bobbles are just a row of wooden pegs now with traces of the old silk clinging to them. I got new lining for the canopy and curtains, blue jap silk from John Lewis, clean and cheap.

The walls are covered with pale blue slub silk bordered by a gilt fillet of a complicated pattern. Nearly all the bedrooms have these fillets in different designs. John Fowler told me they are made of *papier mâché* on wire and that they are Italian.

The sofa at the foot of the bed has never been covered (laziness) but is wrapped in one of those old white cotton bedspreads with patterns made of bubbles of air. I wish I knew where to get this stuff. Perhaps it doesn't exist any more.

Three large dogs share the room with me and my sister Diana says it has a zoo smell. One of them likes sleeping under the bed and does something awful to the springs when he turns over.

The ornaments all seem to be to do with chickens. The best are a pair of Belgian faience hens, with eggs attached and chicks on their backs and under their wings.

In 1941 my aunt gave me three pounds to buy myself a wedding present. I rushed to Peter Jones and got the triple mirror which is on the dressing table.

The pictures are a mixture of old and new, Landseer, Epstein, Allingham, Duncan Grant, Millet, Rosa Bonheur, two Helleus of my mother, and various unknowns. The latest acquisition is some Huggins poultry.

I wake up very early and make my breakfast here. The strident colours of the electric kettle and toasting machine are a blot on the landscape but the comfort of not having to wait for a civilised hour outweighs that. I try not to have it before seven but I can see the time coming when it will be six and then five. It is early in the morning when all is quiet that I look around and realise how lucky I am to sleep in such a room.

The little sitting-room nearby is a complete change from the high drawing-rooms. In the last century a floor was put in so it is half the original height, and gives a mezzanine above. I am glad this was done because it makes the sitting-room of more human scale and the space above is a precious one for hanging clothes, hiding Christmas presents and keeping the mass of things acquired over the years.

There were dingy beige cotton hangings on the wall, a relic of Granny and years ago. It was the headmistress's study while the school was here.

I got dark green watered silk from George Spencer of Sloane Street and they hung it. It is box-pleated every four inches and fixed by a plain gilt fillet I found in the stable loft. After twenty-five years it has faded a bit but there is no harm in that and you only notice it when a picture is moved. The floor is covered in beige felt, which seems better than plain pile where a pattern might be too muddling to the eye. By the fire is a needlework rug with snakes sewn into it.

The paint below the dado, and the ceiling, is dead white; unfashionable, but it is what I like. Most of the furniture came from Compton Place at Eastbourne. It is smaller in scale than the native Chatsworth things and extremely pretty and pleasant to live with.

The sofa and armchair are covered in cotton with a dark green oak-leaf design. The covers are worn out and the piping cord hangs loose from the cushions. You can still get the stuff in any colour except the one I like, which is a warning to buy twice as much as you want in the first place. Extravagant I know, but as Hamish Erskine used to say when he took a taxi instead of a bus for fear of getting lost, it's cheaper in the end.

The writing table is an inlaid English beauty made by Ince and Mayhew, who supplied furniture for the drawing-rooms here in 1786. It is so smothered in letters and ornaments and flowers that I have resorted to spikes to hold papers which really must not be lost. Sometimes I find the bottom letters have answered themselves by being there for so long and with great satisfaction I throw them away.

There are swatches of patterns, architects' plans, more and more writing paper, photographs waiting to be stuck into albums, reference books, farm reports, files, ponies' pedigrees, half-written speeches, lists for tomorrow, and other signs of

Corner of the sitting-room. The inlaid writing-table was made by Ince and Mayhew, who supplied furniture for the Chatsworth drawing-rooms in 1786.

extra-mural activities on the floor. I spend a great deal of time looking for things I have lost and I beg people not to leave an important paper near my room without keeping a copy. On a windowsill is every one of the magazine *Interiors* since it started. The pile is beginning to topple now.

I am no good at indoor flowers and can't do arrangements so I plump for plants in pots, preferably the kind that last a long time. There is a glorious portrait of a woman by Velasquez which I can see from the writing table. The lower half of her is usually obliterated by flowers.

I think all pictures look well on the green silk. There is a strange mixture in this little room. An early Freud, a tiny Millais watercolour, a Boldini drawing of my mother's foot, a Turner of Oxford of sheep on Salisbury plain with Stonehenge in the background, some framed ivory and wax pictures,

a Landseer portrait of the sixth Duke in his box at the opera, the fourth Duke's children in the garden at Chiswick by Zoffany, some Crawhall chickens, Wootton racehorses and Barden Tower by Atkinson Grimshaw. To look at such a mixture every day is pure pleasure.

Books are a bother. They grow in number in the most extraordinary way. I'm all for a bookcase full of books (and there are two such in here, one a blocked-up door which someone put shelves in), but when they fall about all over the place what are you to do? It seems awful to throw them away when you think of what a trouble they are to write. Perhaps I will put a second-hand book stall in the shop.

There are two big boxes where I throw letters from family and friends. I suppose few people write to each other as often as we all do and the quantities are a bit daunting, but I couldn't bear to tear them up.

I feel sorry for the person who has to clear out this room when I have gone. It is encrusted with *things*. It is like the room in Ireland described by Somerville and Ross when they were trying to pack up before moving . . . 'Under *everything* there is *something*'.

The view from this side of the house is one of the joys of living here. Below is the West Garden, with its plan of Chiswick House in golden box. You look over it to the river Derwent and James Paine's three-arched bridge beyond, then a mile or more of close-cropped grass and huge trees and up the hill to the high woods on the distant skyline.

If ever I have a house of my own I will try something different, partly because nothing could be as beautiful as Chatsworth and partly because I should not want to embark on rooms and furniture which have to be looked after.

I expect it will have blockbusting heating, painted floors, office furniture made of tin, filing cabinets with drawers which open and shut with terrifying ease, a shiny red writing table from Rymans and an Executive Chair with a swivel seat covered in beige tweed. The cabinets will be empty because I will have nothing to do. It will feel very odd.

Deborah Devonshire

Daphne Fielding

THE LAUNDRY
Badminton, Avon

L ike Mrs. Tiggywinkle of Beatrix Potter fame,
I live in a laundry—the old laundry of Badminton House, owned by the Duke of Beaufort. It
was built in 1662—a sundial marks this date. The
classical Caroline building stands alone beside a
large reach of water which used to be known as 'the
horse-pond' and is contained by sunken drystone
walling. Here, in what is now my home, the laundry of a succession of dukes and duchesses, their
families and visitors was washed, blue-bagged,
starched, ironed and goffered.

    When I first saw where I was going to live, the

laundry had not functioned as such for many a
year and had become a mere shell—a beautiful
grey fossilised shell. Inside, the ceiling was falling
down, walls were crumbling, and below an eczema
of flaking plaster the old narrow red bricks
showed. Rats had invaded. There were still
broken remains of wooden drying screens that
used to be manipulated by rope-pulleys and hung
with bedlinen and household napery after it had
been washed, scrubbed and boiled in a great
copper. Brick niches, like old-fashioned bakers'
ovens, were built into the walls for the heating of

Looking across and out of the living-room.

flat-irons on red-hot embers. On the far side of the water, clothes-lines were set in an orchard of apple trees.

The horse-pond has now become a crowded duck-pond inhabited by descendants of the white 'Call ducks' brought there by Mary Cambridge when she married the last duke in 1923.

Wild mallard ducks from other waters fly in at dusk. Some of these foreigners have become squatters. They are a rough lot and molest the white Jemima Puddleducks which have crossed with Aylesburys, resulting in a strain peculiar to this pond and which increases yearly despite nocturnal raids of foxes—lords of the animal world at Badminton. But . . . back to square one and how I came to live here.

My son-in-law, David Somerset, is the present Duke. The restoration of the laundry was his project, and he asked that brilliant architect Philip Jebb (Hilaire Belloc's grandson) to submit a plan on which they worked closely together.

I had been living in France for fifteen years and wanted to return to England, when out of the blue came the wonderful offer of the laundry—to come and live there when the restoration was finished and make it my permanent home. I could hardly believe my good fortune.

Philip Jebb's blueprint was to feature one very big room and I was asked whether I would prefer a large bedroom or living-room. Without hesitation I plumped for a big living-room; I like a womb-pocket of a bedroom (with room to swing a Pekingese) and a rather larger bathroom which I can also use as my dressing-room. When the work was nearly finished I moved from France and stayed with my daughter and son-in-law in their house at the gates of the park. While I was staying with them I visited the site most days, clutching Jebb's blueprint which began to crack at the folds. I also made many trips to Bath and London to get patterns of wallpapers and snippets of fabric for curtains, furniture upholstery and loose covers.

I was positive that I wanted the big room to be cream and white. My friend Alan Tagg—one of the best of our stage decorators—told me of a paint he had often used successfully; its colour name is 'Buttermilk'. This has a pinkish glow coming through pale cream; it is lovely.

Furniture removers from England bringing a friend's furniture out to France returned with the empty van crammed full with all my treasures;

Corner of the drawing-room.

none of great value, but infinitely precious to me because I am a sentimental magpie. The provenance of most of my furniture and objects springs from two grandmothers and the *salle des ventes* at Nîmes. All arrived safely at Badminton but when unloaded most of them seemed unworthy of the noble big room which forms the heart of the house. This is almost a double cube but, like all the rooms in Badminton, proved slightly uneven when it came to taking measurements; this, I think, adds a certain charm. It has four double mullion windows with the original lead surrounding the square panes and a French window-cum-door. The ceiling is very high and has a fine cornice—the copy of one in my son-in-law's house in the village; a plastercast was taken from the original.

The windows at the far end of the room have window seats in recesses contained by the thick walls. From these I can observe the duck-pond. The French window on the opposite side of the room leads into a cobbled courtyard where a short roofed-in passage is the approach to my front door; through it a sweep of grass lawn, the big house and another world.

The cobbled courtyard is very French in feeling and viewed through the front door gives one the impression that it will lead to a *pavillon de*

The Old Laundry, with Badminton House behind.

chasse. Before the restoration it was covered by a glass roof and strips of corrugated iron. When I first saw it a lone lavatory stood against a wall and still flushed; its make was 'Niagara'!

The big room has lovely details. In a store-room at Badminton House a beautiful Kent chimney-piece languished unseen. Kent was the architect of the house and this must be contemporary. The last Duke in his great kindness let me have it installed in my big room. It is my favourite thing there. In the centre set between wreaths of fruit and flowers is a head of Diana, goddess of the chase, with a crescent moon in her hair. Swags of full-blown roses and plums hang from two stylised pedestals on either side. There is a Greek key pattern border below the shelf they support. Here I have green glass obelisks and two Jean Petiot figures of a sultan and sultana. Rising above it is a big Regency mirror.

I had borrowed an elegant Georgian fire-basket which stood on legs. It was in keeping with the Kent mantelpiece but eighty per cent of the heat of the fire was lost up the chimney, so I am installing a Norwegian cast-iron stove copied from a classical American colonial design. Either side of it will stand two andirons—cast-iron figures of autumn and winter which marry well with the mantelpiece. I bought these at an auction sale in Nîmes.

Some people are totally unable to visualise the restoration and conversion of a building with prophetic eyes. Many of my friends who saw the laundry in its state of ruin were convinced that the big room would be dark. In point of fact, it is dancing with light which, on a sunny day, reflects off the water onto the ceiling.

My curtains are full and long with deep pelmets. They are interlined with padding and the material is chintz. The design, rather like Chinese wallpaper, has big pink peonies, fuchsia and yellow lilies on a cream-coloured ground. They were made by Yvonne Nettles, the daughter-in-law of the housekeeper at Badminton. Her husband did the carpentry required for this job. All my curtains and pelmets have been made with a *tête flamande* (French heading). I love this because it looks like smocking and reminds me of children's frocks.

The big room leads into the kitchen, which has two views. My back door opens onto the 'waterfront' and a French window onto the cobbled courtyard with its pot plants and window-boxes. It is 'wood fitted' and the colour of a hazel nut. Tiles surround the gas oven range, grill and 'washing-up department'. On the walls I have a Coles wallpaper with a small design of intertwin-

ing flowers. The roller blinds are made in a matching fabric and I have a brown Frigidaire. The floor
is covered with linoleum which fakes Provençal
tiles. I rather wish I had used big cork tiles.

Big prints of fruit which belonged to my
grandmother look well here. I have had them in
the dining-room of every house I have lived in.

When I first saw Jebb's plan I was most of all
delighted by the fact that it showed me I would be
able to go straight out of my bedroom and make
myself a cup of tea at 6.30 am when my alarm clock
rings. This is the time of day that I like best—
when the telephone does not torment and nothing
disturbs.

My tiny bedroom had the ceiling lowered,
as did the kitchen, to keep the heat in. Here I have
a Coles wallpaper with matching material which
hangs from below the cornice to the floor. The
design has prim little bunches of pink lilies of the
valley on an ivory-coloured ground. My bed faces
onto the pond and again there is a window seat
with heating installed below. This is very effective
and unobtrusive. It looks like picket fencing—
'pretty maids all in a row' style.

My primrose-coloured bathroom is the best I
have ever known. It is just opposite my bedroom,
a few steps across a little lobby with a window.
From this and the bathroom there is yet another
view onto a green lawn, the old malt-house where
beer used to be brewed and a part of the stables. I
can look out of these windows and tell which way
the wind is blowing from the weather-vane over
the stables—a running fox.

The bath is huge, panelled in wood stained
mahogany colour and varnished. The carpentry
was executed by a local craftsman. This bathroom
reminds me of one in an old-fashioned yacht or
liner. I particularly like the lights over the
looking-glass and the washing basin (called by the
plumber the 'toilet unit' and all enclosed in wood,
like the bath). These bracket wall-lights have
jointed arms. They are made of brass and designed
by Billy Baldwin. I have a collection of Victorian
shell pictures in octagonal frames above the bath.

A theme of trellis and basket patterns runs
through this little house. It recurs on the floor of
the big room in the design of the Portuguese rugs.
Baskets are everywhere, and happily there is a
wonderful weaver at nearby Acton Turville who
made me a huge square log basket for firewood.

One of the things I like best about the laundry

The primrose-coloured bathroom has a huge, wood-panelled bath, stained mahogany. Above the bath is a collection of Victorian shell pictures.

is the vistas Jebb's plan provided. With one room
leading into another, looking through, I am often
reminded of a Dutch picture. Perhaps above all I
love the pond views from my window seats. In the
spring there are yellow ducklings and moorhen
chicks which take to the water as soon as they are
hatched and look like black fluffy walnuts. A lone
grey heron stands like the ghost of a statue waiting
for fish. The pond is stocked with ancient and
enormous carp which jump out of the water before
an electric storm. No one is allowed to fish for
them. I am particularly fond of the view onto the
opposite side of the pond. The big willows leaning
against each other might well have been painted by
Corot.

My need is to live close by water. I have been
drawn to pond life ever since I brought tadpoles
back from Le Touquet in a jam-jar when I was
twelve. *The Wind in the Willows* was my first
favourite book. It is by my bedside here—the
edition with the Shepard illustrations.

One day a rather affected art dealer was
lunching with my son-in-law and I was sitting next
to him. 'Tell me', he said, 'when you are in residence in your laundry, will you dress as Marie
Antoinette did at Le Petit Hameau? Perhaps like a
laundress painted by Madame Vigée Le Brun?'
Such an idea ruffled me.

'Certainly not', I replied. 'I'll probably be
dressed like Toad of Toad Hall when he was on the
run in drag, disguised as a washerwoman with that

little black bonnet tied under his chin.'

Waking up each morning is an adventure here. I've never paddled my own canoe before and it is a challenge.

I share my pond life with two familiars. A green Amazon parrot who behaves like the geese of Troy, giving warning when anyone approaches and capable of making noises like a pack of bloodhounds, and a young Pekingese who is rather too fascinated by the duck.

Daphne Fielding

The kitchen, looking onto the 'waterfront'.

Christina Foyle

BEELEIGH ABBEY
Maldon, Essex

One of the bedrooms with seventeenth-century four-poster.

My lovely home, Beeleigh Abbey, lies surrounded by twelve acres of gardens on the banks of the river Chelmer. It is a Premonstratensian abbey, built in the latter part of the twelfth century, and it remains in a surprisingly perfect state of preservation. A Tudor timber-framed wing was added soon after the Dissolution, in about 1560. For hundreds of years the place lay neglected, a home for farmers, with the largest room housing their sheep and cows. Then in 1911 Colonel Grantham bought it and beautifully restored it, making it a lovely comfortable home without in the least disturbing the peaceful tranquillity, the legacy of the monks. It is a fairytale place with a romantic history, all of it happy. The monks wore white habits and they bore romantic names—Andreln, living here in 1265, William de Rokelaunde in 1320, Richard de Purlee in 1384. One of the monks knew and corresponded with Peter Abelard. The most loved was a merry monk who is immortalised in the fresco painting of a cock in the monks' warming-room, a reminder that there was lighthearted fun in this religious community.

The patrons too fire the imagination—Henry Bourchier, first Earl of Essex, who was buried here, Isobel, Countess of Essex, sister of Richard, Duke of York, the father of Edward IV who, with his queen, visited the Abbey. We have their portraits in the calefactory, which is the main room. It was the monks' dining-room and we use it as our sitting-room. Its superb vaulted roof is supported by a row of pillars made of Purbeck marble brought in by barge from the West Country eight centuries ago. The huge fire-place is surrounded by a carved stone frieze of six angels, part of the canopy of the tomb of the Abbey's patron Henry Bourchier, Earl of Essex.

All through the winter, and often through the English summer, we have a huge log fire burning. There is a constant supply of logs from our surrounding woodland. The furniture is very comfortable—a big soft sofa, deep armchairs, Oriental rugs laid on rush matting to soften the original monastic austerity, and masses of flowers from the garden and greenhouse.

When we have guests, we entertain in this room. There is a magnificent oak refectory table about fourteen feet long made from two perfect planks of wood from the same enormous tree. Twenty people can be comfortably seated at this table.

We are lucky to have traced the original stained-glass windows from Beeleigh. They had been stored for many years in Westminster Abbey. The windows depict the life of the Virgin Mary and they are now in their original place.

Some of my favourite pictures are in this room. Among them is the portrait of Baretti, great friend of Dr. Johnson and Fanny Burney and also the compiler of a famous dictionary. There is a lovely court scene of fair ladies by Matania, one of my favourite artists, and two wonderful moonlight scenes by Pether Senior. The pictures look very dark, with just the full moon shining, but if a light is shone on them wonderful little figures, woodmen sitting by their fires with their animals, a castle almost hidden in the trees, a lamp shining through the latticed window of a cottage, fishermen preparing their boat for the morning, all emerge from the shadows.

The whole Abbey is so lovely that the less furniture the better. My father's contribution and legacy was the wonderful library. Perhaps mine has been the pictures, a very personal collection. I have been fortunate all my life in knowing artists and many have given me pictures. My favourites are those by the painters of fairy tales, Edmund Dulac and Arthur Rackham. Sir Alfred Munnings gave me a delightful self-portrait and Sir Gerald Kelly a typical charming painting of a Burmese dancing girl. This hangs in my bedroom. Many artists, Doris Zinkeisen, Kitty Shannon, relation of Shannon and Ricketts of legendary fame, and the brilliant Zsuzsi Roboz have painted portraits of me and these are hung discreetly about the place. I love children's books and their illustrators

Christina Foyle's bedroom showing a corner of her four-poster bed.

and have an enchanting collection of Kate Greenaway and Ernest Shepherd originals.

When I find an artist specially appealing, I ask him to paint the Abbey. Nicholas Ridley has recently painted an exquisite picture in his own romantic style, and Felix Kelly, whose work so much resembles that of Rex Whistler, has added to my collection.

We have an art gallery in Foyles where artists and craftsmen exhibit. All kinds of work are shown, embroidery, jewellery, engraved glass, pottery, and from every exhibition I buy something lovely to embellish the Abbey.

Beyond the calefactory is a private chapel used for family weddings and christenings. To reach the chapel, you go through a small anteroom whose use was explained to me by Mr. Enoch Powell. It was where visitors to the monks

Small, heavily timbered drawing-room.

Another corner of the calefactory room.

The Monks' dormitory now housing Christina Foyle's father's collection of books and manuscripts.

🐦 *The calefactory now the main sitting-room with a fine vaulted ceiling.*

used to be put up and was called 'The Slype'. We had always used it as a larder, but when the shelves became rather shabby we had the cupboard stripped out, and there were revealed original wall paintings done by the monks.

We made this place into a delightful small dining-room as it is near the kitchen. There are a circular marble table and very pretty oak chairs with blue velvet cushions. It is here that we have the Felix Kelly picture of the Abbey. Local craftsmen who specialise in church restoration helped me. There was a very small bricked-in window; they enlarged this and built a Gothic frame based on the original design of the Abbey windows and I commissioned John Hayward, whose beautiful stained glass I had admired at the Goldsmith's Hall, to design a window giving the whole history of the Abbey. The result is superb, and one of the most attractive features of our home. Everything is in it, in glowing colours—the early monks in their habits, the canonised St. Roger, King Edward and Queen Eleanor, Henry VIII and his evil friend Sir John Gate, to whom he bestowed the Abbey and who was later executed on Tower Hill, my father's library, and even the sheep and cows which once lived in the main room. A scroll in the corner lists the distinguished visitors to the Abbey. This will make interesting reading in a hundred years' time. How I wish that the monks

An outside view of Beeleigh Abbey.

had left a similar record.

In the chapel, stone plaques list the names of the monks, patrons and secular owners. There is an interesting organ which came from the Foundling Hospital and was actually built in the old organ loft in Manette Street off Charing Cross Road, the home of Foyles. Handel once played on this organ.

The vicar holds services in the chapel on summer Sundays and it is a lovely English scene, with families picnicking on the lawn and the sound of hymns on the evening air.

From the other end of the calefactory steps lead to the Tudor Wing, a charming small drawing-room, heavily timbered, with a splendid open fire-place. French windows open onto a sunken garden with a goldfish pool, and from mid-morning until evening on a summer day this room is bathed in sunshine. The décor, carpets, sofa and chairs are pale pink, giving the room an extra glow. The pictures, a Matania and a Conder fan, blend delightfully with the surroundings.

Above the calefactory is the monks' dormitory, now our library, housing my father's collection of manuscripts and rare books. The room is quite breathtaking in its beauty, with its great roof of chestnut timbers, its early sixteenth century windows looking out over the Essex marshes, and its magnificent library of exquisite bindings. Here hangs the portrait of my father by Dugdale and the enigmatic Chandos portrait of Shakespeare.

This room, indeed the whole house, is so beautiful that very little furniture or decoration is needed. If a room gets shabby and the hangings and carpets show signs of wear, I seek the help of artists. Henry Bardon, who designs the lovely scenery for the Covent Garden ballets and for Glyndebourne, has made a bedroom into a fairytale world of fantasy. He has painted frescoes of poetic scenes—forest glades, winding rivers, hidden away castles and, in the connecting bathroom, gorgeous birds. There is a coal fire and the most comfortable sofa and chairs, the colours of the upholstery blending with the paintings on the walls. The bed is a four-poster made in 1613, and the bedspread was woven by one of the artists who exhibited in my gallery. I found the perfect picture for the room, a wild woodland scene by de Loutherbourg, also a stage artist painting for the theatre in about 1800. To wake up in this room is an aesthetic experience.

In all there are seven bedrooms, four with their own bathrooms, and the beds are Tudor carved four-posters—very attractive and comfortable.

One magnificent bed was built for James I, and in this room we have a collection of books connected with the monarch. These include several very beautiful bindings with the royal arms embossed and most of the books written by James I, who was a considerable author, including his famous diatribe against tobacco.

There is a charming small suite of rooms at the far end of the library which we use for guests. One is a music room with a piano and records and everything to make a visitor happy.

An enormous loft runs the whole length of the building. It was here that my father kept a model railway of steam and electric trains, stations, terminals—everything to delight the heart of an enthusiast. My father and the vicar spent many happy hours here together, and when my father died I gave the whole set to the vicar who was quite overwhelmed. The loft now houses Foyles Anti-

A postcard dated 1903 picturing Beeleigh Abbey.

quarian Book Department.

The Abbey really is one of the loveliest homes in England. Every room is beautiful and the prospect from each window gives delight. Some look over lawns where peacocks strut, others to the river and the marshes, but everywhere it is peaceful and serene. Although so remote, the place is not lonely. Students often stay to study the manuscripts, and book collectors come from all over the world to look at our treasures.

We have cared for Beeleigh Abbey for more than forty years, looking upon it as a sacred trust, and it is my dearest wish that whoever follows us here will feel as we do about this lovely and hallowed place.

Christina Foyle

Diana Gage

THE HOLE OF ELLEL
Cark-in-Cartmel, Grange-over-Sands, Cumbria

The old ordnance maps mark the Hole of Ellel in gothic letters signifying a site of archaeological interest. The Lancashire County Record Department at Preston have no information, so perhaps it was a myth. When we were making an approach to the house, the pickaxe struck a large stone which rang hollow. Hoping for an exciting discovery I dug much deeper than necessary, only to locate an early land drain.

The late Steven Potter who wrote about English place names thought the name Hole of Ellel derived from a Norse invader and was 'Ella's Nook'—'Who and what was Ella you must find out' he said, but no one seems to know. The rest of the address describes the surrounding country.

There may have been an early habitation here. It is sheltered from the north and east, on rising ground, and there was a nearby stream, now part of an underground reservoir.

In the seventeenth century it was recorded that Mrs. Preston from Holker retired to the dower house at Ellel. There are lumps in the field that may have been buildings, so it is possible; though there is another Ellel near Lancaster.

The original back door is now the main entrance. The flooring is half-polished, blue-grey slates.

The Hole of Ellel stands on rising ground and faces south-west. The main part probably dates from the eighteenth century.

The main part of the house as it is now probably dates from the eighteenth century. It was originally a square simple farmhouse; the part to the east was built on at the beginning of this century and combined to make two cottages. It is near my childhood home, and when young we always thought it delightful. Facing south west, across fields and woods, it gives just a glimpse of cottage roofs and the sands and tides of Morecambe Bay over to the far shore of the Furness Peninsula.

I first came to live here as a widow in 1946.

Another part of the sitting-room has charming water colours by Ian Campbell-Gray.

The long, blue-green sitting-room has a fire-place either end.

The main part of the house was inhabited by a grand old lady, Mrs. Fox, who had been there most of her life, so I had the bit on the east side. This consisted of kitchen to the north, sitting-room opposite, to the south. Upstairs two bedrooms and a bathroom.

The kitchen had a small open fire with an oven attached, a grate with cast-iron daffodils. This also heated the water. It was warm and looked quite welcoming but cooking was difficult. Later a dual-purpose cooker was installed. More practical, but the prevailing wind from the west made the cooker roar and shake the house like a liner under stress in a storm. We ate in the kitchen

A drawing by the Viscountess Gage's sister, Mary Countess of Crowford, done in 1946, representing Mrs. Fox who originally lived in the main part of the house.

but guests said they preferred the simpler, old-fashioned atmosphere. Later I had calor gas.

The sitting-room had a good-sized window, bookcases built into two walls and an open wood-burning fire-place. Everywhere painted white. I had lived in a small house in London and the furniture was just right for size here. This room is now a dining-room.

I kept a little visitors' book, and looking back am astonished at the kindness of friends who braved an extremely simple life and came to stay.

In 1947 the other part of the house became available, so it was possible to make it one. Ways through were made on the ground and upper floors. The old walls were three feet thick and consisted of very large boulders filled in with smaller undressed stones.

Central heating was a primary consideration and for months workmen, mostly local, were installing pipes, rendering walls, plastering, painting.

The levels of the two parts of the house are

different, so regretfully the staircase from the east side had to be removed.

The back door to the north opened directly into the kitchen but I made it into the main entrance with a little hall. For flooring the Burlington quarries across the Bay provided beautiful blue-grey slates cut two and a quarter feet square and half polished, which makes them nearly black and gives a good surface.

The remaining staircase is on the north side and direct from the hall, with a long window which goes the length of the house. Very typical of the north country—and there is a window in the garden door to the east so quite a lot of crosslight.

A cupboard door under the stairs opens onto a steep stair down to a cellar which still has the original hooks in the ceiling for hanging hams, and rough slate slabs. It is ideal for storage. For a time I had a smallholding, Jersey cows, Tamworth pigs, Rhode Island Red chickens, an orchard and bees, and the cellar fulfilled a much-felt need. The kitchen sheltered some bereaved piglets for a short time.

The living-room faces south west onto a little terrace. It consisted of two little rooms divided by a passage with what was once a front door. I took away one of the walls but it was not right; so later removed both walls, making a longish sitting-room with a fire-place either end. The garden door is in the middle, its top half glazed, and there are windows with acid yellow curtains either side. The room is painted bluey-green. One wall is books. The pictures, as in most of the other rooms in the house, are by my husband Ian Campbell-Gray.

Finance was always a problem, but luckily the curtains and carpets as well as the furniture from London fitted in all right and have not been replaced until absolutely in tatters. Similarly, when I made a sitting-out place to the west of the sitting-room terrace, slate solved the problem of pillars. It could not be cut rounded, so was dressed in an octagonal shape. Unpolished, blue-grey, lying on the ground, the 'pillars' looked as though I was about to create Kar-nak, but once in place were quite suitable.

After the conversion there were five bedrooms, one very tiny, and two bathrooms—all painted white with chintz curtains.

There were several built-in cupboards but more furniture was needed and I used to go to local sales; at one I was fortunate to get one armchair and three occasional rush-seated chairs for a total of four shillings.

There was a large attic which had the original farm grinders fixed to the beams. It was open over the joists and to the roof and a lot of heat used to escape. At first I thought to seal it, then it seemed ideal for a bedsitting-room for anyone who wanted quiet to read or write. So the roof was insulated, a floor made over the open joists, and a bathroom leading off and dormer window installed. The roof is quite high but slanting, and the recesses make good cupboards. The original beams of natural wood are uncovered and the rest of the room is white. In many of the houses in the neighbourhood the beams are of old ships' timbers. Here, though they have certain curves, they are just ordinary trees.

The attic has a lovely view across the bay, and I like it so much I have made it into my bedroom.

In the sixties I had a job in London and was away a lot of the time. Then I married again and lived at beautiful Firle in Sussex for twelve years. I think the whole of this house could fit into the great hall at Firle.

During those years a variety of people lived here. Most were appreciative and considerate, but inevitably there was a good deal of wear and tear and when I came back in 1983 it was very dilapidated and in a state of confusion. Egg-cups in the attic bathroom, lamps in the cellar, curtains in shreds, furniture in smithereens. Many objects vanished, including a very heavy doorstop, a copper nugget which my uncle had brought back from Alaska—travelling on foot, by horse and canoe in order to join up for the 1914–18 war.

Gradually the house is returning to normal, and is now much as before.

Diana Gage

The large attic is now a bedroom with a view across Morecambe Bay.

The hall is in pale blue, blending with the large tapestry on the staircase wall.

Cynthia Gladwyn

BRAMFIELD HALL
Halesworth, Suffolk

I knew that in the Middle Ages the priest at Bramfield lived 'a bowshot from the church', but recently our Suffolk architect Eric Sandon discovered from documents that this in fact was the house in which he lived. Hence our fish pond.

The church had become enormously rich since East Anglia, leading nowhere, had been spared the troubles of the Wars of the Roses. Then in the sixteenth century with Henry VIII came changes of religion creating dreadful destruction and burnings, so that finally the priest retreated to Mettingham College and the house was acquired by the Rabetts, an old family from the nearby town of Dunwich which was caving into the sea. They lived at Bramfield Hall (as it now became) for nearly three hundred years, until 1899.

The house they took over was a thatched timber-framed building with wattle and daub walls which they encased with Tudor brick. The great hall would have risen to the entire height of the building. Some modernization was done in the time of Queen Anne, including a new porch, but some time towards the end of the eighteenth century the Rabetts must have come into money

A pretty Venetian four-poster trimmed by Lady Gladwyn in the pale pink bedroom.

which enabled them to change its appearance completely. It was stuccoed white and the windows were altered. Evidently this work was carried out by men who had been employed at nearby Heveningham under Wyatt, since windows, shutters and chimney-pieces are almost identical with those on the upper floor at Hevingham. I mention all this because Bramfield is so often described as being an eighteenth century house.

After the departure of the Rabetts it changed hands several times until we acquired it at the end of 1945; we were able to move in early in 1946 with such of our things as had not been bombed and pieces of furniture and pictures lent or given us by our families. Serious redecoration was out of the question. However, there was a good deal of brown paint inside which was extremely darkening with the thick walls, and I remember being dismayed to find that, in those post-war days of austerity, there was no white paint, only cream.

At that time there was still alive a splendid craftsman, our village carpenter Bill Foster, who came to help and who told me much that I needed to know about the house; he had worked for one of the owners, Sir George Vernon, who was nursing the constituency just before the First World War. Bill Foster spoke the most enchanting old English, such as saying that a particular screw was 'not mighty enough' for the sconce he was 'offering up'.

And when he had painted the library yellow he said: 'That will smile at you when you come in.' Of more importance, he was a mine of information about the alterations he had done for Sir George Vernon, who had at once set to work to remove as many of the eighteenth century features as he could.

The white stucco was scraped off the exterior revealing the ancient mellowed Tudor red brick; the mahogany staircase was twisted round so as to give a larger hall and show more of the flagstones; old beams were uncovered; the Victorian chimney-piece in the drawing-room was removed to display the original fire-place behind. In the garden he planted yews.

In 1950 we were posted abroad for ten years, and on our return started making practical improvements and redecoration, now much needed. We employed the excellent firm of Reid of Aldeburgh to carry out this work under the advice of Eric Sandon. I chose all the colours. The hall and passages are duck-egg blue, blending well with the large tapestry which hangs above the staircase. Downstairs are fine old yellow curtains with good pelmets from my father's house in Norfolk. I am not so proud of the curtains to the windows above on the first floor. They are a beautiful old chintz with a bold floral pattern in strong blue, green and red, which I have known all

Bramfield Hall.

my life and never remember in pristine condition. Now they are literally in tatters. But I am attached to them, and four years in New York taught me how characterless rooms can become with continual redecoration. The library, which is at the north-west side of the house, is now a pale apricot and the curtains of the bow window are made of linen of the same shade with a bright red and orange floral pattern. These came from and were made by Spencers in Sloane Street. All the rest of the curtains were made by a wonderful old man, alas now dead, Mr. Comer, who came over from Lowestoft.

Now we come to the drawing-room, which I think is the prettiest room in the house. It is thirty feet long, being two rooms knocked into one, so we get cross-lights; the further end is where the original staircase once led from the great hall to the priest's room above his solar. The beams here are moulded, and an old legend has it that neither bats nor the devil can hang from them. The old fire-place greets you as you enter the room.

I have a predilection for pink, pale pink with a speck of black in it to relieve the crudity. It is a beautiful background for people as well as pictures. With this pink I always like an old-fashioned floral chintz with lots of stronger pink and green which I used to get at an excellent shop, Haynes, near Paddington Station, now unfortunately vanished. The sofas and easy chairs are yellow and other chairs are mostly pink. At the further end of the room, near the piano, is a purple velvet 'Madame Récamier' sofa and one or two other purple chairs.

The dining-room, on the left of the house as you come in, is still pure late eighteenth century. It has three windows looking towards the park and I thought that here we should have some strong colour for a change, so I chose a bright green named 'Gobelin green' which the workmen called Goblin green! The curtains are red damask from Peter Jones made by Mr. Comer. There is a very pretty cornice in this room and a fine marble chimney-piece.

Immediately above is my bedroom. I always have a pale pink bedroom and again a floral chintz, and, alas, a no longer white carpet—shooting boots and dogs have sullied it sadly. I love pretty beds, and my bed here is a Venetian four-poster which I bought in Rome, consisting of narrow gilded iron posts with gilded iron flowers at the four corners. On this I hung, rather than draped, my mother's lace, and nylon curtains. I have a splendid Spanish screen and a dressing table with a rather tattered old muslin petticoat which I cannot bear to change because it belonged to Lady Lee of Fareham.

My bedroom has three windows, and from

A view of the big drawing-room.

where I sit and write I look down on the park and can see any person who may drive up. East Anglia was once an immense oak forest and we still have many fine old trees. My daughter and I have a mania for replanting oaks, and cherishing any small ones which appear in the rough grass. From my room I see all that remains of the celebrated Bramfield oak, a pre-Conquest tree which was a landmark in the thirteenth century and figures in an ancient ballad about Sir Hugh Bigod (who died in 1177). It fell suddenly on a windless June day in 1843.

The house itself looks lovely from the park. Within it is certainly shabby, but at least 'ça ne sent pas le décorateur'.

The late eighteenth-century dining-room.

The large drawing-room has moulded beams and the original old fire-place.

Wilhelmine Harrod

THE OLD RECTORY
Holt, Norfolk

The red-papered 'winter' room filled with books.

M y house was built in the latter part of the seventeenth century as a rectory. It was unpretentious and rambling, but in 1725 a parson with grander ideas added some new rooms inside a pretty five-windowed front with an elegant doorway. Later, another parson diverted the stream which came from a spring on the nearby common to make a pond, and a rivulet which runs through the garden over a neatly cobbled bed. The clergy lived like country gentlemen then. The ones here planted fine trees, copper beeches, oaks and ilex, and a woodland belt for a Sermon Walk; and made lawns and orchards and a walled kitchen garden. By the time we bought the house in 1962 the garden was very wild (more so now) and most of the paint inside the house was a dark chocolate colour; many of the rooms were distempered a very gloomy green. But in spite of the depressing decoration it felt like a very happy house.

It is the fifth house I have 'arranged'—decorated is too grand a word—and I have never thought of employing a decorator or even of asking advice. Not, I hope, from arrogance, but because it seems more natural to let things just happen.

But I have been influenced by the taste of my friends: in the late 1930s by Nancy Mitford—my first drawing-room was pink and blue like hers; by Camilla Sykes, who collected black *papier maché* and lacquer, painted and inlaid with mother-of-pearl; by Roger Hesketh, whose knowledge of the Georgian period is unsurpassed; and by Robert Heber-Percy and Gerald Berners, who went in for fantasy. My houses have never *nearly* approximated to theirs but, nonetheless, their styles have always been, almost subconsciously, in the back of my mind.

We had to redecorate the whole house,

The Old Rectory seen from across the stream.

though we left (probably because the painters didn't notice) the ecclesiastical chocolate on the inside of the hall shutters, and I am glad we still have that. We were lucky about grates. There was only one hideous modern one which we had to remove; the rest are probably very late Victorian, not important but not ugly. The one in the drawing-room is surrounded by tiles with yellow daffodils on them, which was why we chose a yellow Morris wallpaper, plain yellow curtains and Morris chair covers in yellow and green. This is a very cheerful, light room, with two big windows to the east and one to the south, and it is hung with watercolours. I really prefer the room on the other side of the hall, done up much later after a burst pipe in the bad winter of 1978–79. This is a winter room, with only two windows, and it is papered in dark red (the Covent Garden stripe); most of the furniture, bought cheaply at local sales many years ago, is covered in red too. I

was lucky enough to get what was probably the only cheap lot at the Gunton Hall sale in 1981: a bundle of old curtains in striped rep, red on red, with which we covered most of the chairs. A lot of this room, which is semi-oval, is taken up by a big square piano, a Steinway, made in New York in 1878—not a pretty piece and so out of tune that it is fairly useless. It would cost far too much to put it right for a totally unmusical family, but we keep it because there is a vague rumour that it once belonged to Henry James, who knew my mother-in-law. I hate personal photographs anywhere except in my bedroom, but this old piano is very useful as a stand for some amusing old ones with family connections, of soldiering in India and such like.

Surprisingly, this room, though partially lined with bookshelves, was the rectory dining-room; surprising because the food had to be brought through the cold stone-floored hall. So we turned the rectory kitchen into our dining-room and the big rectory scullery into our kitchen. My husband hated kitchen meals, so until lately we have not tried to develop the popular kitchen–dining-room. I do not think it would work here anyhow, as I am such an untidy disorganised cook. I used to have a sofa in my kitchen for my friends to loll on; there are complaints because, to make room for a cupboard, the sofa has now been replaced by a large armchair. The back door leads from the kitchen straight into the garden, very convenient as I nip out to cut cabbage or asparagus while the water is coming to the boil on the Aga. Both kitchen and dining-room are passage rooms and get pretty muddy; the kitchen has an old, uneven floor of wide red pamments, but the dining-room is smarter, with black-and-white plastic tiles. It is perhaps the most successful room in the house; it is low, with a beam across the middle, and was probably the main room of the seventeenth century house. There are two windows facing north, and a glass door on the south side opening into the flower (as opposed to vegetable) garden. The walls are peacock blue, to match one of the colours in the printed curtains—huge scarlet poppies with bright green and blue foliage. When I saw the stuff at Liberty's I loved it, because as well as being a good design it suggested Poppyland to me, which was the name given to this part of Norfolk in 1883 by the journalist Clement Scott who, with Swinburne

The walls of the hall and staircase are hung with family portraits.

and his friend Watts-Dunton, often stayed on this part of the coast. Paintings look good on these walls, and there are either local primitives of boats and the sea by the Sheringham fisherman John Craske who died in 1943, or recent paintings by Jean Hugo, Barbara Robinson, Joan Zuckerman and Hector McDonnell. The old range must have been here as there is a wide chimney, and we bought for five pounds from some gypsies a long,

narrow naïve painting of Suffolk Punches, which exactly fits the opening. Victorian shell and wax bouquets under domes stand on the wide window-sills, together with bright bits of glass picked up for only shillings in the happy days of junk shops.

As a family we never throw anything away, and as none of the rooms is very big, my grand-children have made a museum in the attics. Here are toys, very broken I fear, going back for a hundred years; mementoes (gasmasks, ration books, etc.) from two world wars; kid gloves, spats, white silk mufflers, dance programmes, embroidered baby clothes, Victorian scrapbooks, and much more. Next door is a shell collection and a few old agricultural tools. Like Tom Kitten, my grandchildren, not content with many passages and five staircases, have climbed through trapdoors and explored the whole of the space under the rafters of the black pantiled roof.

Although the main road is very close, it cannot be seen from any window. The house sits right in the middle of its five and a half acres of garden and woodland, and in the spring the east and south windows look onto a sea of snowdrops. From the

The kitchen contains a large armchair for visiting friends.

dining-room and the kitchen windows on the north side, the view is, suitably, of asparagus beds and globe artichokes; and an old apple tree with a huge Albertine rose. Our poor young Rector who, with his wife and four children, has to live in a rabbit hutch, can hardly bear to make me a pastoral visit, so much does he covet the paradise which should rightly be his!

The low-ceilinged dining-room. A naïve painting of Suffolk Punches fits exactly over the old range opening.

A view of Lady Harrod's bedroom.

Corner of Lady Harrod's bedroom.

The drawing-room where the decoration was inspired by the daffodil tiles surrounding the grate.

Mary Henderson

South Kensington, London

We are back in a house we bought over thirty years ago. I still remember phoning from a call-box outside the house agent's office on the Brompton Road to tell Nicko, my husband, that I had made out the biggest cheque in my life—a two hundred pounds deposit (today, alas, this barely pays for a pair of curtains!). We bought our little London house—just before being sent to Vienna—in order to have a home, an English home, a base, an anchor. It has fulfilled this purpose.

Looking round it now I realise that it is very much a patchwork of our lives. The objects, the lamps, vases, plates, pictures, prints and Staffordshire figures, have been with us in our various posts, some acquired on the way, others brought from home. But they—like us—were surprised to find themselves arriving at Pauline Borghèse's palace in Paris (the British Embassy) and then unexpectedly being shipped to Lutyens' stately red brick mansion in Washington (our Embassy in the United States). Yet they fitted in quite happily and our guests found them—and us—'very English'.

The main bedroom where Lady Henderson has used material designed by Bernard Nevill.

One of the major drawbacks to our London house in the past was that, like most houses in the area, the bathroom had been added at a later date. It was built out on the half landing, next to the drawing-room. This meant that if the door were left open, a visitor coming to the front door would have as his first view of our home—a pink lavatory.

On retirement, we both decided we wanted bathrooms leading off our bedrooms on the second floor. After some trouble with the local city council and aid from our architect Nicholas Johnston, the work was carried out. The two rooms on the second floor became my bedroom-bathroom and an attic room and bathroom were added for Nicko; the old bathroom became my study, leading into a conservatory. This Victorian addition came from a new firm called Room Outside who deliver it in pieces which fit like Meccano. Our local carpenter installed it, carefully adding to the bold, white-painted arched windows three Victorian etched glass panels which we had found. The two on the door have a geometric floral design, while the larger square panel at the far end has a stylised urn filled with roses, tulips, convolvulus and fuchsias. Throughout the house early fads such as my craze for wall-to-wall red carpet and white paint have been thrown out. A stone-coloured cord, old rugs and glossy off-white paint have taken their place.

My new bedroom-bathroom is now a favourite room. Four old doors cut off the corners of the bedroom part, leaving it almost octagonal in shape with good cupboard space behind the doors. (The doors and the decorative, early stone religious overmantel were put into the rooms by a previous owner who was, we were told, a curator of the Victoria and Albert Museum.) The scale, of course, is minute, but it was just what I wanted to house my old polished iron bed, my eighteenth century angels (my first purchase in Paris when I was a correspondent for *Time*, before my marriage) and my travelling madonna—a present I have always kept with me since Boris Anrep gave it to me when he was working on the mosaics in Westminster Cathedral. (While I was suffering from vertigo, I remember the aged Russian artist climbing up ladders and stepping lightly on planks with the agility of a ballet dancer.)

The bathroom end of the room is like a Victorian picture album. The walls are covered with photographs—my mother as a young girl in Bedouin fancy dress, my grandparents with my uncles and aunts stiffly posed with potted palms in Alexandria and my grandson's christening in London this year. These and others share the tiny space with my favourite Victorian paraphernalia. I had always wanted a *chaise percée* or comfortable old-fashioned wooden water closet for my bathroom and after a long search I came across a

A corner of the staircase.

rosewood chest of drawers. The top and the two front drawer panels lift up and fold back to become a seat. It was a Victorian commode chair which I have adapted. When closed it matches my Victorian hand basin with its rosewood cabinet base. Just above the chest of drawers is a large photograph of Queen Victoria sitting in a chair. She is pensive and dressed in black taffeta. How clever the Victorian dress designers were—a high neckline hides a sagging chin, a crisp little bonnet covers thinning hair, all so neat and proper. I bought her for two pounds in a market. Along the wall behind the claw and ball footed Victorian bath are antique floral tiles which Nicko has collected; they mostly come from old Victorian fire surrounds. I carefully chose which ones would go where. Some over the hand basin where they greet me in the morning, others on the far end of the bath so that I can see them well as I soak and think and choose my favourite flower. Sometimes it is the pale mauve pansy, sometimes the pink convolvulus, at other times my eye rests on the upright lily. Above the tiles a giant Victorian overmantel mirror repeats, reflects and gives a feeling of space. It was a monster to get up the stairs and I had to measure the space over and over again to make sure it would fit.

The decoration has been influenced by Bernard Nevill's design for the Lutyens gallery in

The claw and ball footed Victorian bath in Lady Henderson's favourite bedroom-bathroom.

A detail from the bathroom which is filled with Victoriana.

The small conservatory filled with decorative plants.

Looking from the study through to the sunny conservatory.

Lady Henderson's pretty dining-room.

Washington for the British Embassy Show Case which I helped to organise. Bernard used his curtains with William Morris rope edges, and tiebacks to cut across the vast long gallery—I have used them instead of doors between my bedroom and bathroom and between my bath and my desk. They are heavy and long, they have rope edges and lie well on the ground, making up for years of despair at the skimpy curtains supplied by the Department of the Environment. The material I have used was designed by Bernard Nevill for his Sekers Country House Collection. Bernard also had a covered window seat in Washington with a view over the Embassy garden—I have a tiny window seat, a view over London rooftops and space inside for my hair dryer! For the walls and double curtains I have used Laura Ashley's burgundy and sand ticking. It makes an ideal background for photos and prints, and I have also used it on photo mounts. Finally, Laura Ashley's lace curtains are a touch of the past and give me privacy, as does the little pull-down blind in matching fabric edged with lace.

Upstairs Nicko has a Victorian bathroom too. It was to be a shower-room but he preferred a bath and quite by chance we found a minute Victorian bath which is now surrounded with rows and rows of his favourite Victorian tiles. He also has a Victorian hand basin and water closet decorated with bunches of wild flowers. As the bedroom has sloping walls there are no pictures. Instead William Morris' hand-blocked briar rose wallpaper climbs up, over the ceiling and down the walls, encircling the room as in a garden bower. Pale apple green yacht paint has been used to paint the floorboards, and from his French window Nicko watches the London sparrows and tits fight over his birdseed nets which he replenishes at breakfast time. (The painted floor, although originating in this country, is an American influence and is used much more there today.)

It was the drawing-room that made us buy the house. We fell in love with its mellow Queen Anne pine panelling—so unexpected in a London cottage. Here pictures that have hung on other walls in other countries are now back in their old places. A naïve eighteenth century portrait of Darwin's grandfather (picked up in the Kings Road on our way to Chile), a Duncan Grant design for Lytton Strachey's library and a jug of flowers by Carrington look down on a large

chintz-covered sofa and chairs. The crisp Baker's all over chintz is new. It replaces the more severe William Morris honeysuckle which we chose years ago when we were younger, and it is the material we selected for our private sitting-room in Washington. On the floor a Persian kelim and a Russian rug are both recent purchases. The Russian rug was probably a nursery rug. It has horses, dogs and birds, and our Staffordshire figures seem to like it very much; the dogs, I would say, are particularly happy.

As you leave the house, on the staircase landing there is an unusual clock. It is a picture clock with the Kaiser Franz and his wife at the opera. The last Holy Roman Emperor is glum, his wife, no beauty, is befeathered, with lorgnettes in hand; a deep red curtain and the two-headed eagle are the backcloth. At alternate hours the clock plays Haydn's 'Güte Kaiser Franz' (which was later adopted as the German national anthem) and a gay gavotte. Nicko bought it in Vienna as a present on the birth of our daughter Alexandra. After being turned out of two hotels because guests were kept awake by our baby crying, we spotted the clock outside an antique shop on our way to a third hotel. We quickly packed it into the car, and such was the charm of its music that Alexandra stopped crying and we were able to stay in the hotel without more trouble.

The simple, weathered pine front door and the blue and white exterior of our house are in sharp contrast with the interior, with its detail, its mixture of periods and jumble of colours. Somehow the new additions now seem as if they have always been there and the old parts of the house have a new and lighter look. The whole blends happily, perhaps because it mirrors a more mature taste and our feeling of contentment at being back in our English home.

Joan Holland

SHEEPBRIDGE BARN
Eastleach, Cirencester, Gloucestershire

Nearly forty years ago I would beg my husband almost every morning that, when exercising the horses, we could go to Sheepbridge Valley, three miles from where we were then living—Westwell, his old home where he was born and brought up. 'You can't want to go there every day,' he would say. 'I do, I could never get tired of it,' I replied; and now that I am here every day, I never do. The valley is intensely romantic and pastoral: the green hills are covered in sheep, there are beautiful beech woods following the natural contours of the land, while below runs the river Leach bordered in spring with white may trees.

The barn stands poised on the lip of the valley, and has a unique history for a present-day habitation in that it was one of the *mutationes*, or staging posts, during the Roman occupation. It is still known locally as 'the Roman barn', and we are the first people to live here since those days. Akeman Street, the Roman road running from Cirencester (one of the four largest towns in Roman Britain) to London, lies fifty yards below. The approach to the barn is down a line of eleven stone pillars, eight of which are classified as being Roman; and for this reason the colonnade is designated Grade I whereas the barn itself, being supposedly only seventeenth century, is Grade II. Walking around we have picked up innumerable Romano-British potsherds and Neolithic and Bronze Age flint artefacts all of which have been authenticated by the Ashmolean Museum and are now mounted as pictures in the kitchen. There could well have been a prehistoric habitation here. The configuration of the surrounding ground suggests that the Romans may have made use of the ditch of a Neolithic causewayed camp, and therefore possibly a religious site, when construct-

The approach to Sheepbridge Barn is down a line of eleven stone pillars, eight of which are classified as being Roman.

Above: *One of the decorative tapestry hangings which is in the main part of the barn.*

Right: *Sheepbridge Barn still retains its atmosphere of ancient peace.*

Looking towards one of the two massive fire-places.

ing Akeman Street, and that the Roman staging post was built within this camp. For those who believe in the so-called 'ley lines' we were told by a learned neighbour—somewhat of a mystic—that we live on a 'power point' where a number of important lines intersect. The children of one of our friends always call it 'the Magic Castle'! It undoubtedly has an immensely powerful atmosphere of ancient peace which we were afraid it would lose in its new role, but this has remained as strong as ever and is invariably the first feature that newcomers remark on.

We bought the barn, which had always lain a

mile or two beyond our own land, fourteen years ago from our neighbour Sir Thomas Bazley, who fortunately for us was finding the upkeep of it an unwarrantable expense on his estate and only wished to sell to a local man, who, as he said, 'was mad enough to buy it'. Indeed, all our friends were of the same opinion, which, when we looked at the tree growing out of the roof and the fourteen far-rowing sows wallowing happily in a foot of liquid manure in what was to be my bedroom, was scarcely surprising. We were tremendously fortunate in our architect and builder. The former, Michael Wright, a young man twenty-five years our junior (now alas dead) and educated in the most *avant-garde* architectural school, was the perfect foil to my husband and Alan Churchill, a local master mason, both of whom were steeped in the immemorial tradition of Cotswold architecture. Alan Churchill had his own, very small firm comprising himself and two boys.

The original building consisted of the main barn, sixty feet long by forty-four feet wide, which became our living- and dining-room, and a small adjoining stable fifteen feet by eleven feet—to be our kitchen—with no windows, in which lived a charming white horse. There were indeed no windows anywhere, and needless to say no fire-places. In order to build on further bedrooms at the back we had to get stone from two derelict cottages, as we were not allowed by the planning authorities to use any new materials. Heating presented a major problem. My husband spent two days at the Heating Centre in London in order to get the most expert advice, and they subsequently came down here to see the site and assess the situation. 'Do not worry,' the manager assured him, 'we will heat your barn like Ely Cathedral.' They finally settled for a somewhat less grandiose conception, that of digging four and a half feet below the barn floor and laying a honeycomb of copper pipes—in fact appropriately enough in the Roman system of a hypocaust—which though expensive to install is economical to run and has the added visual advantage of no radiators. It was naturally dark having only the wagon bays either side, so we elongated the triangular ventilation holes into nine-foot lancet windows which give a suitably mediaeval air; and our architect had the brilliant idea of making

The dining end of the living-room.

practically the whole of the north wall to the left of the fire-place into an enormous window giving a panoramic view of the valley, which inspired the remark of the French Ambassador when staying here, 'Every time you look out of this window you have your own Samuel Palmer'.

Our first priority was to retain the simple and massive feeling of the barn and to have an easily run home for our old age. Therefore we insisted, much to the chagrin of our architect (who had thrilling ideas of having our bedroom slung between the beams of the barn on mobile girders and approached by a rope ladder), on it all being on one level. We have just two self-contained suites of double bedroom, dressing-room and bathroom for ourselves and guests. We also wished to be warm, and have maximum security. To this end all the windows are double glazed. The doors are all treble locked, and some have security grilles in addition to other measures. The small kitchen has a hatch to the dining end of the barn, a wall-mounted oven and electric rings let into the working top. The decoration of the whole house can be very briefly described. There was none, we have employed no decorator, and have had only one idea throughout. This was to use just the colours of the surrounding landscape and the sky, and thus preserve the harmony of the building within its natural setting. The barn room has only greens and greys and yellows, which colouring is repeated in the planting of the garden seen through the windows. The bedrooms are all in varying shades of the blue and white of the sky.

When we bought the barn it was stacked to the roof with bales of straw so we naturally could not see what the floor was made of, which was just as well as it consisted of old railway sleepers and concrete. The stone floors from the derelict cottages came in very handy, but we still had to find more to cover such a large area. My husband had a great stroke of luck one day in Burford, our local shopping town, when he saw one of the old shops in the High Street being gutted and a monumental twenty-five-foot oak beam lying on the floor; this now forms the overmantel to the north fire-place. Concealing a drinks cupboard was no problem; we simply built into the four-foot thick wall to the right of the entrance and in a space eight feet by four feet have ample room for bottles and glasses, with a flower vase cupboard below.

We live entirely in this one huge room, and it is by no means a hardship. It is quite amazingly adaptable, and equally good for our annual charity concert seating a hundred and fifty people plus an orchestra (by a freak ratio of stone to wood to glass we happen to have perfect acoustics) or just the two of us in front of the fire. We built two massive fire-places, one at either end, which take enormous logs that stay smouldering through the night. Having both fires burning most of the winter we only need a minimal amount of heating except in the very coldest weather. The walls are hung with rather beautiful eighteenth century tapestries and silk hangings, but I have a very special sentimental attachment to the stags' heads all of which came from my parents-in-laws' forest in the Highlands where we spent our honeymoon. I can see them reflected in the monumental seventeenth century gilt mirror.

Over the years I have always managed to have those things I consider most important for a 'cosy' atmosphere, even though the vital elements of children and dogs, wood fires, flowers, candles and books have at times been somewhat on top of each other. Here, however, I have infinite scope to indulge all of them. The fires are vast, no flower arrangement is ever too big, books are everywhere, there are three pairs of altar candlesticks, the children have multiplied into grandchildren and the dogs are two immense Old English mastiffs. This is the most ancient English breed of dog, indigenous here when the Romans first came to Britain. They are our most devoted friends and never leave our sides. Other friends in the animal world are a flock of about seventy doves, dazzling white as they circle the barn on a sunny day—a great delight to us, but never more so than when they settle on the roof and their soft murmurings come through to us below.

The best times here are either the spring, when there are hundreds of lambs all over the valley, or the autumn, when the beech woods are at their most sensational; but the very best time of all is a still night with a full moon shining on the Roman columns, turning them from pale grey to pure white, when there is an almost tangible feeling of peace.

Joan Holland.

Betty Hussey

SCOTNEY CASTLE
Lamberhurst, Kent

When young Edward Hussey, my husband's grandfather, decided in 1835 he no longer wished to live in the old castle in the valley, probably because it was both cold and damp, he commissioned the equally young architect Anthony Salvin to design him a new house on higher ground overlooking the view below. The result was a fine house in the revived Tudor style, built from stone quarried out of the hillside.

At the time the new Scotney Castle was built, it must have been the very latest example of modern planning. It boasted one splendid bathroom,

later made into two not so splendid ones divided by a partition through which one could hear everything. Since then we have added a lot more bathrooms. There was adequate plumbing throughout, and a central heating system (now converted to oil) in the main rooms which comes through iron grilles in the floor and works well to this day.

The Husseys were a very conservative family and did not like change, so when I first saw the house it had remained virtually untouched inside from the day it was built. Perhaps not all of it was lovely I must admit, nor indeed very comfortable,

The hall, a typical example of 1830s architecture at Scotney.

Above: *A bust of Princess Alice, a daughter of Queen Victoria, in the library.*

Below: *Salvin's library where books line every wall.*

Right: *A high Victorian bed draped in the original material.*

Above: *Mrs. Hussey's bow-fronted sunny bedroom.*

Below: *Corner of bamboo spare room with a handsome eighteenth-century fire-place from the Old Castle.*

but it was a house with a marvellously happy atmosphere, and above all it was eminently live-able in.

When my husband inherited Scotney there was a lot to be done. Happily in those days we still had our own estate yard to do the work, and as we were already living in a large wing of the house we had the fun of watching it all happen.

The first thing we did was to put the house on the mains electricity, as till then the electricity had been supplied by a grand old engine which chug-ged away every morning, lovingly tended by the family groom-cum-chauffeur. Unfortunately it gave very little light and could not cope with any heating.

Then there was the water system. This was supplied by a spring which was apt to get rather low in summer, and as there was a lot of iron in the water both you and the towel emerged after a bath distinctly sunburnt in colour, so that had to be put on the mains too.

The kitchen was another problem—five passages away from the dining-rooms and enormously high. The upper half is now incorporated into what was our original wing. The new kitchen was moved to what had been the study, a very pleasant, sizeable room looking two ways. The view end of the room is painted coral colour and, as I eat there most of the time, is known as the third dining-room!

When all the essentials had been dealt with, there arose the problem of what to do with the rest of the interior and its decoration. We were determined that the character of the house should be preserved as much as possible, especially the library and the big dining-room, which are panelled in dark oak topped by the original Willement flock wallpaper.

The library to me is the perfect living-room. Books line every wall and there is even a book door. The curtains are a rather faded red serge, with very broad gold patterned stripes. All the furniture was designed by Salvin, and except that we imported some comfortable sofas and chairs, the room is much as it must have been nearly a hundred and fifty years ago. I kept to the warm red colours of the curtains and carpet, and the new covers of the sofas and chairs are a splendid red and white pattern called Ravenna, a design which I believe originally came from Lord Tennyson's home and was suggested by John Fowler. Some of the older covers are a trifle worn, but I rather like a slight shabbiness here and there!

The big dining-room was a trifle daunting. There were a lot of maroon-coloured leather chairs, very worn, the horsehair oozing out of them rather uncomfortably, so we got hides from a friend's deer forest in Scotland to re-cover them with. We kept the hides their natural colour, which is a lovely rich gold and lightens up the oak a lot.

For some reason there was a dearth of curtains in the house, but we were fortunate enough to acquire just what we needed at the great Ash-burnham sale; the red moreen curtains in the dining-room and red Victorian bedroom are both from Ashburnham, as are the green velvet curtains in the hall.

The hall is really very handsome, but we thought it needed something doing to it. The panelling was a curious foxy red, which we had treated, and the fire-place had a smallish grate surrounded by shiny blue and white tiles. It also had its original velvet pelmet draped over it. Luck was with us, as we found a whole heap of marvellous fourteenth century tortoiseshell-coloured tiles lying in the old castle so we brought them up and used them for the rebuilt fire-place, which with its massive iron firedogs looks wonderful, and burns wonderfully well too.

The staircase walls were putty colour hung with numerous small watercolours, blue china and various strange weapons, while on the half landing one was greeted by a rampant, distinctly disintegrating boa constrictor! Weapons and snake now grace the old castle.

A friend of ours, David Style, found us some old rolls of a rather grand, bold patterned wall-paper in two shades of gold, the same period as the house, which looks well on the staircase where some of the family portraits hang. This is not an easy house to hang big pictures in—there is so much panelling, and so many books everywhere—but there is a unique collection of family watercolours from the beginning of the last century which hang in bedrooms and passages throughout the house. Almost all the family on both sides were very gifted artists, and the works they left behind are proof of their talent.

Out of more than twenty bedrooms, there were four particularly Victorian ones, with huge beds and furniture to match. Two of these we kept intact. One of the beds was designed by Salvin, and is so large I always feel he must have thought he was designing a house! However, my own bedroom, and several of the others as well, also my upstairs drawing-room, is furnished in lighter Regency taste from homes we had before we came to Scotney.

The drawing-room is a pretty room with a lovely view of the old castle surrounded by its moat, lying in the valley of flowering shrubs and fine trees below. It has a fine early chimney-piece which must have come out of the old castle when it was 'picturesquely ruined'. The walls are pale grey, the covers lime green and coral, which pick up the colours of the Aubusson carpet. The furniture is mostly black painted pieces, but pride of place goes to a handsome eighteenth century black lacquer bureau, filled with a fascinating collection of treasured family objects.

I have always known what colour schemes I wanted, what wallpapers and covers I needed for any particular room, and we were fortunate enough to have in our home town of Tunbridge Wells a friend and decorator, Merlin Pennink, who could invariably find, supply and make exactly what I wanted.

When we were moving into the house after the war good materials were still hard to come by, so I raided the linen cupboards and found lots of huge old damask tablecloths which I had dyed and used as curtains very successfully. For the same reason my bedroom was curtained with mattress ticking, now changed to something more glamorous!

One pleasant surprise was to find we had a lamp room full of good Victorian lamps still with the colza oil in them; needless to say these are now converted to electricity. An even more exciting find in a locked cupboard was a roll of a dozen ravishing eighteenth century original watercolours, labelled 'Birds and butterflies at the

Brazils'. These now hang in the small dining-room.

We did most of the work and decoration in under six months, but naturally throughout the years other changes and improvements have taken place, such as making two or three flats for household and friends; the whole of the main part of the house, however, is still used and lived in much as it was when young Edward Hussey walked up the hill from the old castle to the new.

Scotney may not be one of the great English country houses, but it has for me all the warmth and welcoming attributes an English country house should have, and whatever we have done to make it easier for present-day living has still left it one of the most lovable and liveable houses I know.

A painting of the library by Billy Henderson.

An array of antlers overhangs the small back staircase.

Susanna Johnston

SHELLINGFORD HOUSE
Nr. Faringdon, Oxfordshire

People tend to groan when one admits to living in an old rectory. It's possible to experience the uneasy feeling of having fallen into some sort of trap; committed a whimsical solecism. Even if this confession does conjure up a horrifying obviousness, our rectory is jolly nice and suits us down to the ground. By lucky chance the house's name was changed when the last incumbent moved out so we can sometimes get away with it.

Shellingford House, stone-faced but partly rendered to protect it from howling gales trapped in the valley by the Berkshire Downs, was built in the sixteenth century. The front door and windows round it were added in the eighteenth century. Other excrescences are early Victorian. Fire-places must have been rearranged somewhere along the line as the house gained stature. In the dining-room we replaced a bogusly fluted wooden surround with a stone one, no longer of service in the tack-room. Behind each fire-place we could see traces of Elizabethan caverns. Alas, they were too big, too broken down and proved too much of an undertaking for resurrection.

The house has had few owners. Rectors lived

Corner of the drawing-room. There is a Victorian-added French window, and the ceiling is divided into elaborate moulded panels.

here for four centuries, until the moment when it was sold by the church in 1924. One of these clerics is good enough to visit us from time to time, providing the statutory ghost. Fortunately he is undemanding and seldom enters, preferring to peer through windows. Perhaps he was a bit of a snooper. When we arrived, the house had for many years been lived in by two elderly ladies. It had never been 'tidied up' and was fairly dilapidated. Our main and urgent problem was to rid it of the stench of cats. Burmese kittens by the thousand must have opened their eyes for the first time in every one of the twenty-odd rooms. I was tipped off—hyacinth bulbs were said to be the answer. I squeezed hundreds into tubs and lugged them into the slimy cellar—holding my nose until they bloomed. This, with the help of a general washdown and various licks of paint, did the trick.

I had no need to seek professional advice since I'm married to an incomparable architect. In fact he was the main problem: how to find room for his T-squares, drawing-boards, duplicating machines and various assistants in a house which would, but for this, have been the perfect size and shape?

The old ladies had cooked in a cupboard. The original kitchen, which looked out to a walnut tree and eleven garages (the ladies were rally drivers of high renown) through a three-light window with stone mullions and arched tops, had become the main maternity home. Hyacinths were screamed for. This is where we did our major work, hollowing out a space in an immensely thick wall under a chimney breast. Inching in girders to support the chimney, thus making a deep alcove, we had room at last for an Aga cooker. With unrivalled skill, Robert Keep of Pendell and Spinage, Stanford-in-the-Vale, carved cupboards from deal which he covered with white stain and a sealer, hoping to prevent them turning yellow. In this, happily, he was successful. Next door we built a pantry where washing-up goes on. The machine can thump away for all it's worth, while we're eating in the kitchen. Victorian bells, whose peals are now unanswered, remain in a high corner of the room reminding us of nurseries and dressing-rooms.

The old ladies' cooking cupboard was bare and I decided to bag it for myself. This met with opposition. It didn't seem right that any one person should hog any one room (other than for sleeping) in so large a family. I promised that if I

The refurbished kitchen with three-arched window.

A collection of china treasures in the study.

was allowed it I would write a book or something. I had my way, wrote a book or two, and honour was satisfied. The window of this room looks out, if you make a sideways squint, past a marble font where birds dip to drink, over a crumbling wall, to the downs, where on a clear day the eerie silhouette of the prehistoric White Horse can just be sighted. My desk is under the window with shelves, housing much-needed dictionaries, running along beside it. These were built, as were others in the house, with infinite patience at weekends and during long evenings by Martin Hedges, whose working day is spent repairing railway carriages in Swindon.

I had a length of curled-up wallpaper (left over from a former incarnation) almost large enough to cover the visible wall space. Even though these expanses were tiny, cheating came into play: paperless gaps behind sofas and chairs. It was well worth preserving this battered and faded floral pattern, reputedly a Voysey design which, I'm sure, the ghost must much appreciate.

Bearing in mind the dictum of William Morris that nothing must be on show in a house 'unless believed to be pretty or known to be useful', I decided to protect my family from the large number of my possessions which fall into neither category: to stuff them all into my study. Years ago I was walking through the town of Street and dallied outside a ragged junk-shop. In among the broken toasters I spotted a tiny china ambulance.

It was utterly moving (not literally so). Shiny white, no more than two inches high, it had a bright red cross stamped onto each of its side-doors. A peak jutted forward, halfway across the bonnet, and on its roof the multicoloured Royal Military College crest was stamped. My passion for First World War souvenirs was established. Now my room is lined with miniature aeroplanes, war memorials, Zeppelins, tanks, battleships and forage-caps. An awful lot has to be hidden away in there: insects from Peru, drawings by me, and orthodontal moulds of children's teeth. William Morris would faint were he to cross the portal. A chamber of horrors. He might cheer up, however, if he were to settle for a while in the hall and find himself surrounded by a wallpaper of his own design. Here he could sit in front of a good log fire

Personal possessions in the study set off by flower-patterned wallpaper.

and never complain that it wasn't useful in a house as ill-insulated as ours. It had been blocked up, but, with the powerful energy of Jack Fox of Russel Spinage, Faringdon, the old firewell was cleared out and a cement surround concocted with great ingenuity in imitation of a stone bolection.

Before leaving the Morris bower, perhaps I should say that although far too stingy and self-willed to dream of consulting a decorator, I am not proof against pinching the ideas of others. I spotted a sample of this golden leafy paper peeping out of a basket carried by my friend Amabel Lindsay, herself a decorator.

The best feature in the house, the seven-teenth century staircase, rises from the hall through two floors in dark oak with immense newel posts. These strain towards each other but never quite meet. The steps are broad and shallow, the whole construction immensely sturdy beneath its balustrading and arcading.

The drawing-room (a good mixture of early and late) owes light to the Victorians, who added windows—two French and one bow. Coarse Elizabethan grapes divide the ceiling into elaborate moulded panels. The walls, rough and bumpy, wouldn't allow for a paper so we sloshed watered-down pink emulsion over them. To begin with I was nervous. So much pink looked like under-wear, but when the pictures were replaced and I had made a hideously expensive mistake in choosing sofa covers, it was fine. The dining-room, seldom used as such, is multipurpose. Here, again, we have built shelves where books of general interest can be used so that there is no real need for anyone to trespass in my sitting-room. In fact it's quite hard for trespassers to dream up an excuse.

Since I'm a compulsive bather and can't bear competition or queuing at any hour of the day or night, we added two extra bathrooms. Better safe than sorry. I was horrified when, sticking hazily to a budget, I learned that it was cheaper to buy baths with geriatric handrails attached in scooped-out slices each side of the tub. They seemed entirely depressing, but now—well! They're beginning to come in handy.

The house boasts a small back staircase. I'm told this is a 'must'. If by gruesome chance we have to sell, no Arab would touch the place with a bargepole unless he could despatch his womenfolk to upper regions by a route other than his own. These ladies might find it a little bloodcurdling, on reaching the top floor, to discover that the somewhat spooky nature of the wealth of black oak balustrading has been extended. On the long wall over the stairs we have arranged a collection of antlers. These were shot, decades ago, by my father-in-law. Warthogs, kudus and dwarf buf-faloes from South Africa look glassily down on frightened guests and children as they cringe their way to bed. Fears are often enhanced by the scream of a screech-owl outside.

As an antidote to this creepiness my personal recipe for indoor jollity is that all clocks should be wound, kept ticking and chiming, and that as

many fires as possible should be kept alight. A fire
in the hall can give the impression of a warm
welcome to unexpected guests however cold one's
blood may run. Being a pyromaniac, I like to be
able to burn things unexpectedly at my whim.
Cigarette packets and sweetie-papers that find
their way around the house look horrid in a
wastepaper basket—worse on the floor. The television is also by the fire in the hall, but I prefer not
to discuss this since it has been the cause of many a
.rupture—particularly at Christmastime—and
might well prove impossible to burn.

Another view of the drawing-room.

The cheerful hall has leafy William Morris wallpaper and a perpetual log fire.

Loelia Lindsay

AN OLD RECTORY
Surrey

I sometimes lie back on my comfortable sofa and gaze lovingly round my room, murmuring to myself, 'I wouldn't change a thing—it's quite perfect'.

I ascribe my odious smugness to the fact that I built the walls around myself and didn't have to fit into other people's schemes. When you inherit or buy a house, the drawing-room is probably the room that has received the most attention and will be most expensive to alter, so that you may have to adapt or disguise; building from scratch, you should have no problems to face.

My chief delight in my walls has been their thickness, which makes it possible to disguise utilitarian comforts of no beauty; but more of that later.

The room is rectangular, measuring some twenty-six feet long and fifteen wide. It has one large window looking onto the garden. Two smaller windows flank the chimney-piece. One wall is entirely covered with books, though therein is concealed the television set, so well disguised by sham books that I sometimes give small children a prize for who discovers it first.

Three favourite pictures hang over the French bureau.

As I am only an evening viewer, my set remains nestling in the daytime behind volumes of Tolstoy, Pepys and Adam Smith.

The important focal point in a room is the chimney-piece; watch how on the hottest summer day people instinctively stand by the unlit fire. So twenty years ago when I built the room I was determined to have a lovely and perfectly proportioned chimney-piece (I still long to be non-U, and say mantelpiece). This proved anything but easy to find. I did not want a reproduction and could not afford a fancy one from a fashionable shop.

After roaming around I was in despair, when someone said they had heard of a good one for sale in a garage somewhere in Fulham. I managed to locate it and saw that it was perfection, but too expensive for me (a pittance at today's prices), so I walked regretfully away. Then I gave myself one of my lectures to justify an extravagance (with practice I'm good at that). I told myself that I would never find such perfection again; that the size, design and colour of marble were all exactly right for the room, that the drawing-room was the only room in the house that was to have a fireplace, and that it would be madness to pass by this chance. I hurriedly retraced my steps, which I have never regretted, and look fondly at it as I write. It is indeed true that one only regrets one's economies.

I had to change the design of the room to accommodate another lucky windfall which had come my way while I was still living in my big house. I had left one room undecorated owing to lack of funds. One summer I was motoring across Ireland to go and photograph Glenveagh Castle on the west coast, when I and the photographer, an antique-collecting buff, spotted a small shop in the middle of a typical Irish village high street. We stopped the car and nipped in. I wish, looking back, that I had bought everything in the shop as it was a treasure trove of unusual objects and the eccentric owner seemed to have no rhyme or reason in his pricing. Poking about in a dirty corner I unearthed four beautiful carved wooden curtain poles, with metal finials like pineapples and with all the original metal rings still on, painted white and gold two centuries ago. They must have come out of a very grand house indeed; I wish I knew which one. I bought them for a few pounds. They were not easy to pack and take

The television is tucked into the bookcase and can easily be concealed.

home, but I managed it. I vaguely hoped I should be able to use them in my unused 'banqueting hall'. I asked my gardener to stow them away somewhere and forgot about them.

When I started building the room I am now describing, I could not think of anything else night and day. How would my furniture fit in, what colour scheme would I go for, what material for curtains and covers? Suddenly I had a lightning flash of inspiration and remembered my Irish curtain poles, which were finally tracked down under a heap of potatoes. My architect, Mr. Ian Grant, had to alter the window positions slightly, but by joining two poles together they were made to fit the big window, while the two smaller ones fitted the smaller windows easily. The pelmets are sewn to the top of the curtains, and so roll back with them when they are drawn at night.

On one side of the main door is a French bureau and over it hang three pictures I am fond of. One is an amusing picture of a bulldog being painted by a monkey. The bulldog is hating his modelling session and has been given a glass of port to cheer him up and get him through his ordeal. Late nineteenth century, I found it in, of all places, Nantucket many years ago. Of roughly the same date is a minor French Impressionist of an absurdly overdressed lady pretending to fish, while her lover is staggering along behind carrying the oars. My third picture is different again; it is of

THE ENGLISHWOMAN'S HOUSE

Above: *One wall of the drawing-room is entirely covered with books. Antique Irish curtain poles were fitted into the windows.*

Below: *Over the 'mantelscape' hang some of Loelia Lindsay's famous needlework pictures.*

a nymph goddess with attendant cherubs, painted on copper with a Verni Martin background.

On the other side of the door is a favourite piece of furniture of mine. I like to think that this little red and gold bookcase originated from the Brighton Pavilion, but I don't fool myself completely. I have travelled around with this slim little bookcase and was determined to move it once more to what I hope is its final resting place. I couldn't imagine where I was going to find a place for it in my overfurnished cottage, but was grimly determined not to part with it. Why I couldn't at once see that I had the perfect place for it I can't imagine. I had hardly entered the house when I found the ideal position, for apart from its charming exotic appearance, it is so exceptionally narrow that it does not stand out into the room, which is just as well as it is between the door and the bar.

The bar is the best of all my disguises; the

The marble chimney-piece, acquired twenty years ago, was an extravagance that has never been regretted. ☞

blameless-looking wall appears only to display a delightful collection of a little-known artist, Lelong. One can only surmise that the painter was very interested in food, as every picture has minutely painted details of enticing cakes, cups of chocolate and bread baked in the most curious shapes. Concealed behind this innocent collection of Lelongs is a very functional bar. There is a small refrigerator where soft drinks can be stacked and ice-cubes made and below is a stainless-steel sink, handy for mixing drinks, which serves the additional function of being an ideal place to do flowers. Under the sink is another cupboard for bottles which seems constantly to need replenishing. Flower vases live on the other side of the cupboard.

In this room I have displayed the best of my needlework. The guided tour will start with the needlework carpet, which adds splendidly to the room. When occasionally it goes off on loan to an exhibition for a few weeks, the whole room changes character and becomes drab. I acquired the design when I found in the Portobello Road a Victorian rug which was almost falling to pieces. I had the outlines drawn on a new piece of canvas and then worked my own colouring from the magpie hoard of wools I have collected over the years. I specially like the big sprays of lilac, which is an unusual flower to find in a Victorian design.

My best work I have grouped on the fireplace wall—a pair of bell-pulls which actually ring bells (though nobody comes) are judged the finest. I did them soon after the war when it was still difficult to get silks and satins. With the help of a kind friend in Paris and the Royal School of Needlework I designed exactly what I had in mind—a mixture of flowers, butterflies and big fat gourds worked to give an appearance of rough skins bursting open to expose their ripe seeds, actually beads of course.

The rest of my little pictures are individual flowers and butterflies; an exception I am fond of is a chameleon sitting on a branch of a flowering shrub in the act of turning yellow to match the blossoms. The chameleon is entirely worked in tiny steel beads, and the background is a deep verdant green. I have specially designed arc lights that I can turn on at night which make the beads glisten like jewels.

I will now describe my 'tablescapes', a new word that amuses me. Can one have a 'mantel-scape' I wonder? If so, I have one. I start in the centre with a very pretty blue and gold enamel clock, on the corners are a little pair of marble busts, and in between stretches a line of boxes of all shapes and sizes, dates and value. I hate glass-topped museum *objets de vertu* tables and like everything living free. Against the wall are a pair of Hodgkins, one picture of feathers and the other gulls' and plovers' eggs.

On another table on a stand is a picture of a deer's head painted by Simon Bussy, also a large ivory nut with gold leaves attached made by the celebrated jeweller Verdura, some mother-of-pearl boxes, a silver snail shell, a miniature of my great-grandfather, a somewhat battered Meissen figure, and last but not least a monkey dressed in full ceremonials, riding his horse sideways and holding a long curved-handled umbrella made of leaves.

On a still smaller table is a bead tray made by me. Inspired by one in the FitzWilliam Museum in Cambridge dated 1680, I determined to try to make a modern version. I was lucky enough to have the exact Sèvres blue beads to do my own initials, entwined like those of Louis XV and encircled by red and gold ribbons with bows. These form the mat at the bottom of the basket which started so humbly as an 'in and out' tray from Rymans. The net-covered sides are thickly encrusted with oranges and lemons, their leaves and flowers—quite a problem to make a bead orange; curiously enough you crochet it.

The remaining wall, mostly window, has two unusual shaped black and gold torchères; behind them on the wall are a pair of gilt Georgian mirrors and on the torchères stand a pair of crystal candelabra. Finally, in the centre is my overladen writing table, from which I am constantly distracted by the bird life in the garden.

In New York, I once asked a famous interior decorator what the fashion of the moment was. 'Serenity', he replied. 'And how do you achieve that?' I asked. By sweeping away all the clutter, he announced. But supposing the owner was very much attached to her clutter of personal possessions? His answer was, 'You don't suppose that I should let her ideas interfere with my creation?'

I should not want to be one of his clients.

Loelia Lindsay

Jean Muir

Kensington, London

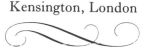

Ten years ago we were living in a flat in Pont Street, full of colour, pattern, ornaments and paintings. Work was increasingly hard. I was dashing backwards and forwards from America, and as the pressure grew, so did the feeling that we should simplify the way we lived. The concept we had of a way to live that would balance the working life was, in a sense, a reflection of my love for the workrooms—the feeling of space around you, good proportions, decks cleared, a studio atmosphere and beautiful light.

As the feeling became a necessity, we began to look for more space and a friend who lived in the building introduced us to a marvellously proportioned flat behind the Albert Hall. It was rather grandly built by a Victorian speculator who ran out of money before the block was completed, so the story goes.

I do not remember that we consciously decided 'We will have a white flat', but that is what it seemed right to do. A good decorator painted it white from one end to the other. The walls of the biggest rooms are lined with a particularly rough hessian as a base for the paint, which gives a good

Ceiling-to-floor curtains veil the bedroom walls. The embroidered bedspread comes from Cyprus.

texture, and there are fine white blinds at all the windows. Alan Irvine, the architect and a fellow Royal Designer for Industry, led us to some good synthetic white flooring he found in France for an exhibition he was designing. It is matt and not cold to touch nor underfoot.

One day when the flat was ready, instead of going home to Pont Street, my husband and I simply came here instead and were joined by our housekeeper Carmen, who has been with us for fifteen years. All we had with us were our tooth-brushes and make-up, and I don't think we went back to Pont Street for five or six weeks. By then, although our old flat held fond memories, it looked far too busy and complicated. We wanted to jettison our possessions, and very, very few things made the journey with us to Kensington.

Here we have only what we use: lovely bare white spaces and one or two essential and move-able pieces of furniture and a good kitchen and bathroom. What we did not want was ever to have to say 'This is the dining-room' or 'This is the sitting-room'. We have ten white calico seating units, designed for visitors to picture galleries, and

these usually go along the length of one wall to make a long sofa though they are moved con-stantly. Our four tables, all alike, were carefully worked out and designed with John Minshure to be linked together or moved apart. Everything

The chair and double seat in the bedroom are in finely engraved Venetian glass, which catches and reflects the light.

Any colour entering the flat stands out immediately. The white calico seating units are constantly regrouped.

rolls smoothly across the floor—tables, chairs and the clinical trolleys where one stacks make-up or linen.

Once you have eliminated all the things you don't like you get down to the bare essentials and the formula that is perfect for yourself. Just as I begin a dress from the proper proportions of the body and resist additions, I have learnt to simplify my life in all directions. If, for instance, you don't want to come home to a clutter of letters, the way to deal with it is not to keep tidying but get rid of the desk itself.

The effect of the empty white spaces is to give a lift to any colour that enters the room. Food

The arched corridor runs the length of the flat.

looks wonderful in the flat, as do books, a pot by Fiona Salazar and Mo Jupp's sculpture. People also stand out—it worries some.

There are two ideas for the flat that we thought through but never completed. The walls of every room are wired for sound, but we never connected up the system. We had plans to project slides onto the walls so that we could have a perpetually changing exhibition of pictures. The one thing we did take enormous trouble with was the lighting, which consists of very small white spotlights placed at intervals around the picture rails, very similar to the lighting in the showroom in Bruton Street. There is a wide and very long arched corridor that runs from the front door to the far end of the flat, and in the evening with the lights turned low it has a cool, classical look to it which reminds me of Greece in late evening: calm, still and free.

The only large room whose purpose is immediately obvious is the bedroom. The bed has a white embroidered linen bedspread made by nuns in Cyprus, and all the walls are veiled by white curtains hung from ceiling to floor. These on one side cover the window, which shines through, and on the other hide a large built cupboard where I hang my clothes and keep my shoes and handbags. Clothes need to breathe not to be crushed.

We have only two pieces of decorative furniture in the flat, and they are both in the bedroom: a chair and double seat in heavy, finely engraved Venetian glass, bought from Christopher Vane-Percy and apparently from the palace of the Nizam of Hyderabad. They repeat and catch the varying lights. On the bed and the chairs are a collection of pillows and small cushions in lace-edged linen and cotton with embroidery and drawn thread work. Most of them were made in my workrooms by sewing together the traycloths I had collected over the years. It is Carmen's particular pleasure to keep these absolutely snow white and perfectly pressed. I treasure a white patchwork cushion made of tiny white moiré triangles starred with small silver sequins, a gift from a good friend, Naomi Langley.

Where a room has a function we wanted it to be completely efficient. A good, well-equipped kitchen and a comfortable, attractive bathroom were essentials. Harry and I are both good cooks and enjoy making our own meals, particularly

The tables are designed to be linked together and moved apart.

when we are in London at the weekends. The kitchen was the only room we thought out and planned in great detail, in consultation with a firm called Kitchen Planners. It was beautifully executed with a bank of well-finished cupboards, drawers and surfaces in black oak, and the central

Fine blinds on all the windows filter light into the flat.

unit accommodates gas, electricity and even calor gas, ready for any emergency. The equipment came from a superb German firm called Poggen-pohl; it has stood the test of ten years and still looks marvellous.

To anyone who saw the flat in its original state, the bathroom would probably be the most surprising room. From a tiny, depressing closet it underwent an amazing transformation when we covered all wall and ceiling surfaces with enormous panels of glass, and found a wide triangular ivory bathtub to fit across one corner, making the most of the floor space. The step in the ceiling, which accommodated part of the structure of the building, adds to the effect of standing in a tall gallery of mirrors throwing reflections back and forward to each other.

The only other rooms in the flat other than Carmen's are a spare bedroom and Harry's dressing-room and bathroom, with a wooden sauna and a wall of books and more books—our great indulgence—opposite the cupboard where he keeps his clothes and fishing gear.

One aspect of the flat which gives me great pleasure is the evening light as it slants in and filters through the fine blinds. I love the perspectives of the view. Surprisingly close, you see the details of the frieze that circles the Albert Hall, and beyond, the Albert Memorial lifts its spires above the trees of Kensington Gardens.

The life that goes on in and around the Albert Hall gives a particular character to our life here. When they raise the immense ventilators in the glass roof you can hear the music quite clearly. From our windows you can look down and see not only the musicians but perhaps the Boys' Brigade lining up with the band, the Institute of Directors, the Salvation Army or the Prom crowds. One advantage of living here is that if we go to a concert we can come home for a drink in the interval. How thrilled I was last year to speak at the AGM of that wonderful institution the Women's Institute.

From the flat, the drive to Bruton Street through Hyde Park, or to our new premises in Farringdon Road through Knightsbridge past Buckingham Palace, Trafalgar Square and along the Embankment, takes us through the heart of London. Depending on what time we leave, the park has a particular cast of characters. At 7.30 to 8 am there are the joggers, and sometimes the tramp with her suitcases of old newspapers. Half an hour later there's the man who does military exercises by himself in a corner of the Gardens, and the horses from the barracks being exercised in the Row, and so much more.

There are other areas in our lives where we accumulate and revise, but the original concept, to find a way of living at home which perfectly suits our London life, found its equation in this flat. We haven't wanted to alter it, we have resisted adding anything, and it has remained a perfectly satisfactory solution for ten years. When will we move on? Who knows? Instinct will tell.

Meredyth Proby

ELTON HALL
Peterborough, Cambridgeshire

When I married in 1974 we lived in London but were allowed the use of a flat at the Hall for weekends. My first memories of Elton are wonderful carefree ones since we enjoyed all the benefits while my parents-in-law had all the worries. I often found it difficult to understand why everyone was so gloomy on occasions, but when my grandfather-in-law died so many problems had to be faced that I could see why. The most pressing one was that, for tax reasons, we open the house to the public.

We came to live here in the summer of 1979 and decided to approach the problem on two fronts. Firstly, to organise the main state rooms so that the public could see them and secondly, to make ourselves comfortable in one corner of the house. This was not as easy as it might seem. Rab Butler is said to have complained that Elton was one of the most uncomfortable houses he had ever

stayed in and I think there was probably some truth in this.

In all our deliberations we were very lucky to have the architects Kit Martin and Bob Weighton. Kit was an old friend of William, my husband, and had been horrified to discover us 'lurking in the basement'. Since we no longer had the necessary help to cope with the original layout, we all agreed that we must move the centre of the household operations, that is the kitchen and associated rooms, up to the ground floor. Bob then spent many hours drawing up plans and we finally decided to put in a new kitchen, laundry room, cloakroom and playroom on the ground floor, new bathrooms upstairs, and to rewire and replumb with new central heating one complete corner of the house.

It was a great relief to see the builders move in in spite of the fact they stayed for nearly a year. We

The re-decorated State Dining-Room which was formerly painted in blue and held only five pictures.

Above: *Alec Cobbe's 1983 design for a picture gallery to be made in the Old Dining-Room of Elton Hall.*

employed a firm of local builders, Bowman and Sons, who are very experienced with old houses and all the problems associated with them. Although I have often described our house as a wonderful architectural muddle, it does have its advantages. Because it starts off in 1475 and rambles on in a delightful way until 1890, it means that there are numerous little corners and turrets which can be made separate from the rest of the building. It was into one of these corners that we retreated while general chaos was going on below.

Everything moved very quickly to begin with; demolition is easier than construction, but at last everything was ready for me to start decorating the rooms. I had once worked for an interior decorator in a very menial capacity, but my job had terminated abruptly when I rushed off skiing with my future husband leaving the company vehicle, loaded with materials, parked on a yellow line. I still had this unshakeable belief, though, that I might be rather good at it, and here at last was my chance to try.

I spent a lot of time rushing up and down to London, carrying little bits of material about. Then I was fortunate enough to come across Anne Harvey, who lives locally, who stocked most of the designer materials that I had been looking at and who could get everything made up. Here was peace at last and I spent many happy hours sitting at her house thumbing through endless books and changing my ideas at least twice a day. I had in my mind the sort of effect I wanted to create. Each room wanted to look distinctive and yet it needed to blend in with the history of the house. I am hopeless at drawing and have never done sketches of a room so I try to imagine the whole effect in my head. However much you plan, though, I think it is the final arranging of a room that can make or break a colour scheme.

It was quite a change for the house to have children living in it again. The last Proby children to be brought up here were the third Earl of Carysfort's family in the 1840s. Since then everyone had been so much older when they inherited that the nursery rooms were not really used unless children came to stay. It was once again necessary to organise the house properly for children. We did the kitchen, playroom, children's bedrooms, our own sitting-room and bedroom and bathroom first. These are essentially bright and cheerful rooms. Some of the materials are modern designed prints,

but the majority are traditional chintz and similar materials. The curtain designs are basically traditional, for example we copied our bedroom pelmets from a nineteenth century design book. We have suffered terrible problems with the proportions of pelmets and it is only by trial and error that one eventually learns. On our tall windows the most successful proportion of pelmet to curtain seems to be between one-fifth and one-sixth of the total height.

Carpeting was a terrible problem, since there was very little of what I call proper carpet in the house. There were endless little bits and pieces tacked together to make an island in the middle of the room, and corridors and bathrooms were covered with the ubiquitous linoleum. My early memories of winter at Elton are full of jumping from one piece of carpet to another in an attempt to get to the bathroom, where one always froze anyway. My answer to this particular problem was to go to the nearest carpet warehouse in Peterborough and order rolls of two or three different-coloured carpet and arrange a date for them to come and lay it. The difference to our corner was phenomenal. Suddenly, we were in a warm and cosy house.

We are now starting to decorate some of the rooms open to the public and our first project has been the State Dining Room. This faces north, and although it has a pretty view looking out across the park to the cricket pitch and Elton church, it is a cold room because of its enormous size (it is twenty feet high and measures forty feet by thirty) and lack of sunlight. It was added onto the house in 1860 but was built very much in the eighteenth century style. In contrast the Drawing Room, which dates from 1475 and faces south, is wonderfully light and sunny. The gilding and decorations carried out in 1860 in the French chateau style still have a tremendous amount of life in them. The contrast between the two rooms was so great that we had felt for some time we wanted to change the former, but we had been so preoccupied with making our own side comfortable that it had had to wait.

The State Dining Room was originally painted in a very deep purple-red and the dado, architraves, doors and eighteenth century fireplace were all woodgrained. The ceiling is very ornate and mostly gilded, and it had bands of different coffee colours and a sort of sludge blue.

We were able to discover most of this by scraping away at the various coats of paint. I do not think the room was changed at all up to the Second World War, but then the house was used initially by a girls' school and then by the Red Cross as a convalescent home. The State Dining Room became one of the many dormitories and the original decorations, except for the gilding, were lost under coats of washable distemper. After the war it was redecorated, but this time in varying shades of blue. Everything was blue, including the doors, dado, shutters and any piece of spare ceiling that wasn't gilded. Since the room was no longer used as a dining-room, it was turned into a museum for displaying books.

Apart from redecorating the room we also wanted to bring it back as a dining-room and display the books somewhere else. We deliberated for hours whether to put it back to red or whether to adopt yellow as the new colour. Among our friends, all the men wanted red and the women yellow. We had to take another very important point into consideration, and that was the hanging of many of our pictures. After the war five pictures

had been hung in this room and there was obviously capacity for far more. We had a lot of pictures sitting in a store-room and quite a lot hanging in rooms which did not show them to their best advantage. Alec Cobbe, who is a picture restorer and a friend of ours, had been pestering us for ages to redecorate the room and hang it in the eighteenth century style: that is, literally covering every available wall space with pictures. This we were very keen to do. A remark by Alec finally decided the colour as well. He was very definitely for red (silk if possible, otherwise paint would do), and when he heard I was still considering yellow he told me that the Duke of Wellington had persevered in a similar vein at Apsley House but as soon as his funeral was over the decorators moved in and changed the room to red. So red it was to be.

We were at loss to know who to contact about specialist paintwork on this scale but were lucky enough to be given the name of a firm who produced Ron Windsor for us. Ron is one of those chosen few with a superb eye for colour. He saved us from one disastrous shade of red and soon had

The recently repainted Marble Hall with the statue of Esmeralda by Romanelly dating from about 1860.

Mrs. Proby's bedroom looking through to the bathroom. The curtain pelmets were copied from a nineteenth-century design book.

The Yellow or Family drawing-room looking through to the Marble Hall. The Aubusson rug was acquired recently to cover bare floor boards.

us organised with the right colour. The invaluable Mr. Kisby, who lives just two miles away, did all the preparation and undercoats and Ron followed him, scumbling the walls and shading the wood-work. The whole effect was then varnished. We have chosen a different, warmer red to the original one and the dado, architraves and shutters are all in shaded off-white. The doors have been wood-grained again and were done by a local friend of Mr. Kisby's who came specially out of retirement to do the job. The ceiling was a tremendous prob-lem. We left the gilding alone but still had to paint out all the blue. After various attempts at different coffee colours and off-whites we at last managed to find the right combination. It is slightly different to the original colours and probably much lighter. We have kept the same curtains and Persian carpet because although they are slightly worn, they are the ones originally made for the room and the cost of replacing them to the same standard would have been very high. The curtains, though, look almost as good as new since they were taken in hand by our great-aunt, Katherine Proby, who has done a superb job in mending them and putting them back to their former glory. One day we hope to restore the dining table, which we found in the apple loft, but at the moment we have to make do with another.

We have now also completed two more rooms, our own dining-room and drawing-room, and we are just beginning to feel at home. It has been nearly five years since we first moved in and I still look around and see so much more to do. I am looking forward to this and am rather glad that for reasons of cost and size we haven't just swept through the house with the same theme in one year. One of the most important things that has been achieved in the last few years is that we are at last beginning to feel it is our home as well as the Family Home. It takes quite a bit of time to put your own mark on four hundred years of predeces-sors and quite a bit of thought not to be too heavy-handed as well.

Meredyth Proby

➤ *The Grand Drawing-Room remains unchanged since it was decorated in 1860 apart from the recent addition of the rug and some rearranging of the furniture.*

Didi Saunders

EASTON GREY HOUSE
Nr. Malmesbury, Wiltshire

There's a good reason why I was almost more frightened than flattered to write this contribution. For let me come clean and confess: I'm an American. And how dare I pose as an authority on the Englishwoman's house?

It's true I've lived in England longer than I've lived in America. And I find it hard to believe that anyone could love their English home better than I love Easton Grey. But I don't pretend to have lost all my American ideas or American heritage, and these are bound to have an influence on my home.

Maybe it was the crazy pioneering spirit—like the one that took my ancestors bumping in a covered wagon to Minnesota—which had me believing I could take on a large, near-derelict house in Wiltshire which had stood empty for five years. Even my mother, who was pretty enterprising, thought it a mistake. When she first walked into the fabulous entrance hall, she said: 'You're mad.' I told her to keep walking, but that didn't help. There were so many rooms, big rooms; and so much that needed to be done to all of them. At the end of the tour, she was in tears.

But at the time I was hardly twenty years old

The drawing-room at Easton Grey House.

and—even worse—had fallen hopelessly in love. How can you talk to someone like that?

I still think, all these years later, that no one could have blamed me for falling in love. Easton Grey is a magical place: a calm, weathered Queen Anne house set in the countryside that everyone dreams about. Very green, very gentle. The river Avon below. And beyond, an unspoilt gem of a Cotswold village. All as English, as enduring, as Shakespeare.

There has been a house on the site since 1236. (Easton Grey was indeed mentioned in the Domesday Book.) And in the reign of Edward II, John de Grey held the manor keep in return for keeping one royal falcon in permanent residence for the king. Not a bad bargain. Later owners included Lord Asquith's sister-in-law, who entertained the prime minister for many summer visits; and the house was also rented as a hunting lodge in the nineteen-twenties by the Duke of Windsor.

One of our first decisions was to keep the bones of the house intact. Inside and out, it's hard to improve on those Queen Anne proportions; and who's going to interfere with an Adam fire-place such as we have in the hall, a free-standing light stone staircase with exquisite wrought-iron banisters, or age-old slate interspaced floors—even though they do take a lot of polishing?

It was in fact my husband Peter who made the whole thing possible. We couldn't afford to take on the house just as a home, but his business proved the lifesaver. The old Victorian broken-down kitchens were converted to offices; and though outside they looked—as they had always looked—a part of the old house, inside they dealt with his expanding mail order business in tweeds and knitwear. This was what helped to support our whole reclamation project.

A business interest may not be part of the traditional Englishwoman's approach to her house. But in this day and age, is it so foreign? Many stately homes are now open to the public; and no one denies that this may be the only way of keeping them upright and in one piece.

Another decision was to be the tortoise rather than the hare in our approach to the endless, echoing rooms in our new home. You can rush around wildly with gallons of white emulsion, trying to make everything presentable. Or you can take one room at a time and say: 'This will be the result I really want.' And although certain repairs to the

roof and so on had to go ahead, and things like a kitchen and a bathroom could not be deferred, we managed to close our eyes to almost everything except 'the one room'.

The reason why the library remains my favourite is probably because this was the first just-the-way-I-want-it room. And for a while, it was almost a complete home. It was here that we played with our baby daughter, ate meals, worked on Peter's catalogues, talked to the plumber; here that I telephoned friends, quivered over bills and

Easton Grey House from the garden side.

estimates, and wrote to my mother to tell her she was right; here that I did just about everything except cook and sleep and have a bath.

If you came to visit me today, I think the first thing you'd notice about the library would be the great sense of light. There's an extravagant amount of window, including the later addition of a big bow window. This is where my overflowing desk stands. Facing south west, it catches most of the sun; and although I know this is a book about houses, not gardens or views, it's difficult to separate them. The garden, dipping down to the Avon valley, feels part of the room; and it's hard to avoid watching our pair of local swans, the kingfisher and the heron. Or to shut your ears to a very busy pair of woodpeckers.

Because of the natural brightness, we decorated in quiet, suedey colours: basically browns and beiges. And I must admit that one American influence was my stepfather's study in his Maryland home, Rolling Ridge. This was done in the most beautiful old green leather, radiating a kind of weathered warmth. And although we couldn't afford such a luxury, we tried to get the same deep, lived-in comfort with the suede effect.

There's a big bookcase, of course, full to overflowing—like my desk. It was made by our then gardener who, we discovered, was a lot better at carpentry than at gardening. On the walls, there are some modern French paintings and two spectacular wood carvings, St. Asprin and St. Agrippa, which once adorned the altar of an old church. They came from a client of Peter's who couldn't pay his bill and gave him the carvings instead.

The library faces south-east, looking down to the Avon Valley, and is always flooded with light.

The free-standing light stone staircase has wrought-iron banisters.

Looking through to the dining-room with its collection of T'ang horses. An original eighteenth-century Chinese wallpaper frames the entrance.

The library curtains have a strong geometric pattern, but still keeping to the brown and beige. I find them restful. They were designed by David Hicks, who has indeed helped us with many rooms in the house. So, too, has another great interior decorator, Tom Parr. And talking of interior decorators, I don't know if this is being American or not, but I've never found it embarrassing, or an admission of failure, to pick professional brains. The best professionals don't move in and dictate that everything must be stone-coloured or pin-striped or whatever. They'll have ideas, of course; but more than anything, they make *you*, the owner, think very hard and work very hard to get the colour schemes and furnishings and pictures and ornaments that *you* want to live with.

Peter and I have always found our advisers a stimulus, mind-stretchers. Added to which, they can be pretty indispensable when it comes to some technical problems. Most of us, for instance, are not used to curtaining big, nearly floor-to-ceiling windows. How should they be designed? What kind of pelmets? Frankly, I hadn't a clue; and without professional help, would probably have made horrendous mistakes.

But I can honestly say that if, after inspection, you don't approve of Easton Grey—don't blame David Hicks or Tom Parr. Blame Peter and me. Because, for better or worse, it's our taste, our

choice. (David Hicks has indeed criticised us on occasions. When he last visited, he looked disapprovingly round the library and said: 'You're ruining this room with all your clutter!')

As we moved on, tortoise-like, from room to room we came on some unchangeable treasures. In particular, there was an original eighteenth century Chinese wallpaper, depicting a Chinese wedding. Like the Adam fire-place, who's going to lose *that*? It was just a question of some restoration.

But most of the walls and ceilings needed a fresh start; and it's hard to feel conservation-minded about old bathrooms or north-facing rooms painted a dark cream. In general, I think our starting point was nearly always colour. We didn't look at a room and wonder: 'Where shall we put our furniture?' The first question was: 'What colour shall we have the walls or the curtains or the carpet?'

Take our dining-room. (For many years a happy ping-pong room for our now four children.) When this became our next project, we began with a large Spanish carpet, woven to our design in Madrid, and everything else had to harmonise. I was delighted to find that an exact replica of some curtains belonging to my mother fitted in beautifully. So did our precious collection of T'ang horses. But that carpet was the boss. That carpet decided what was, and was not, acceptable.

In the drawing-room, we began with a blue-and-white colour scheme and a stippled floor. (This stippling—almost like painting a tapestry on the floor—was another American influence: the idea came from the south of the USA.) Again, it was a question of harmonising everything else with these priorities. Our rare, painted Chippendale mirror was welcome, as was much of the furniture recently inherited from my mother. And we chose some punchy black lithographs at Sothebys, partly because we loved them, but also because we thought they would look their best against the drawing-room's bluey walls. The grouping of chairs and sofas to make for comfortable entertaining, the arrangement of ornaments, small tables and so on . . . all this was important. But it came later.

Moving upstairs, we allowed ourselves brighter, more daring colour schemes. I felt the reception rooms of an old English country house should remain reasonably dignified and traditional; but modern wallpapers, lively paintwork, brilliant Portuguese tiles (again made to our own design) transformed the bedrooms and bathrooms. The ghosts of former owners might blink a little, but it's all such a good antidote to the (frequent) grey English weather, I believe they eventually come to enjoy it, as we do.

There have always been so many things to do. Peter's mail order business has evolved into my Country Boutique and Garden Restaurant, still attached to the house, where I sell mainly women's clothes as well as china, glass and gifts. That alone keeps me busy; and I've often wished there were short cuts in dealing with the house.

Lady Caroline Somerset, in her enchanting contribution to *The Englishwoman's Garden*, wrote that, with a modicum of taste, gardens were easy to create but 'damn difficult to keep going'. With old houses I think we catch it all ways, because they're damn difficult to restore, *and* keep going.

The drawing-room's blue-and-white colour scheme and stippled floor dictated the rest of the decoration and furnishings.

Like old people, they need constant attention.

But I don't want to end on a hard grind note. Apart from the sheer delight of living in Easton Grey—a place which, all our visitors say, takes you out of time into a world very close to an English dream—there have been things all along the line for which I can only say, 'Thank heaven'. But a word of warning. *Be careful about falling in love with a house because it's dreadfully hard to disengage.* You'll get over that devastating Latin lover. But a house remains a lifelong pull on the heartstrings.

If I have to move on to another home, I know the pull will always be there. One way and another, I'll be back and back and back to Easton Grey.

Didi Saunders

Part of the decorative collection of blue-and-white porcelain.

The entrance hall of Easton Grey House.

Anne Scott-James

A Downland Cottage
Berkshire

It is on the face of it absurd that I, who am six feet tall, energetic and restless, should have elected to live in a doll's house. An open-plan studio, with plenty of headroom and space for frenzied pacing, might have been more suitable. But in 1938 I was driving with my mother among the primeval sheepwalks and small, secretive villages of the Berkshire downs when we passed a small, square cottage half-hidden by apple-trees with a board by the gate announcing 'To Be Sold by Auction'. I was about to be married, my fiancé and I lived and worked in London, and we had no money for frills, but I wanted the cottage quite absurdly. It went at auction for four hundred pounds, I was the buyer, and my mother lent me the cash.

The cottage was of brick and tile, built in 1807 (a workman had stippled the date into the chimney), was sited at the top of a small, steeply sloping front garden, and faced west. The view from the front door was charming. It looked onto a triangular green planted with nine elm-trees, with fields of rolling pasture and an eighteenth century farmhouse beyond; to the right, a group of cottages and a Norman parish church. The view is changed now, but not ruined. The pasture is arable (how I miss the mushrooms), the elms are felled, the farmhouse has been gentrified, and the

electricity and telephone people have joined forces to create what Betjeman would call a wirescape. But there are no new buildings, and the parish has planted limes to replace the rook-haunted elms. The church is well preserved, and the hedgerows still blossom with hawthorn, dogroses and sloe.

The cottage was in a primitive state, without water or electricity, and was densely populated with insects and mice; there was an outside privy and an insanitary well. I will not bore readers with the trials and tribulations which are common to all who convert old houses. I made a major mistake in trying to muddle things out myself with a local builder, and if I were starting again I would enlist an architect, but after much trial and error my home was ready. Of course, it has changed in the forty-odd years since I bought it, and I am afraid that neither the house nor the garden is as pretty as it was at first. I had to build onto the house when my children were born, spoiling the doll's house look, and later enlarged the garden to make room for hideous necessities like a garage and a tennis court (now a croquet lawn), but I still like my cottage better than any other house I know.

The two things I want in a home are comfort and a feeling of cleanness. To me, comfort means cosiness, a dreadful word, but I know no other—an open fire, plenty of lamps and electric points,

A nearby group of cottages and the tower of the Norman Parish Church as drawn by Osbert Lancaster.

masses of cupboards, lots of hot water, electric blankets, and a simple kitchen with a minimum of gadgets. I am terrified of machines which slice with razor-sharp blades and I would rather wash clothes by hand than endure the surge and thunder of a washing-machine. These amenities I provided from the beginning. The one comfort I have never managed to achieve is freedom from draughts, and in spite of a double front door and double-glazed windows in the living-room, the inquisitive south-west wind still stirs the papers on my desk.

By a feeling of cleanness, I do not mean the aseptic hygiene of a Swedish house, but rather the freshness of an English farmhouse. I remember with pleasure the whitewashed walls, polished churn and pails and blue-and-white china of a dairy where I was allowed to skim the cream when I was a child.

My style of decoration is, I suppose, a debased and poor woman's version of John Fowler. Of all the decorators of my lifetime John Fowler is the one I admire most, and I feel that his influence has outlasted other contemporary schools of décor, such as the crafts revival of the twenties and thirties. Who now wants tweed curtains or oak settles? I was lucky enough to see some of Fowler's first work in country houses in the nineteen-thirties and was bowled over by its beauty.

His decorations were, of course, of the highest quality and all were exquisitely made, every pelmet a work of art, but anyone could adapt, as I tried to do, the fresh, countrified atmosphere of his rooms. I remember well his ethereal use, in a Regency house in Surrey, of yellow with white, his striped chintz curtains and inviting chaises-longues, the muslin curtains and lampshades and candlewick quilts in the bedrooms—it is significant that many of his fabrics were cotton. I also recall an ivy-patterned wallpaper in the hall, bringing a feeling of the garden into the house. That house was my ideal and I carried its picture in my mind when I set about converting my slummy cottage.

First, being obsessed with lightness, I had the outside painted white, which was perhaps a mistake, for when it has to be repainted the climbers which cover the walls resent being taken down and pinned back again, and can take two seasons to readjust. ,

Inside, I made the rooms, most of which get

no morning sun, as light as possible. Downstairs, there were two tiny front rooms divided by a passage, with a primitive kitchen and larder at the back. I knocked the two front rooms into one, making a living–dining-room twenty-five feet long and twelve feet wide, and had an oak floor laid by a local carpenter, which takes a lovely polish. Since I dislike dust-traps and clutter, I had as much furniture as possible built in, and think this is very important where space is limited. On one side, built-in bookshelves three shelves high run the length of the room, with cupboards let in for games, bottles and glasses. The shelves are, count-

The dining end of the living-room in 1958.

ing from the bottom, fourteen, twelve and ten inches high, so that books of most sizes can be accommodated, including dictionaries. On the other side of the room, a small sideboard was built in at the dining end to take care of silver and table linen. Then I whitewashed the walls and ceiling and indulged my taste for Fowler.

I made the curtains myself of striped chintz in cyclamen pink and white, bought a Regency chaise-longue for ten pounds in Dorchester-on-Thames and had it upholstered in yellow-and-white striped satin, and loose-covered two cheap and uncomfortable armchairs in pale green linen. I bought a white rug for the hearth. But my pride and joy was a refectory table for the dining end of the room, painted in white and apple green, which

I bought at the Colefax & Fowler shop itself for fifteen pounds. Six Victorian dining chairs found in the Kings Road, Chelsea, were upholstered in a green and white ivy-patterned chintz. So there was my living-room, mostly white, with fabrics in cyclamen pink, leaf green and yellow. I must add that I had very few pictures then, the best being an Augustus John watercolour, so I put one or two mirrors on the walls. I already had quite a collection of porcelain, some of it inherited and good.

The kitchen was improved as much as resources would allow, and the larder was just big enough to convert into a bathroom.

Upstairs, a corkscrew staircase led to two double bedrooms in front and a single room at the back, all small, but with enchanting views over farmland or garden. I left them structurally as they were, putting a basin with hot and cold water into each, as the only bathroom was downstairs. We were young and healthy then, and a downstairs lavatory was no drawback. I had roomy cupboards built into each room.

I had the bedrooms whitewashed and made striped chintz curtains for the two larger rooms,

The cottage in springtime.

The light, fresh living-room has simple white walls and built-in bookshelves.

spotted muslin curtains for the single room, tied with large pink ribbon bows. This room faces east and is the only one which gets the morning sun, and I often sit there at sunrise watching hosts of small birds twitter and feed. A favourite bird in summer is the goldcrest, which nests in the Irish yews, and in winter woodpeckers come to peck up insects in the grass. I must mention that all this white would not suit an arachnophobe, for it makes a showy background for spiders. The conversion was just about finished by September 1939, so my enjoyment of the cottage was delayed for several years.

Today, the cottage is larger, with more rooms and two bathrooms, but my taste in decoration remains much the same. The living-room still has white walls (I tried wallpaper at one stage, but it made the room look smaller), but the other rooms are papered, some with French papers, others with Laura Ashley. The stripes have retreated, and the living-room curtains are a sprawly flowered chintz, the couch plain green. I have more porcelain today and many more pictures. The one change I regret is that my green-and-white dining-table has been replaced by a round rosewood table which is too grand for cottage life. (I shall smuggle the original table back one day, for it is safe in our London kitchen.) The rosewood table was installed at the request of my husband, Osbert Lancaster, whom I married in 1967; he is a round-table man, liking to flick his *bons-mots* in circles. He made few other changes, but did design a characteristic Lancaster room upstairs for his studio, a diminutive stage-set with pine ceiling, William Morris wallpaper and curtains, red carpet, and Turkish and mediaeval *objets*. To gain space he had the inspired idea of building out an oriel window, into which he fitted his drawing desk and artist's materials.

Over the years, the doll's house has proved wonderfully flexible, and, thanks to building in and building out, I and my family have never felt cramped.

Anne Scott-James

The dining end where a round rosewood table has replaced the original green-and-white one.

Nancie Sheffield

SUTTON PARK
Sutton-on-the-Forest, Yorkshire

Sutton, which is a Grade I building, was built in the middle of the eighteenth century by Phillip Harland. The architect is thought to be Thomas Atkinson.

Phillip Harland was left five hundred pounds either to build a new house or improve the Elizabethan house already standing. He chose to do the former. My husband and I always thought the money must have run out, as Elizabethan panelling was put back in some of the third floor rooms while most of the other rooms have lovely painted pine panelling except where the Vic-

torians tore it out.

When we had to leave Normanby in Lincoln-shire twenty-three years ago because of its large size, we were delighted to find Sutton, which was all we were seeking: a house of medium size, facing south, with a lovely park, woodlands and a farm in hand. We lived in a small house in the garden for two years, only going back to Normanby on Friday to Monday, while we improved Sutton, making a new dining-room, putting in more bathrooms and installing a lift, as the middle block is of three floors. The dining-room, a major

🐦 *The morning-room is panelled with stripped pine attributed to Flitcroft.*   Above: *Sutton Park from the garden.*

operation, had to be created by removing internal walls in the east wing, with the new kitchen and domestic quarters next door. I knew exactly what I wanted done and we were lucky in having a wonderful architect, Francis Johnson, to help us. He also knew all the good craftsmen, woodcarver Dick Reid of York and plasterer Leonard Stead of Bradford.

We were lucky that all the rooms in Sutton have the windows, doors and staircases in the right places. The doors on the ground and first floors are of mahogany. I think what made my husband decide then and there to buy the house was the beautiful plaster work by Joseph Cortese in the

hall, staircase and the library. We brought four marble chimney-pieces from Normanby which fitted in various rooms very well. As the house faces due south, all the main rooms are flooded with sunshine and look onto the terraced gardens we made.

As all the rooms had to be redecorated, we chose the colours and John Fowler very kindly came down and had them mixed for us, which he did brilliantly. Luckily he liked our ideas. He also did the hangings on two of the four-poster beds and the curtains in my sitting-room. The morning-room was originally the dining-room and has stripped pine panelling which has been attri-

The library is a bright comfortable room with its many armchairs and a sofa.

The beautiful ornate plaster work in the hall, staircase and library is by Joseph Cortese.

A small table in the morning-room displays some of the snuff boxes collected by Mr. and Mrs. Sheffield.

The four-poster in Mrs. Sheffield's bedroom with its elegant hangings by John Fowler.

buted to Flitcroft and was moved to Sutton from a house in Hull. The ceiling has a misty cloud effect which was suggested by John Fowler and which looks very well. There is a collection of treen made by my husband which I have added to. When my husband was alive we were both avid collectors and he contributed greatly to the collection of Chinese snuff bottles in the drawing-room. I started to collect nineteenth century beadwork and fine needlework which I turned into cushions. The morning-room leads into my favourite, the library.

As this is in the centre of the house, we made a window door with stone steps down into the gar-den. I am a passionate gardener and I adore plants from the humblest to the rare. We moved some of the bookcases, designed by Smirke, from the Normanby library and they hold part of that library. The chimney-piece also is one of those we brought from Normanby. I have a big log fire and club fender and lots of armchairs, some of them and the sofa with loose covers in a heavy cotton from Colefax & Fowler called Ravena; the design is in two shades of yellow. The curtains are dark yellow silk. They are seventy years old and my mother-in-law had them in her London house in South Audley Street. Sadly, they are starting to fall apart. The gilt carved cornices above the pel-

Mrs. Sheffield's favourite room, the library, has a window-door leading directly to the garden.

The tea-room whose walls are painted to look like tortoiseshell and ivory.

mets we brought with us, and strangely they only needed to be reduced in size a very little as the windows here are so large. Two years ago I went to Lisbon and designed and had made two large needlework rugs in brown, coral and green; these are laid on matting. The walls of the library are brown and the bookcases and dado off-white. The Cortese ceiling is painted in two shades of white.

Over the last twenty-five years we have collected Imari and early Chinese plates; these are hung in the tea-room, whose walls we had painted in the manner of the eighteenth century to look like tortoiseshell and ivory. This room leads into the hall, and opposite is the porcelain room. As we both inherited small collections we have put them all together in this room. The hall is north facing so the staircase walls are painted yellow with white dado and plasterwork to give an impression of sunlight.

In my sitting-room, which is in one of the wings leading to the Chinese drawing-room in the west pavilion, we put one of the chimney-pieces from Normanby; this was made by the famous

Pedro Bossi. Our son lent us an early nineteenth century chandelier—the facets hang like a waterfall. As it is impossible to hang a chandelier from a plain ceiling we designed the plasterwork with the help of Leonard Stead, which was very interesting and amusing to do. We incorporated some of the motifs of Cortese. The first design was not a great success but the second worked very well.

The drawing-room which leads out of my sitting-room has a very rare eighteenth century hand-painted wallpaper which has the signatures of the artists who worked on it. This paper took three months to restore. On John Fowler's advice we picked out the plasterwork on the ceiling and the cornice in two-coloured gold. Using the lemon gold makes it look so much lighter. The white marble chimney-piece came from my sitting-room in Normanby and looks altogether better here in a much smaller room.

We were amazed how well the furniture from Normanby fitted into a much smaller house. The lacquer furniture came originally from the Japan room in Buckingham House, now incorporated in Buckingham Palace and built by John Sheffield, first Duke of Buckingham, in 1705. The original architect was William Talman, who was a notoriously difficult man; the Duke had a disagreement with him and William Winde took over, which is rather surprising as he was not one of the leading architects of that day. There is a drawing by Giacomo Leoni which came out of the Japan room and shows the original façade hanging in the hall of Sutton. Most of the paintings also fitted in very well, as there is a secondary staircase leading from the centre block to the third floor with plenty of wall space.

There are two things I feel strongly about in interior decoration. I do not like close cover carpets in the downstair rooms, especially in the hall; it gives one the impression of coming into an hotel or a block of flats. Lampshades must be very simple, pleated or plain in white or pale cream, and definitely no fringes.

I love lots of plants in the house in the winter, mostly white and particularly jasmin, narcissi, scented cyclamen and hyacinth, because they smell the best.

Margot Brigdon, who was the forerunner of John Fowler, taught me to get a big scrapbook and pin in pieces of material, wallpaper, carpet, fringes, gimps, etc., for each room so it was clear exactly what the colour scheme would be. So much more convenient for matching things.

Sutton, which is open to the public four days a week from Easter to October, is less well known than the famous historical houses, but it has an atmosphere of being lived in and greatly loved which so many houses do not have. People can relate to it and not feel they are in a museum.

Nancie McD. Sheffield.

An early nineteenth-century chandelier hangs in the drawing-room at Sutton Park.

Janet Stone

Salisbury, Wiltshire

The dining-room, low-ceilinged and beamed.

Reynolds and I had taken ten years of intermit-tent searching to find our perfect Old Rectory in Dorset, and twenty-five years later, when I was widowed, I found myself in the unexpected position of looking for a quite different sort of house, a smaller one this time, and with rather more urgency. Partly because of my passion for cathedrals, I had decided I wanted to live in Salisbury.

I found this house quite by accident. I had been longing for the impossible: water at the bottom of my garden and a view of the cathedral spire. Bicycling across St. Nicholas' bridge I suddenly noticed a charming terraced row of arti-sans' cottages; it looked as if they backed onto the river Avon. Then I noticed a 'For Sale' sign. I turned round immediately and pedalled back to find out more from the estate agents.

First impressions were not so promising. It seemed to feature all my least favourite things. It was an old dairy that had been modernised by a builder in a 'ye olde' way that made my heart sink. It looked like the interior of a pub. Beams had been picked out in chocolate and the walls replas-

tered in bumpy textured whirls. And I don't even
like the genuine thing—the Elizabethan period
has never appealed to me very much. But what a
wonderful shock I got when I saw the two largest
rooms, the drawing-room and the main bedroom
above. They extended to the water's edge, and
through the large bay window at the end of each of
them was one of the most perfect views I have ever
seen: the cathedral spire rising above the willows
on the island opposite.

I bought the house in spite of the oak beams.
The views (which included the mediaeval bridge
of St. Nicholas and the unspoilt red-brick Edwardian terrace opposite) were too wonderful to
resist. Also, the window shapes were right—not
too big, but low enough, which is vital—and the
situation is so incredibly quiet. To be so close to
the city centre and yet only to be able to hear ducks
quacking seemed almost too good to be true.

I have always enjoyed mentally reorganising
and redesigning rooms. Although the mock

*The bay window of the drawing-room extends to the water's edge,
giving a marvellous view of Salisbury cathedral spire.*

The drawing-room furniture is of pale, honey-coloured wood. A large tapestry on the wall has a charming story attached to it.

mediaeval interiors of my house were a bit of a challenge, I realised that several coats of paint would more or less obliterate the beams, and a new layer of plaster would smooth out the Instant Whip whirls. Then the house would begin to come to life. The other general problem was the floor. There was a surprising number of rooms, and long wide passages with acres of cement screed on the ground floor. Mollie Salisbury suggested the perfect solution: to lay fitted coconut matting throughout, downstairs and upstairs, except for the drawing-room and main bedroom which should have fitted squares of rush matting. I particularly liked the idea of rush matting because it echoes my courtyard of a garden, which is laid out in a checkerboard pattern of old paving stones alternating with herb beds.

The marble bust of Mrs. Stone's grandmother in a drawing by her daughter Phillida Gili.

The only snag was that it is not supposed to be possible to fit rush matting. But I persuaded the carpet-layer to bind the edges to stop it unravelling. The effort was worthwhile because it did provide the sort of surface I wanted—softer than tiles or boards—and the natural colour is the ideal foil for my furniture and curtains.

So much for generalities. I will now describe in detail my favourite rooms, starting at the front door.

The hall is microscopic, and filled with a large coloured print and a John Piper painting, both of Lichfield Cathedral, where my father was Bishop. The dining-room has the character of a cottage 'front parlour'—low-ceilinged and beamed—and is filled with small sketches and one large painting by John Piper of mountains in North Wales. The latter was painted on a memorably freezing expedition up Mount Snowdon; we watched while he used moss instead of the sponge he had forgotten to bring. The large round table is one of my favourite pieces of furniture. It is painted in dark green veined marbling and was rescued by me from my friend Richard Stewart-Jones at 100 Cheyne Walk when he was carting it off to the workhouse—'I think they might like it, Jan, what do you think?' Fortunately I persuaded him that our need was greater than theirs. The chairs, with black-painted wood and rush seats, are a relic from my husband's grandfather's school, Stone House. The curtains are hand-embroidered and are really part of the hangings for my four-poster bed.

One proceeds through to a hall where the marble bust of my grandmother stands gravely between two of my husband's paintings and to the drawing-room at the end of a passage.

The astonishing view across the river Avon to the cathedral spire, with the Victorian scene of sheep grazing on the island, is still the drawing-room's most remarkable feature. I decided to plan the room round the colours in my David Jones and Mary Potter paintings. These include a particular pink and green. By a wonderful bit of luck some curtains and a chair cover which I had brought from Dorset had exactly the right colours in them. They are both William Morris designs, known as 'Compton' and 'Pink and Rose'. I had the sofa covered in pale green linen with pink piping. All the furniture is of pale honey-coloured wood: the spinet, which was a wedding present from my husband; the lute, which was made specially for me by Dolmetsch; the Victorian work table left to us by Toddy Vaughan of Eton, the top of which is a checkerboard pattern of tiny cathedral views; the Regency cabinet, filled with my collection of cathedral china; and the round table in the bay window, which belonged to my husband's uncle, Christopher Stone. The wall opposite the bay window is furnished with my husband's collection of 1860s books, with their glorious gilt bindings. I think books make the best wallpaper of all.

I put a long richly-patterned Turkish carpet on the rush matting, and for the first time it is in a setting which does it justice. The standard lamps have modern umbrella-shaped lampshades with a bamboo design on them in pale green.

There were two flaws in this room, both created by the builder, which had to be overcome. The first was a mysterious recess in the wall, made to look like a blocked-up window. It was dealt with simply and beautifully by covering it with a large tapestry which hangs from floor to ceiling. It once belonged to H. E. Luxmoore at Eton, and there is a touching story attached to it. Although he loved it dearly, Luxmoore decided to give it to the Red

Framed book plate designs by the late Reynolds Stone.

Another part of the drawing-room.

Cross to help raise funds during the First World War. Reynolds' mother knew how painfully he missed it and organised a subscription to buy it back for him; it was replaced secretly on the wall where it had originally hung. But her ingenious

The richly-coloured bedroom is also a sitting-room and work-room.

plan was frustrated by Luxmoore, who had developed the habit of carefully averting his eyes whenever he walked past the blank wall. In the end he had to have it pointed out to him. He was so touched that he left it to her in his will.

The second problem was the complete absence of any fire-place or chimney. It was solved by installing a cast-iron log-burning stove called a 'Dragon', with a pipe that goes straight up to the roof through the ceiling and my bedroom above.

If the room succeeds in its effect, it is because of the mixture of colours and shapes which the furniture and furnishings provide; the walls themselves I left the colour I found them, magnolia white.

On the staircase are hung two of my favourite portraits, both large paintings. One is by Furze

and is of Reynolds' grandfather, Edward Stone; the other is a self-portrait of my son, also called Edward Stone.

My bedroom is at the end of a passage lined with my husband's framed engravings. It is, I suppose, my favourite room of all. The views are, if anything, even better than those of the floor below; one is more aware of the curve in the river and the arches of the bridge. In spite of being a north-facing room it is somehow always filled with light; the early morning sun pours in on one side and sets through the big window on the other. The cathedral spire perpetually changes colour according to the weather and the time of day; after dark it is even more dramatic, floodlit against the black sky.

My purpose in designing this room, which is as much a sitting-room and a work-room as it is a bedroom, was to make it warm, rich and cosy. The furniture is all dark, including a Victorian screen, made by my grandmother Ellen Barclay, and my four-poster bed, which comes from Reynolds' family. I chose a dark, glowing design by William Morris called 'Grape' for the bed hangings and curtains. I picked out a plum colour from it and used it, piped with the dark Morris pattern, on the bed valance, the canopy and the cushions on the window seats. I chose two paintings by my husband whose colours are primarily dark green to hang near my bed. This room has one wonderful luxury—it has its own bathroom adjoining it. Unfortunately the builder's taste and mine were not identical. He had put in it a streamlined mushroom-coloured bath and basin, with matching tiles. Something had to be done. I commissioned my son-in-law, the artist and illustrator Ian Beck, to paint a mural all over the walls with a bamboo motif. The minimal amount of furniture is all bamboo and the whole effect is, I think, stunning.

My house is not in itself a remarkable one, nor have I spent a fortune on it. But I have tried to create a place where my family and friends can feel at home, whether they want to work or to rest.

Janet Stone.

Anne Tree

SHUTE HOUSE
Donhead St. Mary, Nr. Shaftesbury, Dorset

We live in the ubiquitous old vicarage. The Church authorities changed its name after the war to Shute House, but it is known to our friends as the 'Dripping Vicarage'. Shute faces north, south, east and west and the East Front has a modest classical front. The house has a curious format, being divided in two halves, the new built around 1720, the old being the remains of a sixteenth century hostelry. The parson who built the new half evidently had grander ideas than his predecessors. This modern part consists of four sizeable rooms, two up and two down and a big staircase lit by a large Palladian window. He must then have run out of money or died, as the old part of the house is modest.

I had little or no experience of decorating as I had moved to a large folly, Mereworth Castle, as a bride, and over the twenty years we lived there had only the odd bedroom to refurbish. My husband was lucky to inherit a lot of furniture and carpets from his parents and over the years his mother has given us endless presents of beautiful things. The decoration of our house was a mutual effort by my husband and myself, and I must add that my

The staircase at Shute House incorporating the vivid blue suggested by the skies in Giotto's frescoes.

husband has an unerring eye for colour and scale.

We started from scratch, the hall with the big staircase being the starting point. While we were househunting we visited Assisi, where we determined that in any future house we might own we must incorporate the wonderful vivid blue that Giotto used for his skies. To this end I purchased as many postcards as possible which included sky. When we bought Shute the staircase was the obvious place to use this blue. We asked Cyril Wapshott to mix the distemper. The colours looked truly alarming in the buckets; bright dark purple, emerald green and lots of brilliant blues. These were applied by sponge on a pale blue background. At first the walls looked like an abstract mural, but the finished ones were beautiful, if a little startling.

To begin with, we had no suitable pictures to

Interior of the drawing-room painted by Michael Tree.

put on the walls to break up the colour, but a year or two later I was lucky enough to acquire a large set of Chinese prints which do the job perfectly. We chose a modern carpet from Colefax & Fowler, made from a design in blue and orange on a piece of Chinese porcelain which was found by Tom Parr in the Wallace Collection.

To the left of the hall are two rooms: a drawing-room facing south, leading to a library through a jib door, facing north. The library was to be my husband's room, the drawing-room, mine. In fact we all live together in a muddle. For the drawing-room walls I chose khaki. I have always liked khaki, perhaps it is a lingering

memory of glamorous officers in uniform during my impressionable years in the 1939–45 war. Anyway, khaki it is and a jolly good background for watercolours and drawings. These we have in abundance spattered on the walls. My husband has collected McEvoy for years. They are decorative and delicate. A pair of mirrors and some mounted exotic butterflies complete the decoration.

On the floor I have coconut matting with fur rugs. I don't like wall-to-wall carpet—it reminds me of hotel suites—but our coconut matting was the greatest possible mistake. It is impossible to make a good job of clearing up a dog mess: you have to get busy with a palate knife and it still leaves a stain.

The curtains, or what remains of them, are very old. They were in a bedroom at Ditchley and are mentioned by Madame de la Tour du Pin in her diary, when she fled the French Revolution and took refuge with her Litchfield relations, the then owners of Ditchley. The curtains are now reduced to faded blue patterned Dress curtains, falling apart and frequently mended with copydex as they are too frail to sew. In the space left over are pale cotton Venetian blinds.

The drawing-room was awkwardly shaped, having a large immovable beam two thirds of the way across the room. This meant that the fireplace was not central. John Fowler had the bright idea of putting up two pillars under this beam, which made the room square, leaving an open annex at the north end. Here is my writing table, faded black-and-gold lacquer. There is a bookcase, lots of potted plants and a tree by a glass door leading to the garden. On the other side we have a coromandel screen, hiding both the door and the drinks tray, an ideal arrangement for those who think the hospitality of the house less than perfect.

We bought a blue, yellow and white French marble chimney-piece, large enough for a big fire and room for a clock and vases on top. On either side of the fire-place are a pair of gilt gesso tables, with Chinese lamps and vases of flowers. Two sofas face each other on either side of the fireplace, covered in gingerbread-coloured cotton, easy to wash and good with the khaki walls. The cushions are in different coloured chintzes, all with the same braid. On the floor is a large pale yellow rug with a rose border, and on top of that a polar bear fur rug.

In front of the south window we put a round table. It has a lamp and lampshade of pleated chintz on it. The tablecloth came from my mother-in-law, and is a winner. It is French and has life-size animals in fancy dress. They are copies from Granville's '*Les Scenes de la Vie Privée et Publique des Animaux*', published in 1842. Opposite the fire-place we have a pair of tables by Johnson, carved gilt branches of oak trees with marble tops; Chinese lamps, again on the table tops, numerous small Chinese fretwork vases, always filled summer and winter with flowers from the garden. I have a mass of flowers in the drawing-room, perhaps forty or fifty vases and, therefore, I do not feel the need to go out in bad weather. As far as I am concerned, the main fault with the room is that the sofas are not long enough to lie out full length and go to sleep.

I have my own little study in the old part of the house. Half the walls are covered with old panelling, sadly painted over at some time. In these panels I have stuck paintings of flowers and leaves from the garden which I have varnished. I have not yet completed the panels as, if I do not finish a painting at once, I have to wait another year to start again with the right leaves.

I collect paintings of animals dressed as humans. On one wall I have a pair of prints of Russian Bear soldiers fighting Napoleonic Frogs. On another wall I have cases of stuffed frogs bicycling, dancing and playing cards. There is also a charming pair of courting stuffed ducks. He wears a top hat, bow tie and binoculars and she has a hat, lace shawl and an engagement ring on her webbed foot. Over the fire-place I have mounted pieces of landscape marble from Florence, and a

A table in front of the drawing-room's south window is covered by a French tablecloth displaying Granville's animals in fancy dress.

fossilised fish which is either forty million or four-hundred million years old; I can never remember which. The curtains came from the Kings Road, nineteenth-century and velvet, with an intricate pattern in patchwork. The rest of the wall space is covered with bookshelves. The middle of the room is taken up with a huge modern writing table that I designed. I covered it with pictures like a Victorian screen. Often the pictures were donations from friends who cut them out from magazines. It has a cork top, a perfect surface on which to pin letters and bills.

I do not anticipate redoing the house and as the years go by I suppose it will get shabbier and more worn like its owner and the next inhabitants will then redecorate from scratch in their manner and their style.

Anne Tree

Above: *Numerous small Chinese fretwork vases are filled summer and winter with flowers from the garden.*
Below: *In the study a large modern writing table is covered with pictures—often donations from friends.*

A well-filled corner of the drawing-room with the door leading to the garden. ☛

Rosemary Verey

BARNSLEY HOUSE
Nr. Cirencester, Gloucestershire

Our drawing-room with its archway into the morning-room is quite my favourite part of the house. I share it with David—and our visitors—but feel completely happy sitting there alone, reading, writing, doing nothing, sometimes thinking of the people who have enjoyed it before us.

The house was built by Brereton Bourchier, the lord of the manor, in 1697 on or near the site of the former manor house. It was built in excellent local oolitic limestone from a quarry on the edge of the parish, the same stone as was used for some of the Oxford colleges. The style was old-fashioned,

with mullion and transom windows. Three years later Bourchier married Katharine Brydges, sister of the first Duke of Chandos, a great patron of the arts. It is not surprising that with such good stone available and his creative inclinations Bourchier decided to build a bigger and grander house, more suitable for entertaining his brother-in-law, and the baroque mansion Barnsley Park was begun.

The 1697 house was abandoned by the family, and in 1762 it became the rectory. It was enlarged in 1830 when an attempt was made to make it look Tudor, and the William and Mary windows survive only on the garden side—luckily

Pale colours in the drawing-room blend with the woven rush matting.

where our drawing-room is situated.

When we came to live here in 1951 the two rooms I am going to tell you about were three: our drawing-room, which was divided in two by cream-coloured panelling, and the dining-room, with white marble fire-place, deep yellow wall-paper and heavy dark red curtains covering the 1830 bow window.

It was in 1958 that we made major structural alterations; we moved out and the builders moved in for the summer. The large old kitchen became our dining-room and erstwhile double doors between the old dining-room and drawing-room were released and opened so making a wide arch-way. The panelled partition was removed from the drawing-room and our three rooms were now opened up into one glorious space, sixty feet long.

We took out the marble fire-place and replaced it with a beautiful pine chimney-piece which David had cleverly acquired when the big house at Draycot Cerne was demolished. It has a central female mask and is thoroughly baroque. Another clever buy he had made was a splendid seventeenth century oil painting of the arch of Titus by Viviano Codazzi. It fits exactly into the space above the chimney-piece and the two together make a striking feature as one looks through the archway from the drawing-room and on through the arch of Titus. The early morning sun catches it and brings the picture alive.

The space was wonderful for children's games, Christmas parties and dancing reels, but at this point we made a series of dreadful errors. We economised on carpets, using existing rugs which could easily be pulled back for dancing. I was ignorant about colours and too busy with a young family to worry about 'stuffs', and would have thought it extravagant to seek professional help. This was the beginning of the post-war Fowler era and we were still 'utility'-minded, good material being in short supply.

We painted the panelling 'eau de Nil'; you can imagine how dreadful it looked. For curtains I bought seventy yards of apricot pink material at a sale in the Edgware Road. It went well with the 'eau de Nil' but definitely wasn't right in the Cots-wolds, and the lesson I learnt was that such a large expanse of plain material looked flat instead of lively. My one wise decision was to have the cur-tains made by a good firm. They were lined, inter-lined and padded in conventional style; more of them hereafter.

Have you ever measured up a room for a carpet and considered the pros and cons of having either wall to wall covering or just an island in the middle with polished boards all round? My advice is 'Don't have the latter'. It is wiser without ques-tion to pay the higher price; you'll never regret the cost but you will always dislike the mean look of a shrunken-looking carpet. Two more mistakes we made—then I can get on to better things. We kept a much too big, uncomfortable and not even pretty Regency sofa. We imagined we had to keep it because it had always been in David's life. Also, I insisted on having a huge grand piano occupying far too much space; wherever we put it, it looked

The drawing-room at Barnsley Rectory before alterations.

overgrown and upset the symmetry of the long French windows. When at last we steeled our-selves to part with these we felt released and were able to start properly.

It was a shame that we had treated this lovely space so badly for so long and it finally came home to us when David Vicary became a friend and gave us advice. Make it into a light, long gallery was his suggestion, keep the colours pale but warm and use pretty flower chintzes. Make the room feel as though it belongs to the garden. There are so many windows it *is* almost part of the garden anyway. As I spend most of my time in the garden, the idea seemed quite natural.

The architectural features around which the decorating had to be done were a seventeenth century stone fire-place with moulded stonework, nineteenth century painted panelling, four large windows and a glass-topped door, all facing south east, and two French windows on the narrow south-west side, added when the Gothic verandah

The amber-coloured walls provide a good background for pictures.

Tablescape of seed pods below a leaf and butterfly collage.

Framed Chinese fans hang in the archway which both divides and unites the drawing- and morning-rooms.

The drawing-room feels almost part of the garden.

was built in 1830.

As this was to become a room associated with the garden, rush matting was the obvious choice. It was made locally, or so we thought, and we ordered it from a mill in nearby Stroud; it wasn't until it arrived that I read the label 'Made in Hongkong'. It has been extremely successful, never shows the dirt as everything possible falls through it, and has a nuance of pattern created by

the way in which it is woven. Compared with good quality carpet it is incredibly cheap.

The curtains were the next problem together with the future colour of the panelling. Thank goodness David Vicary steered us away from pastel shades! The panelling was painted two whites, the mouldings completely white and the flat surfaces dragged with a pale biscuit colour on white. Now that dragging has become a common practice

Looking through the archway to the 'Arch of Titus' above the pine chimney-piece.

there would be no problem in getting it done, but in 1968 it was impossible to find anyone locally who could do it. The painter who was working for us was immensely skilled and eventually, after desperate telephone calls to the wonderful Imogen Taylor of Colefax & Fowler, he achieved it brilliantly. Every wall space, window shutter, door—and almost us as well—was dragged with two whites.

We chose the seaweed pattern in fawn and white for the curtains. It was a momentous decision involving a hundred and twenty yards of material and the curtains would either blend with or dominate the final effect. They had to blend.

Two lucky things happened. I realised we could cover the existing curtains, and as the curtain-makers could not be persuaded to do this I determined to tackle it myself. Fortunately I have always enjoyed a challenge and this one took most of April and the help of two friends, one aged sixteen and the other ten. We laid each curtain in turn on the floor and cut round them. We pinned and stitched and the ten-year-old kept us tidy and put the pins away. All had to be finished in the school holidays so we worked to a timetable, twelve long curtains in three weeks. I made the drapes later. I chose a design from Mario Pratz and with some old sheets and pins I finally arrived at a satisfactory pattern. Each one turned out slightly different and I definitely improved as time went on. The top corners have fat, punched-in 'cauliflowers' and by now these have gathered a considerable quantity of dust, but I dare not take them down as I would never succeed in putting them up again.

Imogen Taylor chose for us some really pretty 'climbing geranium' chintz for the chairs and window seats. David Vicary found me two old rosy-patterned curtains to make into a cloth for a large oval table draped to the ground and some unusual brown flowery chintz for a small round table.

The pictures have been entirely my husband David's choice, except for the piece of Chinese wallpaper which we framed and put over the drawing-room fire-place. We had endless difficulty in finding a picture to fit both the space and the mood of the room. This piece of wallpaper, the bottom section of a panel, is very decorative, with two black swans against a flowery background. Another important feature of the room is a glass-fronted bookcase made in walnut by Peter Waals, a

Dutch craftsman employed by Ernest Gimson, the Arts and Crafts furniture designer. It is fifteen feet long and has six bays beautifully made down to the smallest detail. What is amazing is that although it was designed for another house it fits exactly into its allotted space. The books inside it are especially precious to me—all on gardening.

Corner of the drawing-room with walnut, glass-fronted bookcase.

Sit in the drawing-room and look through the archway and you discover that the atmosphere of the morning-room is quite different. Whereas one is almost part of the garden, the other is very much an indoor room. There are open-fronted book-cases and all along the top shelf are pieces of seventeenth century blue and white Chinese por-

celain. The colour of the walls is 'Hot Sahara', which compliments and sets off the blue china beautifully. Surprisingly there was no cornice, and when this was added it made a great contribution to the completion of the room; my husband wisely insisted that it was deep and bold as possible.

Peter Hood helped us select the materials for the sofa, chair covers and the curtains. The blue of the china had to be repeated but not too strongly. My desk is in the bow window, and as I look out I have a good view of the garden and can contemplate what we will do next in an effort to improve it!

Many years ago Oliver Hill gave us a collage of skeleton magnolia leaves and butterflies and this sparked off in my mind the idea of making a tablescape with interestingly shaped seed pods which we have collected on holidays abroad. They are of every size and shape, some long and thin and others fat and round, and they live on a mahogany table under the collage.

David is always having good ideas and after our ruby wedding he made a blue table and a ruby table each side of the fire-place. The ruby side has the presents we were given on that occasion and the central feature is a charming ruby, velvet-covered workbox given to us by Alvilde Lees-Milne. Another of David's ideas was to have six of my Chinese fans framed with rich coloured backgrounds and to hang them in the archway between the two rooms, the archway which divides the rooms and yet unites them as one.

Rooms like clothes should remain in fashion, though good clothes like good furniture never become unfashionable, but it is essential that the style of the décor be in keeping with the architecture of the house and with the character of the people who live there.

Rosemary Verey

Jane Westmorland

A SMALL MANOR HOUSE
Gloucestershire

We had lived in ten houses before we bought Kingsmead and each one in turn had been destined to be our home for life—where we brought up our children, sank our roots, planted our herbaceous borders, etc. However, for one reason or another we always moved on, until eleven years ago we heard that this particular house was for sale. Over the years we had known it well from the outside and had always coveted it. It must have been built around 1720 and can best be described as a small manor house. From the road all we could see was a particularly attractive and

friendly façade with a wonderful pediment over the front door and, unusual for the Cotswolds, the original harling which had faded to a beautiful colour. The house had the added advantage of proper sash windows.

When we were finally able to look over it we discovered that the original front door was not used; a side door opening into a dark and narrow passage served instead. This gave a most misleading first impression of the house, and when we finally bought it we immediately made a drive up to the front so that one now walks straight into the

The main drawing-room looking towards the garden.

heart of the house—a small panelled hall where, however hard I try to move people into other and larger rooms, everyone always seems to congregate. Maybe because this is where the drinks tray stands. The long passage we originally disliked has been knocked into an adjoining room where we keep the television, books and hopefully our children.

Fortunately, because I enjoy doing it, the whole house needed redecorating; but unfortu-nately, or not, we did not have the money at the time to do it all properly. Consequently during the years we have lived there we have made many changes. The major alteration—requiring at least three or four RSJs—was knocking down an extremely important wall to make a good-sized drawing-room. To me, almost more important than having this large room was the fact that by putting in French windows we could now walk straight into the garden, which in the summer is

Corner of the flower-filled drawing-room.

The small hall is a favourite congregating place for guests.

The lobby filled with garden accoutrements.

The shelves in the drawing-room are filled with books and china.

like having an extension to the house. Much as I love being indoors I always seem to want to get out, which is possibly why there are, to many people, including, I often feel, my husband, an almost ridiculous amount of flowers in every room.

I find it hard to describe how I decorated any of the rooms. Nearly always there were curtains, carpets or something from a previous house that had to be fitted in. I never really seem to have started from scratch, but basically I love all the old English chintzes—roses, ribbons, speckled backgrounds—linen materials, silk cushions. On the whole, traditional, easy to live with and not obtrusive.

Apart from pieces of family furniture there was always the portrait of John, the tenth Earl, who, though wonderful to look at in his dark red cloak, is eleven and a half feet high. He is now in the drawing-room, up to the ceiling and cut into the skirting board. I am sure many people would feel he overpowers the room, but we love him. Also in the same room is a huge and once old-fashioned, but now immensely popular sofa. It originated in my husband's nursery and was once slept on in a London house we had by two of our greatest friends the night before the Queen's coronation!

As to getting the basic proportions of the rooms right, arranging the furniture and hanging the serious pictures, my husband is far better than me. I tend to mind much more about my clutter—the ornaments, the perpetual flowers, the photographs and the dog baskets always seem-

A pretty arrangement on a landing.

Part of a bedroom.

ing to me more important. However, between us we manage to achieve what we like, well-disciplined rooms disguised with all the pieces we have collected through the years.

I think it is fair to say that I have never used a decorator as such and have certainly never given one *carte blanche* to do a room. However, for many years and certainly with this house, I have had the help of a wonderful person. She is a very professional decorator and has always given me invaluable advice, particularly with colours where I can go extremely wrong and over details such as cushions about which I tend to be very lazy.

One thing I consider essential to any house one lives in is to 'personalise' it, not only with the straightforward decorating that has to be done, but with pieces of one's own needlework—cushions, carpets, etc.—hopefully finished, but they even look quite good unfinished in work baskets. My latest enthusiasm is for collage, and I have had the greatest fun in decorating a dark and narrow passage with eighteen-inch borders around the doors and skirtings—the problem being to know when to stop.

In conclusion, I hope that we have created a house that not only our family and our numerous animals enjoy living in, but one to which we hope our friends will always want to return.

Jane Westmorland

The front of the house today.

Peggy Willis

Radway, Warwickshire

Most of the houses in Radway, the village where I live, are built of the Hornton stone, quarried at the top of Edgehill which rises in a long ridge behind the village. It is very like Cotswold stone but more golden and more beautiful.

My own house is built of this stone and stands slightly back from the village street, from which it is hidden by a line of espaliered lime trees. It is approached by a narrow drive winding between high walls and yew hedges and finally widening to become a gravelled circle in front of the house, which from this side (the north) looks like a child's drawing—a square with a porch in the middle with a window each side and three windows in a row above.

It was, almost certainly, a small farmhouse originally, but must at some time have been considerably enlarged, for one of the inside walls is almost two feet thick; this was probably once the outside wall of the house.

I lived here for six months in the summer of 1914 and have the usual distant memories of a garden filled with flowers and perpetual sunshine. I never saw it again till 1957, when I was looking for somewhere to live. On a friend telling me that this house was for sale, I came to look at it, and eventually bought it.

I realised that I should have to make many alterations. In due course I gutted the house, knocked rooms together, made new windows, changed the position of doors, and built on a new kitchen and a small staff flat at right angles to the

Heavy, lime-yellow silk curtains frame the view from the drawing-room.

The drawing-room, its colouring inspired by the English Savonnerie carpet.

The decoration of the blue, south-facing bedroom is based on the Victorian needlework carpet.

original square house, with, above it, approached by an outside staircase, a room rather pretentiously named 'the Studio'; this is where I paint, or work with the many shells that I have collected over the years.

Last, but not least, I built a garden-room leading out of the drawing-room at one end and into the new kitchen at the other.

There had been a garden-room at the house where I lived before, and I was determined if possible to have one again. Luckily, it was quite easy to achieve this since there had been an aviary on the same spot and the foundations were already there. The room is built out from the south wall of the house and is mostly of glass, with big double doors on three sides which, when they are all open in the summer, justify its name by making it seem almost a part of the garden. The roof too is partly glass, with rush matting blinds which are left pulled across on sunny days. The walls are pale coral, covered with a wooden trellis painted grey, up which are trained a variety of climbing plants;

The view from the garden.

more plants stand in pots on the floor.

In the middle of the room is an oval marble table (brought from my last garden-room) large enough to take a luncheon party of ten. I lunch in this room all the year round for it is warm and catches whatever sun there may be, but I don't dine there in winter as the glass doors have no curtains, so that after dark the blackness outside makes it rather gloomy.

The drawing-room is the largest room in the house (two rooms knocked into one) and, like the garden-room, faces south onto the big straggling garden which climbs the lower slopes of Edgehill until it meets the woods dropping down from the top.

The colouring of the drawing-room was inspired by an English Savonnerie carpet which I brought with me from my last home, a carpet of many colours, mostly muted, with a background of dull green, but including bright patches which have been picked up and repeated in the covers and curtains of the room. The furniture is an undistinguished but pleasant mixture which includes a grand piano inherited from my mother, and a number of Regency and Victorian pieces, plus an eighteenth century Gothic mirror and side tables bought especially for the room.

Sanderson Miller, the eighteenth century architect, owned the big house in the village and his granddaughter lived in my house when it was the Vicarage (her husband, a cousin, was the

A view of the garden from Mrs. Willis's bathroom.

Vicar). Mrs. Miller's presence in the house seemed to me sufficient excuse for the Gothic glazing bars I have put into most of the windows and for the row of stone crenellations with which I have bordered the edge of the roof on the south side; these crenellations repeat those with which Sanderson Miller crowned the octagonal tower which he built at the top of the hill, on the spot where Charles I raised his standard the morning of

The garden room has walls covered with trellis and a marble table used for luncheon.

the Battle of Edgehill.

Although the drawing-room is the 'best' and largest room in the house, and although I don't sit in it much when I am alone, it has a pleasantly lived-in feeling about it. I think this is because the door from the hall is always open and so is the glass door into the garden-room beyond, which means that anyone wanting to go into the garden automatically passes through the drawing-room. Also,

the drinks table stands between the windows, so that whenever guests are offered drinks it is in the drawing-room that they are given them. The room is painted a pale grey and has heavy lime-yellow silk curtains framing the green outside. At night they make a big splash of warm colour. I have already mentioned that the furniture is pleasant but undistinguished, because (alas) I have never had an urge to collect furniture whereas pictures

One of Mrs. Willis's shell pictures.

have always been a special interest of mine. Consequently, the walls of this room (and all the other rooms in the house) are postage stamped with pictures of many kinds—for mine is a catholic taste.

Books are also, for me, an indispensable part of the decoration of any room, so the drawing-room has a pair of Regency bookcases at one end and the little sitting-room where I spend my time when I am alone has bookcases built all round it, with spaces left for pictures. A number of small pictures are propped on the shelves in front of the books. This room is painted olive green and has a red sofa and armchairs; the chintz curtains and cushions are patterned in green and red on a white background. The room is full of a great variety of things, my writing desk, the television, the telephone, my photograph books, and a crowd of small objects all of which mean something personal and which I should find it impossible to scrap. The result is clutter, but it is a clutter which engenders a warm and cosy atmosphere very pleasant to live with. I don't like formal tidy rooms.

This and all the rooms are lit by table lamps, with picture lights over the larger pictures. Only the hall and garden-room have hanging lanterns but nowhere are there standard lamps, a pet aversion of mine. The curtains throughout the house are chintz (except the drawing-room), and they are all French headed. None of the rooms are high enough for pelmets. The rooms are all painted, except for the kitchen, the hall and the landings, which have a paper with a big arresting pattern of lilacs. The hall has an ancient stone paved floor.

The rest of the house has neutral haircord carpeting with occasional rugs thrown over it.

My bedroom, like the drawing-room, faces south and it also has a carpet which I brought with me—Victorian needlework in very bright colours, much faded now, with a design of great squares containing bunches of flowers, joined together and bordered by an intricate geometrical pattern. This carpet is very worn and as each new hole appears I buy a white Flokati rug to cover it. Sadly, by now the floor is mostly Flokati. The room is painted blue. The decoration here, too, owes its inspiration to the carpet, and there are pleasantly faded chintz curtains and bed hangings. The bedspread is lace with a pile of lace cushions at the head. The room is quite big, being, again, two rooms knocked together. It is a very feminine room, gets all the sun there is and has a lovely view of the garden and hillside.

The dining-room is only used nowadays for an occasional winter dinner party. It is lacquer red with an oval mahogany table and a set of painted Georgian chairs, their squab seats covered with the same flowered material as the curtains. Round the walls hang the ubiquitous pictures. The only lighting is by picture lights and candles.

I should like to conclude by quoting a verse which Sanderson Miller wrote about his own, much larger, house in the village, but which, I feel, applies equally well to mine:

My house! 'Tis but a small and old one,
Yet now 'tis warm though once a cold one,
My study holds three thousand volumes
And yet I sigh for Gothic columns.

I don't suppose I have three thousand books and I don't aspire to Gothic columns, but I love Gothic furniture and decoration and I much admire the work which caused Sanderson Miller to be considered by his contemporaries the greatest authority on Gothic architecture in the kingdom. I wish he had tampered with my house, which he probably owned, but, sadly, he left it alone and it is impossible to pretend otherwise. I hope, though, that perhaps in time to come someone may look at my crenellations and wonder, was it he who put them there?

Peggy Willis

Elizabeth Winn

A LONDON FLAT

Having always wanted to live in the country with a garden of my own but been obliged to live in London owing to my work, I feel I was very lucky to find a flat, which has now been my home for fifteen years, overlooking a garden square at treetop level. At all seasons of the year there is something new to look at—the bare branches of the large plane trees in the winter, the bursting buds in the spring with the first sound of the lawn mower, and finally the complete oblivion of the houses opposite by a screen of green leaves below the ever changing sky—and to me, nicest of all,

the autumn when the colours change from day to day.

When I first saw the sitting-room, I knew I could make it liveable and cosy. It has three arched-top windows facing north west over the square. There is a built-in breakfront bookcase facing the fire-place, with cupboards below where I managed to fit in my two stereo speakers and store my large collection of long-playing records. Each side of this bookcase are a pair of white and gold Italian tables given to me by my mother which, luckily for me, fitted perfectly into the

The self-stripe white wallpaper in the sitting-room is a perfect backdrop for Miss Winn's many pictures.

spaces.

As I am a compulsive buyer of books, one bookcase was not enough, so I was excited to find a tall, shallow Regency painted rosewood bookcase from Geoffrey Bennison, which is not only pretty to look at but gives height to the wall facing the three windows. To me a room without books is like a face with no eyes.

My other great loves are pictures, particularly watercolours, and I started to accumulate them thirty-five years ago when they were relatively cheap; of course at the time I felt I was being very extravagant, but have never regretted a purchase yet.

For this reason I have kept my walls white with a self-stripe wallpaper. The pictures on each side of the bookcase I have hung in a design, as I have always disliked a row of frames at the same height around a room; they remind me of a picture gallery. Getting the design right is done by placing them on the floor and juggling them around like a pack of cards until one is satisfied with the pattern.

I had no plan of design when I moved into this room. The furniture just seemed to fall into place. The chimney-piece it seems to me is always the focal point of any room, so it is vital to have a comfortable chair each side of it. The chair I sit in is naturally the most comfortable of the two, and it is covered in an old Baker auricula chintz, alas now discontinued. On the other side of the fire-place I have a Victorian buttoned-back chair covered in faded green corded velvet. I wanted the room to look like a country drawing-room and I hope I have achieved this by using subdued colours and simple fabrics.

The floor is close carpeted in a natural colour, but enlivened by a floral Bessarabian rug in off-whites, greens and tomato red on a black ground in front of the fire-place which gives light and colour to the whole room. Incidentally, I had to buy a new chimney-piece as the existing one was too ugly to contemplate living with. Over it I have hung a charming portrait of a small girl in a fur hat by Anthony Devas, given to me by a cousin many years ago.

I think lighting is the most important item when arranging a room for cosiness and comfort. One should be able to read easily from any chair or sofa, so I have acquired over the years five very pretty lamps to produce what John Fowler called 'pools of light'. I am particularly fond of the tomato-coloured Bristol lamp on the left side of the fire-place; it sits on a circular table covered in an old patchwork bedspread bought from Mrs. Hourigan's shop in the Kings Road twenty-five years ago. It is made of pieces of eighteenth century chintz which one longs to be able to obtain today.

I am afraid many people would think my room cluttered, but to me it is important to be surrounded by objects I love and photographs of relations and friends.

I had always wanted a nice writing table and had to make do for years with a cheap pine bureau bookcase I had bought in the country; luckily, about three or four years ago, I happened to pass a shop window in my car on my way home from work and saw what I had been looking for—a Louis XVI cylinder bureau with brass inlay on a marble top with brass gallery. I had a sleepless night wondering whether I should throw discretion to the winds and buy it but I did, and it has given me pleasure every time I write at it, albeit paying unpleasant bills. Above it, I have hung a modern oil painting of a canal in northern England which reminds me of the many happy holidays I have spent on the English canals.

In the centre of the room facing the fire-place I have put my two-seater sofa, covered in an off-white toile, with a small fruitwood table behind it with a tall glass column lamp so that my guests can read *Country Life* if conversation fails. I purposely did not put a bright colour on the sofa as it was important to make the room as large as possible and I did not want it to stick out like a sore thumb.

The curtains I felt should be very plain as I did not want to cover up the arched top windows with fancy pelmets. They are French headed in a plain lime-yellow Sekers fabric, lined only to give them a transparent quality.

My entrance hall has five doors leading out of it—one into the sitting-room I have described, the other four into the bedroom, bathroom, kitchen and study—and two cupboard doors. The cupboard doors had to be disguised, so I removed all the architraves and mouldings and they became flush with the walls. I then papered them into a green and white William Morris wallpaper and hung oil paintings on them. This hall is always cheerful, especially in the mornings when the sun streams in from the open kitchen door which is east facing.

Again there was a problem of where to put my overflow of books, so I designed and had made a pair of low bookcases and asked Maria and Jonathan Brunskill to paint them to simulate the Regency rosewood bookcase in the living-room, picked out with gold lines and *faux* marble tops. Over one of these hangs almost my favourite pos-session, a French circular tole wall clock in a wonderful warm Chinese red. It probably works like a dream, but I have a neurosis about ticking clocks so it has never been wound up.

A very narrow passage about eight feet long leads to the front door, and I have hung in a double row a set of Hogarth's 'The Harlot's Progress'

The dining area of the kitchen. The pine walls are plastered with black-and-white family photographs.

which I bought for a pound each at the end of the war. I framed and mounted these myself when I was working as a humble slave in the Colefax & Fowler studio in 1947, an experience I shall always be grateful for.

My kitchen is small but functional—one half for cooking and the other half the eating area, walled with vertical pine strips and plastered with black-and-white photographs of my family past and present, which makes it very nostalgic for me. On the window ledge, usually flooded with sun, I keep pots of herbs and scented geraniums—this is my secret garden.

The entrance hall and passage to the front door. A French circular tole wall clock in Chinese red hangs over a bookcase painted to simulate the Regency one in the sitting-room.

One of a pair of white-and-gold Italian tables which stand each side of the built-in bookcase.

The sitting-room. A pretty Regency bookcase has a carefully thought out pattern of pictures each side.